A BOX
OF WHITE
CHOCOLATE

FEB 0 8

FEB

KN

A BOX OF WHITE CHOCOLATE

DAAMON SPELLER

URBAN BOOKS

http://www.urbanbooks.net

This is a work of fiction. Any references or similarities to actual events, real people, living or dead, or to real locales are intended to give the novel a sense of reality. Any similarity in other names, characters, places, and incidents is entirely coincidental.

URBAN SOUL is published by

Urban Books
10 Brennan Place
Deer Park, NY 11729

Copyright © 2008 by Daamon Speller

ISBN-13: 978-1-59983-055-1
ISBN-10: 1-59983-055-8

First Printing: February 2008

10 9 8 7 6 5 4 3 2 1

Printed in the United States of America

When Mr. Right isn't even *close* to
what you had in mind . . .

NEW YEAR'S EVE 2002

I

Bailey Gentry

Eleven-o-five. Another New Year's Eve and I'm home alone with nothing going on other than *Who is Jill Scott?* on my CD changer and a pint of Häagen Dazs mint chip. What I need to do is put this ice cream back in the fridge before these hips and thighs of mine get so far away from me that I can't reel 'em back in. Eight years ago, I was a super fit, five-foot-five, 130-pound diva, with an attention-getting apple bottom. (Red beans and rice didn't miss me.) As my late grandma, Lucy Pearl, used to say, a chile was saying som'um. Don't get me wrong, now. I'm *still* saying som'um—just at 160-plus pounds these days. I can still fit into a pair of form-fitting jeans *and* tuck my shirt in because I don't need to hide a fat, unshapely ass. Just the same, I'm not going to fake the funk. I'm straddling the fat fence. I'm about a cheeseburger away from falling over on the wrong side of it.

I'm Bailey Gentry. Born and raised in Washington,

D.C. I guess I'm what you could call a sista going places.
A thirty-seven-year-old, six-figure-earning family attorney
for the black law firm of Jefferson, Bates, and Hankerson, in downtown Washington, D.C. I'm also the recent
proud owner of a beautiful three-bedroom, four-bath
single-family home in the 1400 block of Whittier Street
in Northwest D.C. Besides my height and weight, which
I've already told you, I'm sportin' a short, chin-length-
bob style haircut these days. I've retired the cornrow extensions I had been rocking for the longest. People tell
me I favor that actress Elise Neil from the sitcom *The
Hughleys*. I think I have a wonderful personality, too. I'm
intelligent, attractive, funny, adventurous, self-sufficient,
and very spunky. Oh yeah. I'm also manless. Sure, I
know I'm not the only thirty-seven-year-old black woman
in the District of Columbia who hasn't had her prize
package knock on her door or buzz her intercom—but
that's sure not easing my pain any.

I love black men something awful. Love 'em in all their
hues: dark brown, light brown, beige—navy blue. As a
teenager, my jones was for those butterscotch pretty boys.
Remember Christopher Williams? Al B. Sure? But I
haven't been on that trip since graduating from Roosevelt
High School in eighty-three. These days, I'm on that dark,
Godiva chocolate trip. If someone gave me a pencil and
paper and told me to draw a picture of my ideal brotha—
from a physical standpoint—I'd draw them a picture of
Morris Chestnut from that movie *The Best Man*. Lawd have
mercy! That's a black man beyond fine. He's *foin!*

I don't know about any of you ladies out there, but my
search for a good black man, my kind of Mr. Right, has
been like the proverbial search for a needle in a haystack.
I'll spare you most of the gory details and just tell you
about my three most recent attempts. . . .

2

Victor: The Cat's Meow

Victor had a way of making the kitty purr that no other man has been able to match, before or after. Unfortunately, this happened to be his *only* skill. Vertically, the muthafutta was next to useless. What's a "muthafutta" you ask? Exactly what you think it is. A *muthafucker.* It's just that the latter is a rather crude word, and as a lady, I try to refrain from its usage as often as I can. Got it? Good. Let's move on.

I met Victor at Republic Gardens. This cool-as-can-be, hole-in-the-wall nightclub on U Street in downtown D.C. The year was '96. I was thirty-one at the time. He was twenty-three. Yes, I took a brief detour into Similac country. Sue me. It wasn't like I knew the brotha was a young'un when he stepped to me. He sure didn't look like one. Lisa, my best friend, and I were waiting in line to get in the nightclub. Victor was standing in line a few feet ahead of us. He was about five-eleven, 180, cleanshaven, with a really cute LL Cool J–like dimple in his left cheek. He wasn't what I'd categorize to you as fine, though he was certainly above average. What really got my attention was his gear. He was dressed in a crisp, white, collarless shirt and blue, plaid-patterned slacks that hung a bit baggy on his body. And just below the cuffed hems of his funky blue plaid-patterned slacks were a pair of polished black loafers. (I *always* check out the shoes.) I can get weak at the knees for a well-dressed man.

Victor couldn't keep his eyes off me. He kept looking back from his spot in the line and checking me out. Can't say I blamed him, though. Dressed in a belly-exposing double-ring top with matching stretch pants and a pair of "do me" pumps on my feet, a sista had it going on that night if I do say so myself. He wasn't that dark Godiva chocolate I'm feeling these days. Had sort of a caramel tone to him. Like a Snickers bar. I told Lisa I was definitely backin' it up on this bruh if we got on the dance floor together.

When I finally reached the entrance of Republic Gardens to pay my ten dollars and get in the club, the guy collecting money at the door waved me on. Said a guy in a white shirt had described me, told him what I was wearing, and said he was paying for my admission into the club, too. When I got inside, Victor was standing near the entrance waiting for me.

"Did you pay my way in here?" I asked, batting my big brown eyes at him.

"Is that a problem?"

"Not at all."

"I'm Victor, by the way."

"Bailey."

"Well, just don't stand there, Bailey. Let me buy you a drink."

Lisa cleared her throat. I had forgotten just that quick that I wasn't here alone.

"Oh, I'm sorry. Victor, this is my friend, Lisa."

"Nice to meet you, Lisa," he said.

"Same here," she replied.

I asked Lisa if she'd mind me steppin' off for a minute. I know it was kind of cold leaving her two minutes after getting in the joint, but hey, Lisa already had a man, okay? Tonight, she was going to have to recognize the plight of the less fortunate.

Following a glass of Hennessey and a bit of small talk, Victor and I got down to business on the dance floor. And yes, I backed my ample junk-in-the-trunk up on him just like I told Lisa I was going to. Victor felt kind of large-and-in-charge if you know what I mean. Had a sista curious as George, wondering if he was carrying a bazooka in those funky blue plaid-patterned trousers of his. I gave him my number before leaving the club. He said he'd call, although I didn't believe him. You know the drill, ladies. If a man says he'll call you, he won't. Didn't matter. I wasn't pressed. I met him in a nightclub. Never the best setting for a love connection in my book anyway.

Well, surprise, surprise. Victor did call me. The very next day, in fact. Said he was dying to see me and wanted us to hook up that day. Now, I don't typically go out on a date with a guy the very next day after meeting him. (Just one of my little dating no-nos.) But what the hell? I was game. Willing to try anything once. What I wasn't game for was Victor's *idea* of a first date: coming over to my place and watching TV. (That brings me to another one of my dating no-nos: inviting men over to my house before getting to know them.) However, still in the spirit of trying anything once, I gave him the green light to come on over. Besides, Victor didn't strike me as a possible psychopath or anything. I asked him what time I could expect him. He said around 3:00 PM. That was, if I didn't mind picking him up from the Silver Spring Metro station, because his car wasn't running. *Say what?*

Naturally, I'm a bit taken aback by this request of his. I agree to pick him up anyway. Not sure why. That's a lie. I know exactly why I agreed to do it. A sista was bored out of her friggin' skull and really needed some male company! Victor said he'd call me on his cell phone when he was boarding the Blue Line at Addison Road. After he called, I timed my departure, knowing it would only take me about fifteen minutes to get to the Silver Spring station and at least thirty minutes for him to get there. I don't know where Victor actually was when he called me, but I doubt he was boarding the Blue Line at Addison Road like he said he was. I say this because I waited twenty minutes after his call before *leaving* my house, made it to Silver Spring in fifteen, then proceeded to sit in the park-and-ride another *thirty minutes* waiting for him to show. Eeew, I was fuming!

Anyways, Victor finally shows up and nonchalantly gets in my car. No "Sorry I'm late" or "The train was delayed"— nothing. But, he's looking good and smelling good. So much so that I quickly put aside my current annoyance that a) I had to pick him up from the train station and b) that I've been sitting in a park-and-ride a half hour waiting for him.

Chill, Bailey. You know how our people are when it comes to being on time. Leave it alone.

On the drive back to my condo, Victor asked if we could stop at a 7-Eleven. Said he was hungry and wanted a snack—"unless you've got something in the fridge to eat at your house," he said.

Say what?

I dropped him off at the 7-Eleven, feel me? I waited in the car. A minute or two later, Victor came out of the store and rapped on my car window.

"Um . . . can you loan me five bucks? I got two wallets at my crib, and I must've grabbed the wrong one when I broke out. I've only got about seven dollars on me and I still got to get home later. Man. How could I be so stupid? Sorry, Boo."

Boo?

Frankly, I was beginning to think *I* must've been the stupid one here. This muthafutta was really beginning to pluck my nerves. I was two seconds from driving his ass right back to the Metro station and forgetting about this so-called date. Anyways, I give him a five-spot and he goes back into the 7-Eleven. Returns shortly with two hot dogs and a large soda, gets in my car, and immediately starts throwing down. Doesn't even bother to ask if it's okay for him to eat in my car. Worse yet, doesn't even bother to offer me anything. And *my* money paid for it! Can you beat that?

Chill, Bailey. Leave it alone.

Next, I stopped at Blockbuster and rented a video. *Forrest Gump.* Didn't get to catch it in the movie theater, and neither had he. Once we got to my place, we preceded to get comfortable on the floor in front of my Toshiba 35-inch television. Victor got bored with the flick almost as soon as I put the tape in the VCR. (He obviously had other things in mind.) He asked if he could give me a back rub. Told me he's *famous* for his back rubs. That was the best suggestion to come out of his mouth so far today. Shit. He *owed* me a back rub for his earlier aggravation.

Victor's hands felt so good on my neck and shoulders.

From there, he slowly and methodically worked his way down to the bottom of my feet. Woo, Lawd, that mess got me horny. Pretty soon, I had forgotten all about *Forrest Gump,* too. That's because we were suddenly too busy tonguing and groping the hell out of one another. My hands went on a search to that place where I thought Victor might be hiding a concealed weapon. Found it. Yanked it out. *Day-um.* Victor had a bazooka indeed. And wouldn't you know. Just like that I couldn't remember any of what this man did to pluck my nerves just a short time ago.

Let me pause right here because I already know what some of you must be thinking. *Bailey Gentry, you sound like a fast, loose, floozy.* I'm not. Trust me. I'm a very intelligent black woman. In my professional life, I'm a whip. A hell of a young lawyer. I'm equally as sharp in most other aspects of life. *Most* others, I said. It's just that when it comes to men, I'm no different than a whole lot of you otherwise intelligent black women out there. I can do some *stupid* things. Got it? Good. Back to the story.

I was only partially naked at this juncture. Before getting butt-naked, I asked Victor if he had any condoms. (I may do stupid things at times, but I'm no dummy.) Bruh pulls a Trojan from his wallet with the quickness. Of course I found it interesting that Victor had no *money* in his wallet, but had plenty of *condoms* in it. Anyways, Victor and I never made it to my bedroom. We got butt-naked and busy right there on the floor in front of my Toshiba 35-inch TV—and *Forrest Gump.*

Now normally, this is the part where I'd tell you how ashamed I was for acting like a teenager and giving it up to this dude on our very first date. And normally I would—if Victor hadn't hit every spot just right! Ladies, this youngster had some kind of G-spot-locatin'-radar on that bazooka of his. His sexual prowess had a sista's toes curlin'. He hit it so good that when we finally finished going at it, I got up, went into the kitchen, and starting cooking dinner for him. Made *breakfast* for him the next morning, too!

It's kind of funny how great sex can make a woman forget all the inadequacies of a man. Then again, maybe it isn't really funny at all. And maybe "forget" isn't the adequate word here. *Overlook* may be the apropos. I say this because great sex had me overlooking a whole lot of shit where Victor was concerned. Too much.

For starters, I learned shortly after that first date of ours that God's gift to intercourse didn't even have his own place. He neglected to tell me that he shared his "crib" with a sister of his. In fact, the crib *belonged* to her.

And remember his car that was supposedly not running the day he asked me to pick him up from the metro station? Turns out, that belonged to his sister, too. And furthermore, the car *was* running. His sister simply wasn't letting him drive it anymore because he had gotten two speeding tickets and had a fender bender all in a span of two weeks.

Obviously, Victor and his sister weren't getting along too well in the weeks prior to us meeting. So naturally, he was spending more and more time at my place. I think I began feeling sorry for him. Or was I feeling sorry for myself? I don't know. Either way, I got it in my head that I wanted to be that "super sista" for Victor. You know that sista who helps a struggling brotha get his act together. That sista who takes "nothing" and turns it into "something." I started reasoning: *I'm a lawyer, I make good money.* My condo was big enough. Two bedrooms; two full baths. Furthermore, after many twelve-hour days at the office and coming home to no one in particular for

longer than I cared to recall, it felt good to come home
to a man—even a man who was less than ideal. Guess I
don't have to tell you what I ended up doing next, do I?
That's right. I let Victor move in with me. For that dumb
decision, I would end up supporting his sorry ass for
months. Why? Because I also learned something else
about Sweet-Dick Vic: The muthafutta couldn't keep a
job if his life depended on it!

Victor worked in construction, drywall being his
specialty—or so he claimed. Yeah, that's right, I even
gave the "professional black woman/blue-collar man"
thing a try. (A stretch for me, since I've always preferred
professional men.) But "Get a job today, lose a job tomorrow" was Victor's MO. And I'll be damned if it wasn't
the fault of "the man" every time that muthafutta found
himself out of work. "The Man" didn't know how to talk
to him. "The Man" wasn't giving him his proper respect.
"The Man" was against him from the jump. I got so tired
of hearing that bullshit!

One day, I secretly called Victor's sister. You know,
hoping she could shed some light on her brother—my
new man. She shed some light on him all right. Told me
he was pulling that same disappearing employment shit
when he was living with her, offered me her sympathies
now that he was "my problem," and hung up on me.

Look. Don't get me wrong here. It's not that I'm in-
sensitive to the struggle of the black male. Not at all. And
it's not mind-boggling to me that Victor *could* have been
having problems with "The Man." (By the way, as you
might suspect, "The Man" in this context refers to those
white folks that are running things.) I deal with "him"
everyday, too, and I hate it! But you know what? Bailey's
got to eat. Bailey's got to make her mortgage payments.
Bailey's got to pay back those student loans that got her

through law school. In other words, a sista does what a sista's got to do—in *spite* of "The Man."

Not my Victor. This was a concept totally foreign to him. And why wouldn't it be? He had no worries living with me. He had a roof over his head, food in his stomach, a firm Sealy Posturepedic to sleep on. He drove my car more than I did—and didn't even put gas in it half the time! This young'un was cold *chillin,'* you hear me? He wasn't *trying* to exert himself. It was nothing for me to come home in the evening and find Victor in the same position he was in when I left him earlier in the morning. Call him from the office and ask him to get dinner started, take out the garbage, or draw me a bubble bath when I came through the door exhausted and stressed, and you would think I had just asked him to give me a pint of his blood.

During those rare times when the brotha did have employment to go to, he'd break me off a little chump change for the cable or the phone bill—but that's about it. I didn't push, though. I was afraid that if I asked him to contribute more that he might leave. I didn't want that. Despite it all, I had become shamelessly addicted to the way he was putting it on me night in and night out.

So, if he wasn't carrying his weight under my roof, what was he doing with his money? you ask. Buying clothes. Victor would be in Georgetown almost every weekend, steppin' back in my house with shopping bags full of slacks, shirts, shoes, sneakers, designer sweatsuits. Mind you, *nothing* for me. Can you beat that? This muthafutta didn't have a pot to piss in or a window to throw it out, but no one would ever suspect as much if they saw him walking down the street. I sure fell for the illusion. Hook, line, and sinker.

Eventually, things with Victor became totally unworkable.

Not even great sex could make up for his lack of . . . well, *everything* else. I could have kicked myself for dating somebody like him in the first place. Here I am, an ambitious, responsible, attractive black woman with a career and goals. I deserved better. I should've listened to my girlfriend, Lisa. She told me Victor was nothing more than a male prostitute. That if I told him to bounce he'd simply find some other sista's kitty to tickle, turn her out, and presto! Have another woman taking care of him.

I finally came in out of the fog and put Victor's sorry ass out, almost a year from the day I met him. Went back to being manless. Hallucinating about good sex instead of having it.

3

Keith: Fast and Slow

Next up was Keith. An Adonis: six-foot-three; dark, good-looking, and articulate, with a great job as a mortgage banker. He worked out religiously and had the sexiest six-pack going on. I met him in a Safeway supermarket near my condo in Silver Spring. (Good thing I wasn't in the store looking busted that afternoon.) I was perusing the produce section when I spotted him squeezing some tomatoes. What a sight it was. It was the summer of '98 and steamy as all hell outside. Keith was clad in sweat shorts and a muscle shirt, showing off that gorgeous body of his. And I was just as turned on by what he *wasn't* wearing: A wedding band. Although, as fine as this man was, I'm not sure that a wedding band would have got in my way that day.

I'm kidding. Really.

Grandma Lucy Pearl used to say that a girl can't play cutesy all the time. There are moments when she's got to leave that passive, traditional stuff behind and grab the bull by the horns. That's exactly what I did. I made the first move. Took a deep breath, walked right up to this fine specimen, and struck up a conversation with him.

"You must be a man who's concerned with what he eats," was my opening line to him.

"I try to be," he laughed.

I took that as a good sign. He didn't look at me like I was retarded or ignore me all together.

"So do I," I replied. "Although I'm naughty every now and then. Love my Häagen Dazs mint chip. I'm Bailey, by the way."

"Keith. Nice to meet you. You live around here, Bailey? Don't think I've ever seen you before."

"I was about to ask you the same thing, Keith."

"I don't, but my kids do. They live over on Greencastle Road with their mother. We're divorced."

"Oh. Sorry to hear that." (Hmph. Like hell I was.)

"It was definitely for the best."

"You must work out quite a bit, Keith," I said, admiring his sexy body.

"I do a little som'um-som'um."

"Looks like you've been doing more than a *little* som'um-som'um to me," I giggled.

"I'm going to take that as a compliment, Bailey. So, you still didn't say. You live around here?"

"Yes, I do. Over at the Vineyards condominiums."

"Okay, I know where those are."

An awkward moment of silence followed, neither one of us knowing what to say next to keep the conversation going.

"So um, how 'bout you?" Keith asked, breaking that silence as we moved out of the produce section and into the canned-goods aisle. "Married? Kids?"

"No kids, never been married."

"Get out of here."

"What? Is that a good thing or bad thing?"

"I think it just means some lucky man hasn't snatched you up yet." That made me blush.

"Nope. Mr. Right hasn't knocked on my door or buzzed my intercom."

"Huh? . . . Ooh, I get it. That's funny."

Another moment of awkward silence.

What 'chu you waiting for, Keith? That was your cue to crack for the digits.

Instead of doing the very thing as I hoped he would, Keith turned his attention to a three-cans-for-a-dollar special on Del Monte peaches.

"Wow, this is a good deal. What do you think, Bailey?"

Groceries were the furthest thing from my mind right about now. Bruh was taking too long. I reached in my purse and took out a business card and pen.

"Let me give you my card." I scribbled my home number on the back of it. "Why don't you give me a call if you're ever in need of some legal advice . . . or even if you're not."

Keith placed my card up to his face and read it aloud.

"Bailey Gentry. Attorney-at-law. Jefferson, Bates, and Hankerson. Family law, huh? So, uh, you handle divorces and stuff like that."

"That and then some."

"Too bad I didn't know you when I was going through mine," he chuckled. I wasn't sure how to respond to that remark. "I'll give you a call, Bailey."

Now, that's what I wanted to hear. Although, "Here, take my number, too" would have been an even nicer thing to hear.

"You do that," I told him. "Maybe you can give a sista

some workout tips. I think I need a little inspiration to get back in the gym myself."

Keith gave me the once-over from head to toe.

"I hope you don't mind me saying this, but from where I'm standing, you don't look like you need a whole lot of time in the gym."

I didn't know whether he was being truthful, or just gassin' me up. Either way, it was all good. Ladies, this one seemed *real* promising.

Things got off to a rousing start for Keith and me. For one thing, our first date was a *real* one. We had dinner at Houston's on Rockville Pike. Keith had the roasted chicken, and I had the Chicken & Friends. In addition to that handsome face and sexy body, the brotha's conversation was all that, too. This was not another Victor. Keith had it going on vertically. And it was so refreshing to discover we had a few things in common right off the bat. Keith owned a condo, too; we were both professionals, we were the same age, thirty-three; and both Geminis.

During dinner, Keith got serious on me for a minute. Scared the mess out of me is more like it. He told me he really believed in honesty and that there was something I should know about him up front. I think my heart stopped beating for a few seconds. Keith told me he was seeing someone. Whew! Believe it or not, I was actually relieved to hear that 'cause for a second there, I thought the brotha was going to tell me he was gay or bisexual. Been there, done that, and got the T-shirt already. Anyways, I didn't fret Keith's revelation. What for? He took my number when I offered it to him, didn't he? He called me when I asked him to, didn't he? The two of us were in Houston's having dinner, weren't we? Please. How committed could he have been to this chick he was seeing? Whoever she was.

Keith and I didn't work far from one another in downtown D.C. A few days after we had dinner, we started meeting at lunchtime and working out at a health club on M Street whenever our busy schedules permitted. If not at work, then Keith would come over on the weekends, and we'd work out in the gym at my condo complex. I loved watching him pump iron. Gave me goose bumps! Sometimes I'd catch myself daydreaming about him at work. Daydreaming of us making sweet love under the sheets. Daydreaming of us making pretty babies together. Keith had me glowing. I had finally met a gainfully employed brotha, straight, drama-free, the right height, weight, and skin tone—dark chocolate. Yes, the total package. (Not an easy thing to find in D.C.) And this woman he was seeing? Well, all of a sudden, things weren't quite "working out" between them anymore. (Hmmm, wonder why.) Keith and I were spending so much time together that unless he was a magician capable of being in two places at the same time, he wasn't seeing anybody but me now. Everything was just perfect.

Well, almost everything.

Not to seem overly picky here (although if you ask my girlfriend, Lisa, she'll say I *am* overly picky) there was one thing I found disturbing about Keith. To use an analogy here, if the speed limit of our relationship was fifty-five, I was in the left lane doing seventy. Keith on the other hand, was way over in the right, sputtering along at forty-five. What I'm trying to say is, the brotha was "affectionately slow." Slow about kissing me. Slow about touching me. Slow about you name it. In nearly six weeks of dating, Keith hadn't even made an *attempt* to feed the cat. I wasn't going to press the issue, though. Sure, I took the bull by the horns that day in the supermarket, but I wasn't about to do the same when it came to the two of us being intimate for the first time. That was something *he* was going to have to initiate. Well, that was the plan, at least until one afternoon following a workout at my condo complex.

Keith and I usually showered at the gym before heading over to my place, where I'd make lunch for us. On this particular day, there was a plumbing problem in the facility so we had to shower over at my place instead. Oh darn! What a (pleasant) inconvenience, huh? When we got to my place, I asked Keith if he wanted to jump in the shower first. He insisted I go first. So, I did. As the warm water caressed my body, I lathered up, closed my eyes, and put my head under the shower nozzle. I fantasized that Keith would bust into my bathroom and rip back the shower curtain. I'd drop the Ivory soap in surprise, cover my small, perky breasts, and let out a faint scream. With a feverish look of passion in his eyes, he'd peel my hands away from my breasts, step back, and marvel at my naked body, soaking wet and covered with soapsuds. Next, he'd get out of his sweaty workout clothes and join me in the shower where he would proceed to ravage me from head to toe.

Wooo, Lawd, did that fantasy get a sista horny. I quickly finished up in the shower and patted my body dry. Wrapped a small towel around me—which barely covered my breasts and ass—and admired how cute I looked in the mirror before stepping out of the bathroom.

"Your turn," I shouted to Keith. "Let me get you a towel and washcloth." If you could've seen the look on that man's face when he got a glimpse of me dressed in only a Wamsutta towel. It was just the reaction I was hoping for. I handed Keith a towel and washcloth.

"Have fun," I told him.

Why tease him like that, you ask? Simple. I wanted him in that shower fantasizing about me the way I had just been about him. I wasn't done just yet, either. For the proverbial "cherry on top," I accidentally on purpose let the towel I was wearing come loose and fall to my ankles. (*Oops!*)

That sure got Keith's slow ass to pick up the pace. Without saying another word, he pulled my naked body into his, letting me feel his hardness as he slipped his tongue into my mouth. After savoring the sweet taste of each other's mouths for a few moments, I helped him get out of his sweaty workout clothes. I wanted Keith right then and there. Just like he was. Sweaty and funky. I think he was a little too conservative for that, though. Not a problem. I simply jumped back in the shower with him and scrubbed his sexy body from head to toe. After that, it was off to my Sealy Posturepedic.

Okay. If you're figuring this sounds too good to be true, you're absolutely correct. *It was.* Keith turned out to be an *enormous* disappointment. Horizontally speaking. The sex was . . . well, in a nutshell, p-a-t-h-e-t-i-c! Keith only knew one speed in bed. *Fast.* Kind of ironic given how *slow* he was in the execution of other aspects of affection. There was never ever any foreplay with bruh. And when I say never, a sista means *never!* Keith would just dive into the pool whether it had water in it or not. That's so not cool. And the sex was always predictably unpredictable. Sometimes he'd blast off in two minutes flat. Other times, he'd bang away inside of me for what seemed like hours. Two minutes, two hours—didn't matter. The affect on me was always the same. *Zilch.* Oh, and that "bigger is better" theory? Fuhgitaboutit. Nothing's more irritating than a brotha with a yardstick and not a *clue* what to do with it. Call me crazy, but I'd rather have a bruh with a Twinkie, a little technique, and a whole lot of imagination any day of the week.

Since Keith wasn't getting the job done via, shall we say, "conventional" methods, I figured it was time to try a different approach. A sista ain't never been too prissy to get on her knees and handle her business. Feel me? I will say, to Keith's credit, he was always willing and ready to reciprocate me in this regard. Regrettably, his reciprocation was equally p-a-t-h-e-t-i-c! A few times there, I thought he was going to *literally* eat me out. Mess around down there and gobble up something I needed for real!

Oh, why me? *Why me?* I mean, what were the odds of a perfect, physical specimen like this man turning out to be a complete *dud* in the sack? I was really feeling him, too. Keith moved me mentally and was easy on the eyes. Damn was he easy on the eyes. I thought about it . . . and thought about it some more. Maybe I was just being silly. Had my priorities all screwed up. I mean, sex isn't everything, right? At least I had a *good* black man, right?

Bad sex and all, I really think on some level this relationship would have still worked for me if not for Keith's one and only misfortune: being next batter up after I had been sexually turned out by Victor. Keith just couldn't make the kitty purr. Not even a little bit. So despite his vertical aptitude and impressive packaging, like Victor, I had to kick him to the curb, too. A few days shy of his ninety-day probation period. Boy, did it hurt to do so.

4

Myron: He's Gotta Have It

Then along came Myron, the last relationship I was in, three years ago and counting.

Myron was an online hookup. Met him on one of those black websites; "black-something-or-another." Don't even remember anymore. Frankly, I wasn't too keen on the whole Internet thing. Trying to meet someone in that forum always reeked of desperation, in my book. But desperate times call for desperate measures. And a sista was feeling . . . well, you get the idea. So, I joined the site and set up a personal profile complete with photo:

Thirty-four-year-old, single black female, attractive, sexy, 5'5, 150 lbs. Seeking single professional black male in the D.C. metropolitan area for a serious and monogamous relationship. Must be between the ages of 30 and 40, 6' or taller, and weight proportionate to height. My interests

include reading, dancing, going to plays, and dining out,
to name just a few. Luv to hear yours. No photo, no reply.

I was pleasantly surprised when I logged on to my
computer three days later to discover that I had received
over twenty responses to my personal ad. I poured myself
a glass of wine, sat down in front of the computer, and
one by one began reading through them with excited
anticipation. A few I'd described as "chain replies."
Idiots just on the prowl for some e-booty. Delete. Got a
few reponses from brothas in correctional facilities
across the U.S. (Whoa. Internet access in prison?) While
I felt for those bruhs doing time, there wasn't a whole
hell of a lot they were going to be able to do for me, now,
was there? Delete. Got a few responses from men as old
as Methuselah. Delete. Instead of attaching a photo like
I requested in my ad, some e-mailed me saying things
like, "You won't be disappointed when you see me," or
"Click on this link and blah, blah, blah." Just attach a
damn photo already! Delete. Now some did include
photos of themselves—*in their birthday suits.* Can you beat
that? These as you can probably guess were also pretty
vulgar in nature. Telling me how they want to stick their
this and that in my this and that. Yuck! Pervert muthafuttas. Delete.

By far though, the most intriguing response came from
a guy named Myron. He described himself as a professional black male, thirty-eight years old, six-two, 210
pounds, tall, dark, and handsome. *Yummy,* I'm thinking
before opening his JPEG and kinda hoping this brotha *is*
in his birthday suit. Just kidding. (Uh, not really.)

I eagerly opened the attachment to see how accurate
Myron's self-assessment of his appearance was. Let me
say right off the bat that he was fully dressed. He looked

tall in the picture. Dark? Yes. Handsome? Mmm, no. Myron wrote in his e-mail that he lived in Laurel and worked as a systems analyst for a software firm in Rockville. *Cool*, I'm thinking. *A professional brotha and a local one at that.* That said, I opted not to jump the gun and judge him solely on a single snapshot. Maybe he just wasn't the photogenic type. Or maybe he was simply the beneficiary of a bad camera angle or something. Anyways, Myron and I began e-mailing each other back and forth pretty regularly until we both felt there was enough interest to warrant a meet-and-greet beyond cyberspace.

I suggested a very public place. Happy hour at Jasper's in Greenbelt. I've heard too many horror stories about women disappearing without a trace after clandestine meetings with guys they've met online. A sista wasn't going out like that. I even brought Lisa along for additional security. (And as an excuse to make an early exit if I wasn't feeling this dude.) Myron did look a little better in person than he did in his photo. He was still a long way from eye candy, though. He didn't have the fashion sense of Victor and definitely not the body of Keith. And he'd either sent me an old photo or purposely underestimated (or flat-out lied) about his weight. He was a bit on the overweight side, though I couldn't be too critical of him on that note. This was right around the time I was beginning to put on a few unwanted pounds myself. Besides, a guy can be a little chunky and still have it going on, can't he? You know, like that singer Gerald Lavert. Ladies, is he one fat, sexy teddy bear or what?

I could tell Myron was a little disappointed that I'd brought Lisa with me. Especially, since I didn't tell him I'd be bringing a friend. The three of us got a table and ordered an appetizer of chicken fingers and fries while we got acquainted. I was pretty impressed with Myron. He could hold a decent conversation, spoke clearly and articulately, didn't use words that aren't words, like "conversate," or mispronounce words that end in "ed," like "look-did" instead of "looked." He talked mostly about his job and balanced the conversation nicely by showing a sufficient interest in mine as well. He was also very cordial to Lisa, even though I know her presence was bummin' him out. That right there told me he knew the art of making lemonade out of a lemon-like situation. A half hour into the date, Myron had me at ease. I felt totally comfortable enough to give Lisa her cue to split. I could go one-on-one from here.

In next to no time at all, Myron had grown on me to the point where I knew I wanted to be in an exclusive relationship with him. And all that stuff I said about his appearance earlier, fuhgitaboutit. The brotha was even beginning to look *good* to me. The feeling was mutual— not me looking good to him, that was never an issue— his wanting an exclusive relationship, that is. Vertically, Myron and I were clicking. And while I'll admit that he was no Victor in bed, he was handling his horizontal responsibilities creditably enough. No sexual horror stories to relate like there were when I was with Keith.

In a nutshell, things were going good. Better than good. Naturally—given the way my love life tends to go—that just meant something was about to go wrong.

It all began the evening Myron invited me to a house party in D.C. Said it was time for him to show me off. Good. I felt like being shown off. We had been together for about two months at this point, and this party would mark our official steppin' out as a couple. Myron told me the guests at the party would be a mix of his friends and business associates and that they had these type of get-togethers every month or so. He said they were always casual, laid-back affairs. So I wore a pair of hip-huggin' jeans that accentuated my getting-plump yet still sexy ass, tied my long braids in a ponytail, and dabbed on just a touch of makeup.

The two of us pulled up to an apartment building in the 600 block of G Street SW around 8:00 PM and took the elevator up to the sixth floor. Myron rang the doorbell of unit number 619. A thin bro with really neat dreads and a salt-and-pepper goatee let us in. Guess it was his place. To this day, I don't really know. We stepped inside an immaculately decorated apartment done up in the dominant color scheme of almond and burgundy. There was leather furniture throughout the pad that smelled brand-new, and big live plants set off nicely by an impressive array of African art that adorned the walls. Coconut incense filled the air, cool jazz played on a top-notch Harmon Kardon sound system, and on a chic glass coffee table in the middle of the room lay a mouth-watering array of hors d'oeuvres.

Myron took me around the room and introduced me to everyone. I'd say about a fifty-fifty mix of guys and dolls. Myron's circle of friends ran the gamut of professional occupations: lawyers, CPAs, bankers, computer geeks and geekettes. At first, I was quite impressed with this room full of professional, articulate black people. However, my good initial impression changed quick, fast, and in a hurry. That happened right around the moment they broke out the reefer and began getting sparked. And just like that, I found myself in a room full of professional, articulate *potheads*.

One of the numerous joints being passed around the room found its way to my honey's lips, as I sat next to Myron on the sofa consuming one Swedish meatball after another. He took a long, slow drag and let out an "aaah." (Guess it was some very *good* weed.) Myron never told me he smoked—cigarettes or anything else. He didn't even *look* right smoking. Anyways, when he finished puffin', he stuck the joint in my face like he *knew* I was with it, too. Now, I hadn't smoked weed since trying it for the first time my freshman year in high school. I remember the day vividly. One toke and I was hacking and coughing like I had tuberculosis.

"You smoke, Bailey?" Myron asked.

(Now, is it just me, or do you think that's a question he should have asked me *before* sticking that shit in my face?) What I should have done at that moment was answer his question with an emphatic "no." Instead, I caught a sudden attack of teenage-like peer pressure at thirty-something. Ain't that a trip? Not wanting to appear the lone "L7" in the room, I took a toke—and began hackin' and coughing like I had tuberculosis all over again, the same way I did back in high school. I was *so* embarrassed. Wished that I could have blinked my eyes and disappeared like that chick on *I Dream of Jeannie.* Served my ass right, I guess.

In retrospect, I could have probably dealt with Myron and his buddies smoking a little weed every now and then—if that's *all* they did. Unfortunately, it was only a prelim. The hors d'oeuvre before the main entrée: coke—and I don't mean the stuff that comes in red aluminum cans, either. I may as well have been in a room full of pigs there was so much snortin' going on. To say I was appalled by this scene would be an understatement. But you want to know what appalled me even more? How blasé Myron and his friends were going about it. They kept right on eating, drinking, and conversing like doing coke was hardly a thing. And Myron?

Let me tell you. His ass had a rolled-up dead president under his nose going to town!

Ain't this a muthafutta? I'm dating Pablo Escobar.

I tried hard as I could not to let my shock and dismay show on the outside. Inside, I was furious. Furious at Myron for not telling me about this little thing that he does. Furious that he didn't at least give me a heads-up that drug use would be going on at this party. Furious at his utter lack of respect for me at the moment. Most of all, furious at all these professional, articulate black people defiling their bodies. In thirty-four years on this earth, I had never been friends with, dated, or socialized with anyone who used drugs of any kind. And in case you're wondering, peer pressure wasn't getting the best of me twice in one evening. Nothing was going up my nostrils but oxygen.

The ride home in Myron's Land Cruiser was pretty quiet. I doubt he even noticed that I was perturbed with him. I wanted to hold my tongue—but that's awfully difficult for me to do. (I'm a *black* woman, remember?) Part of me was hoping he would apologize or at least explain what I had just witnessed. Neither of those things happened, so I *had* to say something. Still very angry and confused, I was cautious of my tone and measured my words carefully.

"Myron."

"Yeah, baby?"

"I didn't know you did coke."

"I'm just a recreational user," he said. "Only do it now and then. But don't worry; I don't mess around with any *serious* drugs."

Now maybe I'm just naïve. Or perhaps I was really a blonde underneath those cornrow extensions. But duh! Is coke not a *serious* drug? Recreational or not, I was not thrilled. *Think, Bailey, do you really want to stir the pot when things are going so good between you two? Chill. Let it go.*

Against my better judgment, I did just that. I refrained from questioning Myron any further about his "recreational" drug use.

Allow me to digress a moment. As a family lawyer, I listen to sordid stories of marital discord, child-support issues, abuse, and more, daily. And though I love what I do, there are some days quite honestly when I'm just not in the mood for it. Such was the case one particular afternoon. A client of mine canceled her appointment, which gave me an unexpected break in my day. Boy, did I welcome the downtime. You see, I had Myron and that party we attended heavy on my brain. I closed the door to my office, kicked off my Via Spigas, took a legal pad out of my desk drawer, and drew a line down the center of it. To the left, I jotted down the reasons I was with Myron. The first thing I jotted down was that he was a black man—a must—because nothing but a black man would do for me. He treated me very well. We both wanted marriage and at least one child. He was gainfully employed, owned a home and car, and earned a six-figure income. And, he wasn't intimidated (like a lot of black men I've come across) by a black woman who had a home, car, and six-figure income also.

On the right, I wrote down things I *didn't* like about Myron. Found myself writing the same three words over and over from the top of the page to the bottom of it: *Myron uses drugs.* Clearly, this exercise confirmed that there was only one issue in the way of my being totally happy with this man. And in this day and age of relationship drama, just one sounded pretty damn good to me.

I glanced down at the legal pad and what I had just written on it again. Moved my eyes back and forth across the page and questioned if I should let that one negative on the right nullify all those positives about Myron on the left. Next—and I hate to say it—I fell into that old, destructive pattern of "sista behavior." I'm sure more than a few of you ladies can attest. It goes something like this. After searching long and hard for that needle in a haystack (that good black man), you finally find one that seems to be the perfect match for you. Then, out of the blue, you learn something about him that "just ain't right." But because the pickings to find this man were so slim to begin with, rather than face it, you look for an excuse—or excuses—to make that something about him that "just ain't right," seem "perfectly okay." Sound familiar?

For starters, I never even told Lisa about Myron's little drug habit, and I tell her everything. I didn't because I knew she'd only give me some sound and rational advice I really wasn't trying to hear. After the fiascoes with Victor and Keith, I *really* wanted this relationship with Myron to work out. Like Bobby Caldwell sang: *what we won't do for love.* I convinced myself that Myron wasn't a drug user because a drug user is the kind of guy I would *never* be with. My rationale? He said he only used the stuff *now and then.* If Myron were a real drug user, I theorized, he'd be smoking crack and selling his furniture or stealing money out of my Coach bag in order to buy more. Of course, he wasn't doing any of that, which only helped to support my ridiculous reasoning. I knew in my head and heart that it didn't make a darn bit of sense. Is a man not a rapist if he only rapes now and then? Is a man not a murderer if he only kills now and then? Of course not. My boyfriend was a clean-cut, white-collar drug user. Plain and simple. And it was time for me to get my head out of the sand and deal with this. Good thing I did because it soon became evident that Myron's drug use wasn't as "recreational" as he would have me believe. Our relationship would get to a point where he couldn't seem to get through an entire week without doing some lines.

The straw that broke the camel's back occurred when we were having sex, of all things. Right smack dab in the midst of gettin' it on, Myron inexplicably stopped, excused himself, got out of bed, and ran into the bathroom. I didn't know what to make of his peculiar behavior. Maybe he wasn't feeling well, was the only explanation I could think of. I clasped my hands together under my head, lay back in bed, and waited for him to return, hoping my coochie wouldn't get dry before he did.

Five minutes go by. Ten minutes go by. Myron's still in the bathroom. Concerned, I got out of bed to check on him. You wouldn't believe what I saw when I opened the bathroom door: Myron sitting on the toilet and snorting coke off of a small piece of aluminum foil. I cold lost it!

"Uh-uh. You'd rather hit *that* than hit *this*?" I screamed, directing his attention to my big, naked, voluptuous, round, brown ass. In a fit of reactionary anger, I slapped his white, powdery lover out of his hand. Boy, was that the *wrong* thing for me to do.

"What the . . . you see that on the floor, Bailey? That shit cost me money!" Bruh was hotter than July.

"So what are you going to do about it?" I asked, with much 'tude. "Get on your hands and knees and sniff it off the bathroom floor?"

"What is your fuck-*ing* problem, Bailey?"

Note, he didn't say "fuckin'" problem. He said, "fuck-*ing*" problem. As if he wanted to make sure I got the *full* emphasis of his question. Before this moment, Myron *never* talked to me like this.

"*My* problem? Baby, why are you defiling your body with that shit?"

"Don't act like it's a surprise to you."

"No, it's not a surprise—anymore. I still don't like it."

"Then why haven't you voiced your opinion about it? You do about *everything* else."

Bruh had a point there.

"You're right, Myron. I should have voiced my displeasure with your little habit weeks ago. But I didn't. So, I'm doing it now. And I'm going to start off by saying I felt you disrespected me big-time at that party when you and your friends decided to get drugged up in front of me. Did it ever occur to you *that* might have made me uncomfortable?"

"I'm sorry about that, Bailey. I should have said something to them. I wasn't thinking. But, I'll repeat myself. You should have pulled me aside and voiced your feelings at that time. Not now, *weeks* later. All I can tell you is that what you saw that evening has never been a big deal to me or my friends. It's not like we do it all the time."

"What's *all the time*, Myron? 'Cause lately, you can't seem to get through a week without putting something up your nose."

He looked at me like I was the craziest bitch he had ever laid eyes on. Sucked his teeth, got up off the toilet, walked back into the bedroom, and stretched out on the bed where we had been making sweet love just moments earlier.

"This conversation is over, Bailey. I don't answer to you. You're my girlfriend, not my *wife*. Understand? Besides, I was doing what I do long before I met you."

"So what are you saying, Myron? You're going to keep on doing it?"

"That'll be *my* choice now won't it? Let me ask you

something. Is my 'little habit,' as you call it, keeping me from functioning day to day? Has it stopped me from performing on my day job—or my *night* job? Is it causing me to treat you any differently? Allow me to answer that for you. No, no, and no. Everybody's got a little som'um-som'um they like to put in their bodies to make them feel good. Yours happens to be ice cream. Mine happens to be coke and weed, okay? At least I can say my little som'um isn't going to my thighs!"

No he didn't. . . .

"Get over it, Bailey," was Myron's final word to me on the matter.

I got over it all right. Got over Myron, too.

Eventually.

5

Lisa Parker-Taylor:
My Best Friend

That's enough with the most recent losers in my life.
Y'all are getting me depressed all over again.

I just got off the phone with Lisa a short time ago. She
and I have been best friends since the third grade. We
grew up together on the same block of 13th and Hamilton Street, NW, in D.C. Lisa's got a flawless honey-brown
complexion and wears her hair in one of those short, natural boy cuts. I think she resembles Jada Pinkett Smith,
myself. She'll disagree vehemently with you if you tell her
that, though. As if looking like Jada is a *bad* thing. She's
real petite, about a size four, no more than a buck ten
soakin' wet, and with a set of titties on her that belong on
a woman twice her size. I swear I don't know how that girl
stays upright hauling around that amount of luggage on
such a tiny frame. She began developing those things
pretty early on in life—like in elementary school. Oh

man, how the neighborhood boys used to tease her merci-lessly back in the day. Nowadays, men just gawk and drool over them (and she loves it). I tell Lisa all the time: I wish I had just *half* of what you're working with. She in turn wishes I could break her off a piece of some of this ass I'm towing around.

After graduating from high school, Lisa went south to Spelman to study finance. I opted to stay closer to home and pursue a law degree at Howard. Lisa wasn't feeling "Hotlanta" as much as she thought she would. So after two years, she dropped out of college, came back to D.C., and took a job as a mortgage processor with Fannie Mae. Our relationship picked right back up where it left off. It was though we were never apart.

Boy, were we two young divas back in the day (or at least, no one could tell us we weren't). We worked hard and played even harder. Never met a party we didn't like. We'd practically open and close the Ritz nightclub on E Street every weekend. And we never missed any of those local outdoor festivals in the summertime like The Taste of D.C., the Black Family Reunion, or Artscape, held up in Baltimore. We just loved struttin' around like peacocks, and driving guys crazy in an array of sexy sum-mertime outfits that accentuated our finer assets. And we were some kind of picky when it came to brothas. Not the least bit ashamed of it either. We dated pretty regu-larly and would break some of the luckier guys off a little som'um-som'um from time to time. But don't get it twisted. We were hardly hoochies, okay? Just two vibrant sistas enjoying their womanhood to the fullest extent possible.

Like most young women our age, we each had our prize package in mind. Lisa's was landing a professional athlete clockin' seven figures, so she could quit her job, have a few babies, and start her own catering business out of their six-bedroom mansion somewhere in an exclusive gated community in suburbia. She scuttled that box of heaven quickly enough when she figured out what other sistas with a similar craving already knew: Nine out of ten seven-figure-earning black athletes prefer white women.

My prize package wasn't quite as over-the-top as hers. Least, I don't think so. I simply wanted some dark, Godiva chocolate, six-three or taller, better than average looking, white-collar, with loot equal to or greater than mine. Hmmm. Do you think that's asking for too much? Hope not, 'cause a sista's *still* waiting for that particular box of chocolate to knock on her door or buzz her intercom.

I must admit, when it comes to men, Lisa's been a lot more flexible than I have over the years. She's never been afraid to step outside of her comfort zone. She's always been the voice of reason in our friendship, too. Lisa believes that a person's soul mate only comes along once in a lifetime—twice, if they're really lucky. Everyone else is just passing through for one reason or another according to her. She also had these words of wisdom for me when it came to men: "Don't get caught short, Bailey. Mr. Right doesn't always come to us the way we think he will. What we got to do is *recognize* the package however it comes, or else one day we're going to find ourselves sitting around frustrated, getting fat, and bitching about why it is we ain't got nobody as our biological clocks tick, tick, tick away."

That frequent—and I do mean frequent—admonition of hers always seemed like a whole lot of "what-eva" and "tell it to somebody who cares."

Lisa, shut up already!

Surely that was not going to happen to me. I used to

scoff at things other sista's would lose sleep over. The proverbial "black-male shortage" for one thing. Couldn't tell me I wouldn't get what I wanted, when I wanted it, how I wanted it. Right about now, though, as I'm knocking on the door of the big 4-0, I'm beginning to believe that Ms. Yacka-dee-yack may have been on to something after all.

Lisa's got what I want. Something as hard to find these days as the solution to a Chinese calculus question: a good black man. She and her boyfriend Maurice finally tied the knot five years ago after living together in Largo, Maryland for several years. She met her Mr. Right in the café car of an Amtrak train, of all places. This occurred when the two of them were headed back to D.C. from separate business trips in New York. Mo, as we call him, was hardly what Lisa had in mind. At a mere five feet, six inches, Mo, she found, was vertically challenged. Lisa *never* dated guys under six feet. She's five-two, so, she's eye-to-eye with Mo when she's in a pair of her Stu Weitzman's. That took her some getting used to. Furthermore, Mo was light skinned. Lisa was cuckoo for cocoa puffs. Yet, to hear her tell it, bruh was a smoothie. She said she was unexplainably turned on by the way Mo confidently rolled up on her in the café car of the train that day. He didn't come at her with any of that okey-doke bullshit she was so tired of tired-ass brothas slinging her way. After offering to pick up the tab on her ham-and-cheese sandwich, he walked Lisa back to her seat on the train and actually gave the passenger sitting next to her twenty dollars to find somewhere else to sit. She thought that was so cute. She found Mo's conversation from Penn Station to Union Station that afternoon totally stimulating—rare for a lot of the brothas she had been meeting. He was three years older than her, worked as an account executive for an advertising agency, and owned a home.

Yes, Maurice Taylor was a lot fairer than Lisa liked, and six inches shorter than she preferred. Still, he was handsome, employed, and oozed that all-important thing we sistas crave in a man: *Potential.* As Lisa put it, bruh had it going on vertically *and* horizontally. My best friend can be a prima donna at times, but she's never been anybody's fool.

Now, let me say that Mo's not perfect. He has his moments. (What man doesn't?) He can be a piece of work at times and get on Lisa's last friggin' nerve—mine too. But since that day they met on that Amtrak train, I know he has always made Lisa feel like the most important woman in the world. Now if only shorty had a brother six to eight inches taller for his wife's best friend, ya think?

Yes, Lisa's been with me through some crazy if not enlightening times. One time some eight years ago particularly comes to my mind. What a whirlwind chapter it was for me—personally *and* professionally. Met a man who showed me that love and relationships can sometimes be as daunting as removing the lid on a box of the unknown. And a client who made me see that you may be surprised at what you find when you do.

I just wish I had the time to tell y'all all about it. Wait. What am I saying? It's New Year's Eve and a sista's got no particular place to go. I've got nothing but time.

That said, settle in and get comfortable, while I take y'all back to that point in my life and tell the story of how it all went down.

MAY 1994

6

Jefferson, Bates, and Hankerson

There's one thing about being a family-law attorney: It certainly gives one an interesting insight into the trials and tribulations of relationships. For a minimum of three days out of the week, I was seated behind my desk listening to the sordid details of couples who, once madly in love, were now bitter enemies putting one another through all sorts of hell. Frankly, it could get kind of depressing. When I was fresh out of law school, this career choice had me telling myself I'd *never* get married. I don't feel like that anymore. Every now and then I simply have to remind myself that I'm an attorney whose job is to provide people with the best legal services regardless of my personal feelings. That's what they pay me a good penny to do. And besides, their issues don't *have* to be mine, right?

My client demographic was mostly female, twenty-five

to thirty-five years of age. Most seeking a divorce. Truthfully, I don't understand how some of those women got hooked up with the fools they now came to me to get rid of. Then again, maybe I shouldn't be that surprised. It's not like I hadn't been with a few straight-up fools myself. Guess my saving grace had been that I hadn't married any of them, or worse, had their babies. Grandma Lucy Pearl used to say that the only thing worse than not having a man at home is having a *crazy* man at home. And boy, was she speaking from experience. Grandpa Milton, her late husband, was one crazy muthafutta. (God rest his soul.) Man, when I think back on all the stories she used to tell me about him before she passed away. Whew! They'd make my head spin. That ornery man made my grandmama's marriage a living hell for forty-four years.

Don't know about you, but it seems to me that women back in my grandma's day sure put up with an inordinate amount of shit from the men in their lives. Husband's having affairs, multiple babies out of wedlock with multiple women, squandering hard earned money, drinking too doggone much. Had to be some *strong* sistas to turn the other cheek to all of that just for the sake of keeping the family together. Divorce wasn't an option back in those days. When folks stood before a minister and said "I do," it was truly "until death do us part."

Hmph. Not those Nineties sistas that waltzed in and out of JB&H each week. Oh, no. They came in here with much 'tude. Weren't putting up with nothing—family or no family. Case in point, my client who was waiting out in the reception area to see me one day. Her name was Rose Braxton. I hit the intercom and asked Monifah Jenkins—JB&H's flirtatious and ghetto-fabulous receptionist—to send her in.

"How are you today, Mrs. Braxton? Please, have a seat."

"Thank you, Ms. Gentry."

Mrs. Braxton was in her late twenties, like me. About a size-six frame, tight and curvy in all the right places. Cocoa-brown skin, high cheekbones, and gorgeous brown eyes that made me jealous they didn't belong to me. The hair and nails were hooked. Made me wonder what type of a man would want to mistreat such an attractive woman.

"What's been going on since we last spoke, Mrs. Braxton?"

"Same ol' same ol'. I'm just trying to get away from my husband, Ms. Gentry. He's a nutcase. Has my nerves on edge twenty-four–seven."

"Sorry to hear that. I was going over some notes from our initial consultation. I understand you're seeking sole custody of the child you have together."

"Correct."

"Your son's name and age?"

"Andre. He's five."

"Are you absolutely opposed to a joint-custody agreement with your husband?"

"Ab-so-lute-ly!"

"May I ask why?"

"Where would you like me to start?" she sighed.

"Anywhere you'd like, Mrs. Braxton."

"For starters—in addition to all his other bullshit—I've learned my husband has fathered three other children besides the one he's had with me. And that's three *during* the course of our marriage, I might add. One of those kids is the same age as our son. Can you believe that shit? That nigga had me and some other bitch pregnant at the same time!"

I wanted to say to Mrs. Braxton, that yes, I could believe

it. I'd heard that and much worse sitting behind this desk. Of course, that would have been inappropriate. Sort of like her tone at the moment.

"Uh, Mrs. Braxton—"

"Can you call me, Rose, please? That 'Mrs. Braxton' is beginning to work my nerves. That's *his* name. It's not gonna be mine too much longer if I can help it."

"Very well. Rose, while I understand your frustration, as your lawyer I'm going to have to ask you to cool it with the name-calling, okay? I'd hate for something like that to slip out of your mouth if we're before a judge."

"I'm sorry."

"Do you know whether or not your husband is providing financial support to any of these other children you claim he's fathered?"

"I doubt it. He's hardly supporting me and my son."

"What is your husband's occupation?"

"Drug dealer."

"Your husband's a drug dealer."

"Correct."

"He has no formal job."

"Oh, he's got a 'formal' job, if that's what you want to call it. He works at the post office. He's still selling drugs, though."

I made a note of that on my legal pad before resuming my questioning.

"Are you seeking child support or alimony?"

"Yes."

"Which?"

"Both."

"During our initial consultation, you mentioned that you felt your husband was stalking you. Tell me more about that, please."

"Well, I asked him to leave the house, and that's when the physical and verbal abuse started up all over again—"

"He's been abusive towards you in the past?"

"Has he. It got so bad that one night I planned on waiting until he went to sleep, getting a knife out of the kitchen, and pulling a *Lorena Bobbitt* on his ass. I was seriously gonna cut his—"

"Uh, I get it, Rose. I get it."

"Oops. Sorry again, Ms. Gentry. It's just that . . . that man makes me so . . ."

"I understand. Really, I do. Why don't you sit back, take a deep breath, compose yourself, and finish telling me about this stalking business." I handed Rose a couple of tissues to intercept the tears that had begun forming in the corners of her eyes.

"Like I was saying, Sydney, my soon-to-be-ex-husband, refused to leave the house when I asked him to. So one day while he was at work, I called in sick, packed up as many of my personal belongings as I could, and Andre's, and went to stay with a girlfriend of mine."

"Where does your girlfriend reside?"

"In an apartment complex on Eastern Avenue in Takoma Park."

"Okay. Continue."

"Somehow he found out I was staying with her. So he starts popping up over her house at odd hours of the day and night demanding to see me. If I didn't oblige, he'd make a public nuisance of himself until he got his way. It got so bad one day that someone in my girlfriend's apartment complex called the cops on him. After that, she told me I couldn't stay with her anymore. The constant drama was more than she signed up for. She didn't want any problems with other tenants in the building, or the management, for that matter. Can't say I blamed her."

"So, where are you living now?"

"I'm renting an apartment in Forestville."

"How's that working out?"

"On my salary alone and with a young child, it's tough. Real tough. But at least he doesn't know where I'm staying. But I've got another big problem."

"What is that?"

"Sydney's come up to my job a few times looking for me and demanding that I tell him where me and Andre are staying. Luckily for me, he hasn't been acting like a belligerent fool when he does. Not in front of my coworkers anyway. So far I've been able to hide the reason for his frequent visits to my place of employment. I don't need those folks at my job in my business like that. But I don't think I'm going to be able to keep the real reason for his visits a secret for too much longer. I'm really getting worried, Ms. Gentry. Sydney's fool ass already got me kicked out of my girlfriend's place. I'm afraid he's gonna get me fired from my job next. I can't afford to lose my job over this shit. Can I take out a restraining order on his ass?"

"Given that he's already demonstrated a pattern of physical abuse towards you, yes, you certainly can. Have you ever called the police on him when he's gotten physical with you in the past?"

"Yes, I have."

"Good. That's going to help your cause."

"Look, Ms. Gentry, I just need you to do what you gotta do as soon as possible to get me a divorce and full custody of my son."

"I will do everything in my power to make that happen for you, Mrs. Braxton . . . uh, Rose."

7

Tony Gianni

That evening I was dressed to thrill and looking good enough to eat at the Urban League fund-raising party held at the National Press building in downtown D.C. I was there with a few coworkers from my law firm. It was like an all-out Ebony Fashion Fair going on. Men in their finest power suits; single-breasted, double-breasted. Even saw a few three-piece suits in the house. The ladies were equally rockin' with their hair done up and wearing their finest evening attire. I was clad in a brand-new evening dress I bought from Nordstrom specifically for this event. A black, asymmetrical, off-the-shoulder number that hugged my ample backyard provocatively— yet tastefully.

Let me tell you. It was Switzerland up in that camp— lots of chocolate. Surely this was the type of event where an attractive, single sista such as myself could meet a hand- some, educated, articulate, single black man. No doubt

there were plenty that fit this criteria in attendance. Not a
one of them was trying to knock on my door or buzz my
intercom, however. I caught plenty of them giving me the
eye, staring me up and down, zoning in on my voluptuous
ass and thick, luscious lips. I even tried giving a couple of
the really cute ones my womanly "it's okay to approach
me, I won't bite" gaze. Either those bruhs didn't get it or
simply lacked the confidence to step to a sista. Too bad. I
wasn't about to make the first move just 'cause these
wimps had rejection phobia. Come to find out, I wasn't
alone in my frustration. It was a hot topic among a syndi-
cate of sistas gathered in the ladies' room.

"What's up with all the men in here tonight?" inquired
a short Nia Long lookalike.

"Yeah," followed another woman. "Why are they all
standing around with their hands in their pockets like
they're posing for *GQ*? I bet if we were in here looking like
some video hoochies on BET they'd be all up in our grills."
The two women gave each other high fives to that.

"Fuck 'em. The best-looking ones are too damn short
anyway," said this one giant girlfriend, who had to be at
least six-foot-six in her stiletto heels.

"Naw, I think they're intimidated being in a room full
of black women who probably have houses bigger than
they do, as much if not more money than they do, and
drive nicer cars than they do," chimed in a thick but
shapely sista rocking a Caesar-style haircut—and rocking
it well indeed. (Not every woman can pull that look off.)
Everyone, including me, roared with laughter when she
said that.

After applying a fresh coat of my trademark bronze
lipstick, I left the ladies' room and headed over to who
had become my main man for the evening—the bar-

tender. That's when I was approached, as I took a sip from my second glass of Hennessey for the evening.

"That shade of lipstick really looks good on you."

I glanced up to find the compliment coming from a truly unlikely source.

"Uh . . . thank you. Bobbi Brown," I replied, surprised as all hell.

"Pleased to meet you, Bobbi. I'm Tony Gianni."

"No, no. The lipstick. *It's* Bobbi Brown. I'm Bailey. Bailey Gentry." I shook his hand while discreetly perusing his exterior.

"Gianni. Is that Italian?" I asked him.

"All day, every day," he replied.

This gentleman stood about six-one, 180 to 190 pounds, with a very nice build. Pale, blemish-free skin and jet-black hair cut short and neat. He somewhat resembled a young Al Pacino from back in the early *Godfather* movies. Besides being one of my favorite actors, I've always thought "Michael Corleone" was one good-looking white man. Now, you know I love my black men. But a sista's got to give credit where credit's got to be given. This white boy was all that and a bag of chips! *Where did you come from?* I wondered to myself silently. Tony looked as though he had just stepped out of a male model shoot dressed in a charcoal gray, pinstriped, one-button single-breasted suit over a white shirt and solid-yellow tie. On his feet were a pair of fierce lace-ups—Kenneth Cole, I bet. Two thumbs up! (A man's shoes have got to compliment his outfit, in my book.) I subtly peered around the room looking to see if any other sistas in the house had gotten a glimpse of this fine Caucasian specimen. After all, this was a very black event, and Mr. Gianni was sticking out like a very sore thumb. The next thing that came to mind was this: *That figures.* With a plethora of *black* men in the house, a lone *white* guy would be the first to step to me.

Tony and I talked for most of the evening. A very pleasant conversation at that. I briefly thought back to Lisa while we chatted. Recalled how she told me she was turned on by Mo's conversation the day those two met. Seems like a lost art, doesn't it? Good conversation, I mean. Too many men these days just want to talk shit to you. And the sad thing is, half these dumb muthafuttas actually think they're saying something! Mm, mm, mm. If they only knew that good conversation can get a woman's panties wet, too. But I digress. . . .

Tony and I talked about a bunch of stuff during the evening; politics, sports, music, even soap operas. The *Young and the Restless* is his favorite. Mine, too. I came to find out that he likes jazz, too. I'm into "smooth jazz" myself. You know, Kenny G, Najee, and any other "Gee." Tony said what I listen to isn't jazz at all, but "elevator music." Said I needed to get into some "real" jazz, like the Yellowjackets, Weather Report, and Chick Corea. (I had no earthly idea who any of these artists were.) He was even up on the latest rap and R&B.

And speaking of R&B, as we chatted, the DJ was spinnin' some good R&B. There were a lot of folks on the dance floor getting their groove on. Tony asked me if I'd like to dance. My first inclination was to politely decline his invitation. White guy? Dancing? Hmmm. Sounded oxymoron-ish to me. Look, a sista can *move*, okay? I really didn't want to get on that dance floor and have to put a hurtin' on this white boy. Didn't want him to get out there and start flip-floppin' like a fish and embarrass me either. But the Hennessey in me said, *Why not?* Well, wouldn't you know? Tony actually had some rhythm, for a white boy. In fact, he had more rhythm than a few of the brothas I saw out there getting their groove on. I was impressed. I'm guessing so too were a few other sistas who couldn't seem to take their eyes off the two of us as we fittingly danced to Tony! Toni! Toné!'s, "Feels Good."

Following our dance, Tony got me another glass of Hennessey. Talking with him, I got the impression that hanging out with black folks wasn't out of his norm. There may have been two or three other white faces in the crowd of over 300 people that evening, and he certainly didn't seem like a fish out of water. He went on to tell me a lot about himself in such a short time. Said he was born and raised in Philadelphia, the son of Italian immigrants who came to the U.S. in 1954. An only child, he came along nine years later. I quickly did the math in my head and figured out his age. Thirty-one. Two years older than me. Growing up in Philly, Tony said he witnessed a considerable transformation of his neighborhood. By the time he entered middle school, it had turned from a predominately white one to one that was predominately black. His parents loved the home they made and the neighborhood so they didn't join the exodus. Therefore, from the age of twelve, he had been immersed in black culture.

After attending college at Villanova and working for an investment company on Market Street in downtown Philadelphia for two years, he moved to D.C. in '88 to take a job with the government. A human resources gig at the Federal Reserve. Said he was currently renting an apartment in the midst of the bohemian residents of Adams Morgan—the "Greenwich Village" of D.C. Shared his place with a black college buddy of his named Derrick, who was originally from D.C. That's who he was here at this event with.

Later on in the evening, Tony introduced me to Derrick.

I was hoping Tony's roommate was one of those cuties I was attempting to make subliminal contact with earlier. He wasn't. Derrick seemed cool, though. Just wasn't my type.

Anyway, by the time the clock struck midnight, I was ready to bust the joint. Get out of my dress, my heels, crawl into bed with my only lover at the moment—Häagen Dazs mint chip—and watch *Late Night with David Letterman*. I made the rounds and said good-bye to my coworkers. Nearly gave all those tight-lipped brothas in the house a collective middle finger on my way out. Of course, I said good-bye to Tony and thanked him for keeping me company. As far as I was concerned, the time he and I spent talking was simply two people passing time. Not sure he saw it that way, though. He asked for my number as I was about to leave. My first thought was to give him a typical blow-off line like, "I'm sorry, I can't. I'm seeing someone." But Lord knows that wasn't true. And well, after three or four glasses of Hennessey, a sista's apt to give her number out to just about *anybody*.

Maurice had gone out of town on a business trip. That made the moment ideal for me and Lisa to do some girly stuff together—like shopping. I picked her up at Mo's house in Largo, and we rode out to Pentagon City Mall in Virginia. A little shopping was just the diversion I needed from the case I had begun to work on—a real humdinger. A divorce, child custody, and domestic violence matter all rolled into one. After three hours of shopping, I dropped Lisa off, grabbed some Jamaican takeout from Negril, then headed back home to get back to work on the case. Got home around seven. As soon as I put the key in the door, I heard my phone ringing. I dropped my bags on the floor of the foyer and raced into the kitchen to catch it before my answering machine picked up. I figured it was Lisa calling to say she had left something of hers in one of my shopping bags. (She's got this bad habit of doing that every time we go shopping.)

"Hello?"

"Hi, may I speak to Bailey?"

"This is she."

"Hi, it's Tony. The guy you met at the Urban League party a couple of weeks ago."

Tony?

Truthfully, I had all but forgotten about him. Guess I did give him my number. Couldn't believe he was actually calling me, though.

"Oh, hi, Tony, how are you?"

"Fine. Have I caught you at a bad time?"

"Uh, sorta. I just walked in the door from shopping with my girlfriend."

"Oh, okay. Wanna call me back when you get settled?"

"Uh, sure. I can do that. Hold on, let me grab a pen and get your number." I took a pen and a piece of paper out of my kitchen drawer.

"Okay, give it to me."

"202-555-9661."

"Got it. I'll call you back shortly, Tony."

I hung up the phone in the kitchen, grabbed the cordless out of the bedroom, and raced into the bathroom 'cause I had to pee like nobody's business. While handling my business, I speed-dialed Lisa.

"Guess who just called me?" I said, full of curiosity and intrigue.

"I don't know. Who?"

"Remember that white guy I told you I met at the Urban League party?"

"Nooo. Get out."

"Yeesss. Why is he calling me, Lisa?"

"'Cause you gave him your number, maybe?"

"I know, but I just did that to be doing it. I didn't *expect* him to really call me."

"Whassup with you, girl? You give a guy your number, he doesn't call you, and you get upset. You give a guy your number, he does call you, and you wonder why he's calling you. Maybe he's digging you. Did you back that big ass up on him while y'all were dancing? You know them white boys get turned on by that. Their women don't have big booties. Big titties maybe, but not big boot—"

"Lisa!"

"What?"

"Shut up. I was at a respectable function. Not the Ritz nightclub, thank you very much. Besides, he's Italian, and some of those Italian women have plenty of junk in the trunk, too."

"If you say so. I suspect he's got a thing for brown sugar. I mean, you did meet him at a black function, and you said he seemed kind of cool for a white guy."

"Cool and fine."

"*Fine?* Now you didn't mention all that. Uh-oh, let me find out—"

"Don't you even go there, Lisa. You know I am not down with the swirl."

"The swirl?"

"That pudding in the supermarket where the chocolate and vanilla flavors are all entwined together."

"Ah, that's right. You're strictly a chocolate-lovin' kinda gal, aren't you?"

"And don't forget it!"

"So, what's this guy's name anyway, and what did he want?"

"His name's Tony Gianni. And I don't know what he wanted. I was just getting in the door when he called. I told him I'd call him back."

"Well, you know I'm a nosy kinda heifer, so call me back when you're done speaking with him, and give me details."

"I will."

After getting off the phone with Lisa and leaving the bathroom, I went back into the living room to retrieve my shopping bags from the foyer. I emptied them out and tried on a few of the items I bought at the mall again. The fuchsia Steve Madden sandals and a pair of white short-shorts from the Gap. No, not Daisy Dukes. My ass is a little *too* big for those. A sista ain't trying to stop traffic, feel me? I ate my curried shrimp and rice, then curled up on my living room sofa reviewing some notes from the Rose Braxton case and a few other miscellaneous items from work. Got so engrossed that by the time I put my work down it was already well past nine. I was spent. Ended up falling asleep right there on my sofa. Never did call Tony back.

8

Let's Do Lunch

Ring . . . ring . . .

"Hello?"

"What the dilly, girl? It's been two whole days. Don't keep me in suspense. What did the Italian Stallion want?" Lisa rambled on, barely taking a breath.

"Don't know. I never called him back."

"Why not?"

"I forgot. I'm not sure if I'm even going to call him back."

"Why not?" Lisa asked again, sounding like a broken record.

"How 'bout this? Why don't I give you his number and you can call him, 'cause you seem far more interested—"

"Excuse me. I've got a man. But if I didn't . . ."

"What's the point anyway, Lisa? I'm hardly trying to get with this dude. And please don't ask why not again."

"All right then, I'll ask you a different question. *What's your problem?* You said he was—and I'm quoting you—fine. You love a good-looking man, don't you?"

"I do."

"You said he dressed nice. You love a fashion plate, don't you?"

"I do."

"So then, I'm going to ask one more time. What the dilly, yo?"

"Stop being silly, Lisa. You *know* what's up."

"Ah . . . this lack of interest on your part wouldn't be because this Tony happens to be white, would it?"

"Uh . . . *yeah.*"

"Bailey, I know you've got your preferences. Everybody does—but hang on! You have got to loosen up a little. *Helloo.* Haven't you been reading *Essence*? Watching *Oprah*? The odds are not in our favor in that harsh, dating world out there."

"I don't care. I can't be like Gumby, all flexible and whatnot, like you. It's not in my nature. Just 'cause you settled for a short man, don't expect me to do something similar," I joked.

"Watch it, heifer. Don't make me have to come over there and pimp-slap you. That short man you're referring to happens to be my future husband."

"Oh? Mo's been promoted from boyfriend to husband-to-be status, has he?"

"Shyytt, I hope so. We've been together five years already. But let's not get off the subject at hand. We're not talking about Mo and me. I've got mine. I'm trying to help you get yours. So what if this white boy isn't a possible love connection? You can still go out and have a good time with him. Look around. I don't see anybody else taking you anywhere."

"Gee, thanks, Lisa."

"Have you ever heard of the term 'friends,' Bailey? This guy might be a cool cat to have in your corner for whatever reason. You just never know. I always say a woman can never have enough quality male friends in her life. But I know all I'm saying to you is going in one ear and out the other. You see, Bailey, this is the reason your ass is still—"

"All right already. I'll call him back."

"When?"

"As soon as you stop fussin' at me and get off the phone."

"Got it. I'm gone. Call me back."

Let's pause here a minute. Y'all think I was acting a little stuck-up, huh? Oh, cut a sista some slack. I just didn't want to go through the trouble of turning Tony down if I found out he was interested in me. I already knew the feeling was *not* going to be mutual.

Granted, I could have been jumping the gun. Maybe that wasn't the reason Tony called. Oh, of course it was. He *had* to be interested in me. I found the piece of paper I placed in my kitchen drawer with his number on it and dialed him.

"Hello?"

"Tony?"

"Speaking."

"It's Bailey Gentry. Sorry I'm just getting around to calling you back. I've been kind of busy."

"That's cool. But you know, for a minute there I thought you forgot about me."

"Naw, nothing like that." (Okay, I lied a little.)

"I've been thinking about you, Bailey. I really enjoyed talking to you at the fund-raiser."

"Same here, Tony."

"In fact, I had such a nice time that I want to take you

to lunch. Your favorite spot. Whatever and wherever that may be."

"Lunch?"

"You sound surprised."

"I am a little bit. No, make that a lot of bit."

"Why? You're a very attractive and interesting woman. What kind of man wouldn't want to take you to lunch and get to know you better?"

I wasn't quite sure how to respond to that. I was too busy blushing on the other end of the phone.

"Oh, wait a minute. Am I steppin' on somebody's toes here?" Tony asked.

"Huh?"

"You didn't mention anything at the party about being involved with anyone. I just assumed . . ."

"Neither did you, if I remember correctly."

"Ain't that something," Tony chuckled. "Well, all's clear on my end."

My turn. Now how do I let him down gently and get out of this?

I didn't have to think about it but a second. That's because I could subconsciously hear Lisa's big mouth in my head saying, *Go to lunch with him, Bailey. Go to lunch with him!*

"I guess we can do lunch—just lunch. I'm really not looking to get into anything—"

"Ssssh," Tony cut me off before I could finish. "Just lunch it is. Promise. I won't propose to you while we're eating."

That got me laughing.

"Better not."

Okay, I admit. Maybe I was taking this all a bit too seriously. Tony did seem like a really likable guy. And he had a sense of humor. I really dug that in a man. And you know what else? His voice sounded a lot sexier over the phone than it did in person. Made me think he probably gave good pillow talk.

"How 'bout this," Tony said. "Over the next twenty-four hours, why don't you think about where you want to go and when. I'll call you back at roughly this same time tomorrow. You let me know what you've decided, and I'll make it happen."

(Did I mention I also liked a take-charge kind of man, too?)

"Sounds like a plan, Mr. Gianni."

Tony and I ended up having lunch at the Front Page restaurant in Dupont Circle. And actually, I had a very good time. Far better than I expected. Although I downplayed just how much when I told Lisa about it. I didn't want to hear a bunch of her I-told-you-sos.

Tony had me in stitches the whole time with his silly sense of humor and corny jokes. When he wasn't giving me his stand-up routine, he was telling me all about his vacation to Italy last spring. His third trip to the land of his ancestors. I was so jealous listening to him talk about his sojourns through Rome, Venice, and Sicily. Italy's the one European country I've always wanted to visit myself. It seemed so romantic. Listening to him more than confirmed that notion for me. I almost wished that I was there with him to share in the experience.

Almost, I said.

Tony was a complete gentleman during our lunch date. No come-on lines and no shit-talking. Casually dressed, he looked just as handsome as he did in that fab suit he wore the evening we met. He had been cleanshaven that night. This day, he was sporting a few days' worth of shadow. That made him look even sexier. (I love that.)

Would you believe it if I told you our lunch date was followed by two more dates? A movie and dinner? Go figure, huh?

This is not to imply that I was totally comfortable going out with a white guy. Quite the contrary. I found myself feeling especially uncomfortable whenever we were in the presence of "my people."

During our dinner date at Smith and Wollensky's, not far from where I worked, there was this brotha seated at a table directly across from ours. Chocolate-brown, bald, muscular, drop-dead fine. My kind of Mr. Right material, feel me? Anyway, he was dining with some white chick. A blond-haired, blue-eyed, straight-off the-cover-of-*Cosmo*-looking white chick. Granted, I should have been used to seeing the swirl; it's played out relentlessly in the Washington metropolitan area.

Just the sight of those two stuffin' their faces and making googly eyes at each other was nearly enough to make me hurl my grilled lamb chops. I diverted my attention from Tony for a second and glanced over at "my brotha." Our eyes met, and he gave me a "how you doing?" nod of his head. Before I could catch myself, I had already rolled my eyes at him. Now fortunately, Tony's face was buried in his plate of prime rib at that precise moment, so he didn't catch any of this. No doubt bruh received my silent memo to him:

With all the black women in this city, you couldn't find one to bring to this restaurant, my bro-tha?

Crossover muthafuttas. I can't stand 'em!

Anyway, after getting that out of my system, I turned my focus back to my own date. Holy cow! I forgot so quickly that *I* was dining with a *white* guy. Suddenly, I was a bit embarrassed by my hypocritical behavior toward bruh just a second ago. Just a *bit* I said. I glanced over at him and his white chick again. I guess he was waiting for me to do that very thing, 'cause he was staring me dead in my grill when I did. Wasn't hard to read his mind, now was it?

Bitch, you've got some nerve!

What-eva, homie.

This here was apples and oranges. Dude and his white chick definitely had a lovey-dovey vibe going on. Tony and I, on the other hand, were just friends. Totally platonic. Furthermore, despite a couple of dates, Tony was nothing more to me than a diversion; someone to kick it with until that ideal box of chocolate knocked on my door or buzzed my intercom. When it came to white men, I just didn't get down like *that*.

I still enjoyed Tony's company, though. And why not? He was funny, a great conversationalist, and easy on the eyes. In fact, there had been many moments when he made it real easy for me to *forget* that I was out with a white guy.

JUNE . . .

9

Boyz in the Club

Tony went back to Philly for a while to visit his folks. That was good. I needed a break from him. Don't get me wrong. I'd been enjoying his company, but he had also been running interference. A sista needed to get out and meet some *black men*.

In his absence, my resumed search for my kind of Mr. Right hadn't been going too well. I'd passed the time mostly playing third wheel with Mo and Lisa and hitting nightclubs here and there. I know a lot of women don't like doing that. Hanging out with a couple when they're dateless, that is. I'm one of them. But you know, every now and then, I believe it can actually be a very good method to meet someone. Everyone knows men are like sharks in social settings where women are present. And let's face it. If showing up at a throwdown with your girl-friend and her boyfriend doesn't reek of "blood in the water," I don't know what does. A few nights back, brothas must've really smelled the bait, 'cause they were all over me like white on rice.

Unfortunately, a few nights back they also all happened to be a bunch of jive-talking knee-grows trying to fill me with as much alcohol as they could in hopes of getting me in bed before I could call them out on just half the bullshit they were telling me. One right after another. Each one more pathetic than the previous one. Call me a skeptic, but there's no way you'll ever convince me that it's even remotely possible for one out of every two brothas you meet in a club on a given night to be moneymaking entrepreneurs with their own business. *Puh-leeze.* Do these muthafuttas think we ladies are really that stupid?

I present to you Exhibit A: "Charles the Entrepreneur," I'll call him. He slithered over to our table right after Mo and Lisa got up to dance. Bruh was tall like I like 'em and not half bad-looking. Dressed in black from head to toe. A large Jesus piece swung from his neck. Charles smelled like he had taken a bath in a tub of Joop cologne.

"Wassup, sexy?" was his opening line. That right there put him behind the eight ball with yours truly. A simple, "How are you, Miss" or "Hello, I'm Charles" would have been a much more effective approach.

"Bailey."

"Excuse me?"

"My name. It's Bailey. And you are?"

"My bad, my bad." (Fake laugh followed.) "I'm Charles. Pleased to meet you, Bailey. So, why's a fine, sexy thang like you sitting here all alone?"

Did he just call me a Thang? Mo, Lisa. Hurry back. Please!

"Gee, I don't know, Charles. Why is a fine, sexy *thang* like me sitting here alone?"

"I think I may have an idea."

"Really? Enlighten me. I'd love to hear your thoughts."
This ought to be interesting, I mumbled under my breath.

"Because you haven't found the kind of man you need yet."

"And what kind of man might that be, Charles?"

"A tall, dark, handsome, intelligent, moneymaking brotha who knows how to treat you like the beautiful black queen you are."

"Let me guess. You're just the man for the job?"

"Bingo."

Okay. The brotha wasn't short on confidence. I liked that. Maybe I could overlook his tacky opening line, and work with him on the fragrance abuse thing.

"Let me get you another of whatever it is you're drinking, Bailey," Charles said. He summoned the waiter over and ordered another Hennessey for me. Five minutes into our conversation, it became regrettably apparent that Charles was all flash and no substance. I found myself more engrossed with the Jesus piece than anything flowing out of his mouth.

"So, what do you do for a living, Bailey?"

None of your damn business, I nearly slipped up and said. "I'm an attorney. And you?"

"I have my own business."

Okay, so I'm, like, sitting there waiting for Charles to elaborate . . . still waiting . . . and waiting. I'm running out of patience.

"Uh, that sounds great, Charles. And what is the *nature* of your business, may I ask?"

"I, um, I'm into various moneymaking ventures. You know, all types of entrepreneurial shit and whatnot."

Entrepreneurial shit? Ooo-kay, Where's that waiter with my drink?

"Here's my card, Bailey. Maybe we can discuss some *bizness* opportunities . . . among other things," he said, giving me a wink.

He handed me a blank white card that merely read CHARLES STOKES ENTERPRISES with his *pager* number on it. That's it. No street address, phone number, cell number, or other relative information on it to expand upon whatever this "entrepreneurial shit" was that he was supposedly into.

I glanced at my watch. This knee-grow's time was up already, feel me? Besides, Mr. Too-Much-Cologne-Wearer was beginning to make my eyes water. I peered over his shoulder in an attempt to locate Lisa and Mo and I spotted the two of them boogeying on the dance floor. Couldn't get Lisa's attention. She was in another world, jigglin' her big titties nearly out of that low-cut top she had on. I did manage to get Mo's attention, though. I tried motioning him to come back to the table with my head and eyes, but dummy didn't get my clue. Instead, he started grinning at me and gave me a thumbs-up. The waiter finally came back to the table with my Hennessey. I guzzled it down as quickly as I could without choking, thanked Charles for the refill, told him I'd call him (*don't hold your breath*), and excused myself to reunite with my friends. The first thing I did upon doing so was pop Mo upside the head with my purse.

So it was my first day back to work after the weekend, and I did meet someone. A real cutie-pie in fact. Not in a club, but on the train platform at the Farragut North Metro station during one of those irritating evening delays. Folks were packing into subway cars like sardines, so a sista decided to take a lemon of a situation and make lemonade out of it. I made sure I positioned myself in such a way that would leave me and Mr. Cutie-Pie wedged up nice and tight against each other when we boarded the Red Line train for Silver Spring. His breath didn't stink and he smelled good, too. Not at all overbearing like Charles the Entrepreneur. *Versace Blue Jeans*. I know that scent anywhere. During our conversation into Silver Spring, I didn't ask Mr. Cutie-Pie what he did for a living. (I've been told that doing so can be a turnoff to a man two minutes into an initial conversation.) I did tell him that I was an attorney, however. The conversation went south quickly thereafter.

For the record, I didn't volunteer that particular piece of information regarding my livelihood. He *asked*. But hey, it was cool. That kind of thing was nothing new to me. Being a young lawyer in my twenties, I found myself constantly trying to downplay my secular and financial status in order not to come across too intimidating to certain types of brothas I met. But right then and there, I made up my mind that I wasn't going to do that any longer. This episode brought me a brand new philosophy toward brothas who had issues dealing with that kind of thing: *Fuck every last single one of y'all*—pardon my French. I refused to tiptoe on eggshells for the sake of the black male ego anymore.

As soon as Tony got back from visiting his people in Philly, he called and asked if I wanted to pick up where we had left off. Given my headway—or lack thereof—in my good black man pursuit during his absence, it should come as no surprise that I readily went along with his suggestion.

"I mentioned you to my folks while I was home. Why

don't you give some thought to coming with me to Philly the next time I go back there?" Tony said to me at lunch over a plate of chicken scaloppini at the Cheesecake Factory. "We can make the rounds on South Street, eat some cheesecakes, hit the waterfront. Oh, and I'll take you to my favorite Italian restaurant, Dante & Luigi's, and to one of my favorite jazz clubs on Broad Street. You can even meet my folks before we head back."

Right then I started to ponder something for the first time: What the hell was I getting myself into? As I said before, I was *hardly* trying to get caught up in the swirl.

"Really? You told your folks about me?"

"Is that a big surprise?"

"A little. Did you tell 'em I was black?"

"No."

Didn't think so, I thought to myself.

"Let me ask you something, Tony. Have you ever dated a black woman before?"

"Is that what we're doing? Dating?"

"Well, it's not like you're my man . . . look, stop messin' with me. You know what I mean."

"Yes, I've dated a black woman before. Why?"

"It's just that since you have a lot of black friends and move in black circles . . . well, I figured you may have."

"You figured correct. And you know what? There's a certain black woman sitting across the table from me tonight who—"

"Don't go there, Tony. I don't think you can handle this brown sugar." (One day my mouth is going to write a check my ass can't cash.)

"That remains to be seen," he responded, brimming with confidence.

"Tony Gianni." (I loved calling him by his full name.) "Before the quality of this conversation deteriorates any further, can we get back to what we were originally talking about?"

"You're no fun, B."

"Anyway . . . so what *do* your parents know about me?"

"Just some *meaningful* stuff for the time being."

"Such as?"

"Mmmm, how 'bout that you're the first girl I've thought enough about to mention to them in a while. You know what that means?"

"No, Tony. What does that mean?"

"It means I sense something special about you. But hey, if meeting my parents makes you uncomfortable, don't sweat it. It was just a passing thought. That's all. Now as far as coming to Philly with me one weekend goes, that's something I *really* want you to think about. We can do the town. Me and you. It'll be a blast. I promise!"

You're damn skippy meeting your folks makes me uncomfortable, is what I wanted to say to Tony. But listening to the sincerity in his words coupled with his whole vibe towards me since the first day we met, I couldn't. It had been quite a while since a man wanted me to meet his family. Even longer since a man told me I was special, and I sensed he wasn't saying it simply because he wanted to jump my bones.

"I've got no problem with meeting your folks. I look forward to it."

I was lying through my teeth.

10

Matters of Loyalty

"Say what? He wants you to come to Philly with him?" Lisa asked as we stood at the cosmetic counter at Nordstrom in Montgomery Mall.

"That's not all. He even told his parents about me."

"You sure you didn't back your big ass up on him that night y'all met?"

"Will you get serious for a minute? What am I going to do?"

"What do you mean, *what am I going to do*? You're *going* to go to Philly with him."

"Am not."

"Are too."

"Why in the world would I want to do that, Lisa?"

"Because you'll probably have a good time. Life is short, girl. Have fun. Tony's offer sounds good. July Fourth is right around the corner, and what could be more fitting than spending it in the City of Brotherly Love?"

"Spending the Fourth in the City of Brotherly Love with somebody else."

"Somebody black, I suppose?"

"Exactly."

"Let me get this straight. You're telling me you'd rather have a boring time with a brotha than a great time with a white guy?"

"That's a dumb question."

"No, it's not."

"Yes, it is."

"Why?"

"Why you had to phrase it *that* way, huh? Why can't I have a *great* time with a *black* guy?"

"Whateva, Bailey. But I'm telling you now. Maurice and I are going out of town that weekend, so we can't be your Plan B again if you mess around and get stuck with nothing to do and nobody to do it with."

"Where are you two going?"

"Mo's taking me to the Poconos for a little romantic getaway."

"Get out. That sounds nice. You got a good man there. He doesn't know how to rescue a sista when she's in distress, but he's a good guy. Think you two will ever get married?"

"I'm not even thinking about that."

"Really? Why? But before you tell me, are we done here? I'm getting hungry, Lisa. I want to go to the food court and get something to eat."

"I need to check out some eyeliner real quick."

Ten more minutes at the cosmetic counter and we were finally on our way to the food court to get some grub. Lisa and I got dual plates of bourbon chicken with jambalaya rice and grabbed a table.

"So, you were saying . . ."

"About?"

"About the possibility of you and Mo getting married?"

"Oh yeah. I'm not pressed about it, Bailey. Things are good. We're living together—"

"Something you said you would *never* do as I recall. I believe your exact words were, 'My mama didn't raise me like that.'"

"She didn't. Life is funny that way, Bailey. We sit around at various stages of it talking about what we're gonna do and ain't gonna do, then something or someone happens along and we start thinking differently. Feeling differently. Start making all kinds of amendments to the master plan—get it? Amendments? Some lawyer lingo for your ass."

"I get it, Lisa."

"Five years ago, I wouldn't have given a guy like Maurice the time of day. A short, light-skinned dude? Puleeze! Uh-uh. You know how I used to get down."

"Boy, do I."

"There was a time when I never would have dreamed of shackin' up with a man without a ring, either. But here I am, shackin' up. And doing so with a man that's not *even* what I had in mind."

"Be honest with me, Lisa. Ever feel like you wished you had waited? You know, for the kind of guy you *did* have in mind?"

Lisa paused to contemplate my question.

"What I had in my mind, Bailey . . . I'm not sure if 'he' was even real, to tell you the truth. On the other hand, the man that I have is very real. And the longer Mo and I are together, the more I believe he *is* what I had in mind all along. My prize package just didn't come to me in the type of box I was expecting it to. Let that be a lesson to you. Don't get caught short, Bailey. Mr. Right doesn't always come to us the way we think he will. What we got to do is *recognize* the package however it comes or else one day we'll find ourselves sitting around frustrated, getting fat, and bitching about why it is we ain't got nobody as our biological clocks tick, tick, tick away."

"Mmm-hmm. Right, Lisa."

"What's with the philosophical question anyway? You're thinking about Tony, aren't you?"

"Why does he have to be *white*, Lisa? Can you feel my pain here?"

"I truly can."

"You know I love my black men. I want to support *them*. Cherish *them*. Nurture *them*. Build a black family with *them*."

"You're preaching to the choir, girl. There are times when I want to get down and kiss the ground for having found a good *black* man."

"We're a beautiful people, Lisa. All this racial intermingling stuff . . . I don't know about that. Bottom line for me, I'm staying loyal to our men. No matter what! And I believe every black woman should do likewise."

"Really."

"Really!"

"Even at the risk of your happiness or theirs?"

"What 'chu talking 'bout?"

"Look around you, B. There are a lot more of us than there are of them. And after you sift through the ones that are in jail, gay, got bad credit, bad teeth, or are just straight up canines, it doesn't seem like there's a whole lot left for us to choose from. And the way they're killing each other every day from Southeast D.C. to Compton, California; black men are going to be *extinct* pretty soon. Tell me. What are we going to do then? Sistas might not have any choice but to—"

"Watch me, Lisa. I'm putting my fingers in my ears. I'm not trying to hear that kind of s—"

"Oh stop it. So what are you telling me? That you'd rather be *alone* than step outside of your race?"

"Who said anything about being alone? I'm only twenty-nine years old. I'm intelligent, attractive, funny, adventurous, self-sufficient, and very spunky. I've got plenty of time to find my prince. I don't care how many bruhs out here aren't prospect-worthy. I'm a good catch. I am *not* going to be alone. Besides, the thought of me settling for a white man . . . oooh girl, gives me the heebie-jeebies. I don't think I could be happy with anything *but* a black man."

"Suit yourself. But as far as that plenty of time stuff goes, time has a way of creepin' up and whizzin' past your ass before you knew what hit you. If Mo and I ever part ways—and I hope that never happens, 'cause I love that man—I'm not going to be as quick as you to say I won't cross over if things start getting hectic. Of course, having said that, if I'm gon' do *wrong*, I'm gon' do it *right!* Top shelf all the way. I'm not crossin' over to the other side for some fuddy-duddy. Some average-looking, run-of-the-mill Joe. Uh, uh. He's going to have to be fine, very sexy, and have much more than some lint in his pockets. He *will* be held to a higher standard!"

"Amen to that!"

We cracked up and gave each other high fives. Folks in the food court were beginning to stare at us and our silliness. That's when Lisa stopped laughing and got serious for a moment."

"I just had a thought, B."

"What's that?"

"Do black men ever sit around the table with each other talking about how loyal they want to be to us?"

11

Guess Who?

I was in my office preparing the summons for Mrs. Braxton's divorce petition when Monifah buzzed me to say that there was gentleman in the lobby waiting to see me. Said he had a gift for me, but wouldn't give his name. Hmm, a mystery man? Here to see *moi*? Bearing a gift? Oooh, I just love surprises—but a sista was going to need an itty-bitty more detail before coming out from behind this desk. I buzzed Monifah back.

"Yes, Bailey?"

"Who is this gentleman?"

"I can't tell you, I said. He wants to surp—"

"I get that, Monifah. Can I get a hint? One?"

"Aw'aight. Just one."

"Have you seen him come to this office before?"

"Nope.

"Are you sure?"

"If he had, I'd *remember* him," she exclaimed, chewing gum like a cow all up and through my ears.

"What's he look like?"

"That would be *two* hints, Bailey."

That would be two hints, Bailey . . . Oh, shut up!

Clearly, I was wasting my time fooling with Monifah. I got up and made my way out into the reception area to see who this Mr. Guess Who was. I was clueless . . . well, that is until two-thirds of my way down the corridor. That's when this disconcerting thought hit me: *Tony?*

"Oh hell no. Please don't let it be *him*," I mumbled under my breath.

No such luck.

"Tony? Hi, what are you doing here?"

He was dressed awfully casual in a short-sleeved shirt, denim shorts, and Adidas on his feet. "Hey, B. How are you? Look, I know I'm dropping by unannounced and I promise never to that again. Scout's honor. But I just had an urge to surprise you with a little something."

Tony handed me a gift basket filled with an assortment of lotions and bubble bath products from *Bath & Body Works.*

"T-thanks, Tony. I-I wasn't expecting—"

"I know you weren't. Just call me Mr. Full-of-Surprises. All day, every day." Monifah cleared her throat—loudly.

"Tony, this is our reception—"

"*Administrative assistant*," she quickly corrected me.

" . . . our administrative assistant, Monifah Jenkins. Monifah, my friend, Tony."

"Nice to meet you, Tony," she said, extending her hand to him and cheesin' like a mouse.

"Nice to meet you, Monifah. And thanks for not giving me away. I overheard you on the phone. I know Bailey was trying to get you to do that very thing."

"No, I wasn't."

"Yes, you were."

Shut up, Monifah.

I needed some privacy.

"We can go back to my office and talk, Tony."

"Actually, I can't. There's some place I need to be, shortly."

"It can't be work, judging by how you're dressed."

"It's not. I took a vacation day today."

"Okay. Well, um, let me walk out to the elevator then."

We exited the large glass doors of the office suite and stopped in front of the elevators.

"Thanks for all these wonderful bath products," I turned to Tony and said after pushing the down button for him. "This was a surprise indeed."

"A pleasant one, I hope."

"But of course."

"Enjoy the rest of this gorgeous day, B. We'll talk soon?"

"We'll talk soon."

Tony stepped onto the elevator and disappeared from my sight as the doors closed.

Monifah was on the telephone when I returned, still smackin' her gum like a cow, and get this: simultaneously filing her two-inch fingernails. Judging by her body language, she was on a personal call—again. There's one in every office, isn't there? I mean that one employee who has all the other employees wondering how they manage to keep their job from one day to the next. But I digress.

I heard Monifah tell whomever she was yappin' with to hold on as I walked past her en route to my office.

"Bailey?"

"Yes?"

"Hope you don't mind me saying so, but Tony's *fine!* I didn't know you were down with the swirl."

Uh-uh.

I tossed her my best "you-really-oughta-mind-your-business" look, and kept right on going. Soon as I reached my office, I closed my door, sat on the edge of my desk, took the card out of the envelope that was attached to the basket, and read it.

> *Bailey,*
> *. . . Because you told me how much you look forward to a hot bubble bath after a long hard day at JB&H. Enjoy!*
> *—Tony G.*

I opened a couple of the lotions and took in their aromas. The mango and mandarin was my favorite.

Following my talk with Lisa the other day, I had come to the conclusion that it was best for me to start distancing myself from Tony—effective immediately. Sure, we went out a few times, had a few meals together, shared some laughs. Be that as it may, the last thing I wanted to do was lead him on in any way. Give him the slightest impression that there was a chance of something romantic happening between us. I already felt like I had gotten a bit too comfy with Tony. Opened my big mouth and said a few things I probably should have kept to myself.

Yes, I heard all of Lisa's yacka-dee-yack about the surprise box, package, and all that jazz. But here was the deal. Tony was strictly a "placeholder" in my book—albeit a fine, sexy, Caucasian one. *And what is that,* you ask? Well, ladies, he's that guy in your life that's fun to go out with. Fun to kick back and guzzle a few beers with. He's so easy to talk to. You're so comfortable around him that you can talk to him about almost anything. He's good-looking,

too, so you hardly mind being seen in public with him.
Yet, despite all these great things about him, you're never
ever, *ever* going to let him feed the cat. Now part of the
reason for this is because a guy like this is probably gay as
well. (In which case he's not hardly thinking about feedin'
your cat anyway.) If he does happen to be cut from the
heterosexual cloth, he is what he is because of this one
thing that permeates your thoughts whenever the two of
you are together: *I can't wait till I meet a guy I can be in a
REAL relationship with!*

All right. I know what some of y'all are thinking. Oh
yeah, there's a guy in my life like that right now. A placeholder, mmm-hmm. But dang, girl. I'll at least break him
off a li'l som'um-som'um from time to time. Let him
tune me up every 3,000 miles or so. Wrong, ladies. That
man you describe is *not* a placeholder. That's a "fuckbuddy." There *is* a difference.

Candles and a glass of Zinfandel set the perfect mood
as I soothed my tired body in a hot tub full of bubbles. I
closed my eyes and momentarily drifted off into dream-
land. Imagined this relaxing bubble bath being courtesy
of some tall, fine, chocolate brotha who'd come to pay
me a visit today instead of Tony. Next, I thought of how
ridiculous my previous thought was. Tony's gesture was
sweet. Sweet as the Zinfandel I was sipping. It was the type
of thing that would normally have me grinning from ear
to ear. But I wasn't. Couldn't. This was getting a bit weird,
to tell you the truth. A white guy was making all the right
moves with *me*, Bailey Gentry, the consummate anti-
white-guy kind of black girl. We needed to talk. I needed
to put the brakes on any moves Tony might have in mind

before this thing began turning in a direction impossible for my feelings to go. Feel me?

I set my glass of wine down on the rim of the tub, picked up my cordless, and dialed his number. Gosh. Had it memorized already. Tony answered. Sounded groggy.

"Did I wake you?" I asked, without identifying myself. As if I was the only woman who ever called him.

"Who's this?"

"Bailey."

"Oh, hey, B. Yeah, I must've dozed off."

"I um . . . I'm calling to say thank-you for the bath products again. That was very sweet of you."

"You're very welcome. What are you doing right now?" he asked.

"What else? Taking a nice hot bath in the bubbles you got for me."

"Can I come over and join you?"

Silence.

That caught me off guard like a pickpocket in Dupont Circle. It was the last thing I expected to hear come out of his mouth. And he sounded *so* sexy when he said it, too. Tony's voice was . . . was . . .

"*Nooo*, you cannot come over and join me."

"Why not?"

"Why would you want to?"

"Have you ever taken a bubble bath with a man before?"

"Not that that's any of your business, but yes, I have."

"Enjoy it?"

"Did I."

"Then perhaps I can be of assistance in creating that feeling all over again for you."

"Are you getting fresh with me, Mr. Gianni?"

"You want me to stop?"

Silence.

"Anyway, I'm calling you for another reason, too. I need to talk to you about something," I told him, changing the subject.

"I'm listening."

"I'm not going to beat around the bush, Tony. I want to know where this is going?"

"By 'this,' would you be referring to me and you?"

"Exactly."

"I don't know, Bailey. Where would you like it to go?"

"Don't answer a question with a question."

"Fair enough. I won't beat around the bush with you either. I liked what I saw the moment I saw it. And when I see something I like, I prefer to let things flow. Let what's going to happen or not happen unfold in a natural way. So, to answer your question, I don't have a clue where this is going. But I'm very excited to find out where it *could* go. Now, can I ask you something?"

"Go ahead."

"Do you share my feelings?"

That was it. My chance to nip this in the bud. Tell Tony *my* truth. That I'm a black woman and you're a white man. And in my world that means I could *never* share your feeling on this particular subject. Now, I don't know if it was the bubble bath, the wine, or some combination of the two, but I couldn't say it. It was as if the words were stuck in the back of my throat and I couldn't cough 'em out for the life of me. And here's a question. Why did listening to Tony tell me what was on his mind in that smooth, seductive cadence of his have a sista playing with her coochie underwater? Why was a conversation I initiated with the intent of turning things off suddenly *turning me on*?

"Bailey?"

"Huh?"

"You still there?"

"Yes, Tony Gianni, I'm still here."

He laughed.

"What?"

"I love the way you say my name."

I giggled.

"Are you gonna answer my question or not?"

"Your question . . . right. Do I share your feeling?"

Okay. I was ready to do it now. Took a deep breath. *Here it goes . . .*

"Honestly, Tony, I really think we ought to—"

"Wait. Hold that thought, Bailey. I just got a call on the other line. You gonna hold?"

"Mmm-hmm."

12

Till Death Do Us Part

"This summons commences the filing of your divorce. . ."

Rose Braxton sat across from me looking expressionless. That chippy, fiery 'tude she carried into my office during her last appointment wasn't there today. Her brown eyes looked a shade of blue. Her high cheekbones appeared to droop. Her hair—so impeccably styled—wasn't looking quite as "hooked." Same goes for her attire. Rose was clad in beat-up jeans and a Nike T-shirt.

"You are referred to within it as the plaintiff. Your husband, Sydney, as the defendant . . ."

I'd gone through that particular spiel more times than I could count since I'd been practicing family law. It always brought forth a mix of emotions as varied as the people I represented. It was at this juncture that some clients sat across from me sportin' big, Kool-Aid smiles on their faces. They were just happy to finally be on their way to that long-sought escape from a husband or wife they could no longer love, live with, or cherish till death did them part.

Then there was the opposite reaction. The body language that spoke of sadness. Pain. Defeat. And what I call the classic, "I can't believe it has actually come to this" look.

"Stated are the grounds for which you are seeking this divorce: Adultery, in this case . . ."

I didn't see any relief on Rose's face. No sadness either. What I saw in her eyes was an entirely different emotion.

"Relief you've requested in this divorce is alimony, child support, and full custody of your five-year-old son, Andre Braxton . . ."

An emotion I hadn't come across in that situation before. Fear.

"I've made note that you aren't requesting any ancillary relief. Meaning money, property, and the like. Is that correct?"

Rose paused, looked around my office at the décor. Her eyes locked in on my law degree that hung proudly on the wall. She stared at it hard.

"Yeah, I think so," she said, without looking at me. "If I decide I want anything more, I'll let you know."

"It doesn't quite work that way, Mrs. Braxton. You may not get to include or request anything else once this summons has been filed with the court. Judges like to have all the issues in a divorce proceeding up front. No eleventh-hour surprises."

She shrugged her shoulders.

"Well, in that case, I guess you've covered it all, then." Her mind was obviously someplace else.

"How about this, Mrs. Braxton—"

"Rose."

"Rose. Because I've given you a lot to absorb today, I'm going to hold off filing this petition for a few days. In the meantime, I want you to look over this pamphlet." I slid the pamphlet across my desk to her. "It's a comprehensive listing of the types of ancillary relief parties can request in a divorce action such as yours. Once you've read it over and are certain that I've covered everything you're looking for, I'll proceed with the filing. How does that sound?"

"I have a question," she said.

"What's that?"

"When is Sydney going to find out about this?"

"He'll be notified of your intention to end the marriage by a process server. That person will hand-deliver a copy of this summons to him at his residence. Or we could have him served at his place of employment—"

"No! Don't do that. Just give it to him at our home. Please."

"I take it your husband doesn't know you're filing for divorce?"

"No, he doesn't."

"Are you feeling afraid for your safety?" I already knew the answer to that. For legal reasons, however, I needed to hear it straight from my client's mouth.

"Damn right I'm afraid. I told you, he's a *nutcase!*"

"In that case, I think we ought to look in to getting you an OFP immediately."

"O-F what?"

"Order for protection. Remember? You inquired about that during your previous consultation."

"Oh, yeah."

"Let me explain to you what it's designed to do. Essentially, the OFP is a legally enforceable document granted by a judge that sets restrictions on what level of contact, if any, your husband can have with you and your son. It most surely will specify that he remains a certain distance from you. The order will accomplish a few things. First, having one means you're no longer a helpless, easy target for him. It puts the police, judges, et cetera, on your side in the event that your husband continues in his past abusive behavior towards you. Secondly, if he violates any of the terms set forth in the order, he makes himself subject to arrest and imprisonment. That's the upside. Here's the downside. For some men, subjecting them to a restraining order only *increases* their attempts at harassment. There's a chance your husband could turn out to be the type to completely ignore an OFP *despite* the ramifications, for him, of doing so. Getting hit with one of these could make him feel like he's losing control: control over your marriage and more importantly, the control and intimidation he's currently exercising over *you*. Statistically speaking, it is at the very moment when a man like this is served that he's most apt to 'go off' so to speak, and come after you with the intent of doing some type of harm."

"You're scaring me, Ms. Gentry!"

"I don't mean to scare you, Mrs. Braxton. Nevertheless, this is a potentially scary situation we're dealing with. Let's not pretend otherwise. I would be grossly negligent in my duties as your attorney if I sat here and tried to sugarcoat this for you. The best predictor of future behavior is often past behavior. And if you say this man's been physically abusive to you in the past . . ."

Rose began to cry. I passed her the small box of Kleenex that sat on the edge of my desk. I swear I could hear her begging me in silence, *Bailey, save me. Please save me.* I was a bit afraid for her myself. Just the same, I exuded a calm, cool exterior. Something I learned in law school. No matter what the obstacle or circumstance, always make your client feel like you're in control.

I tried to imagine how Rose Braxton ended up in this place. What kind of man was her husband? I needed to know exactly what she—no we—were working with, so I did something I'd never done before with any of my clients. I turned the meter off. Allowed Rose to just take her time and talk to me openly and freely. Tell me how her personal fairy tale went so wrong.

13

Be Careful What
You Ask For

"I suppose I was going through a metamorphosis of sorts," Rose remarked as I handed her a cup of freshly brewed Columbian java from the office coffee maker. "Until I met my husband, all I had ever dated were clean-cut, nice-guy types."

"What was wrong with that?" I asked.

"I found them all too one-dimensional, boring, easy, and predictable. I needed a challenge. A thrill. Or so I thought."

Rose went on to relate in detail about her relationship with Sydney—a thug type. How she met him at a time when she was young and vulnerable. How he gave her anything she wanted materially, but next to nothing emotionally. She talked about his habitual unfaithfulness to her. How he would build up and tear down her self-esteem according to how it suited his agenda at a given time. Most shocking however, was when she revealed that he had actually been physically abusive toward her long *before* they were ever married—but she married him anyway.

"Maybe I should have you tear up those divorce papers and forget about this whole thing. Just take my punishment like a woman, 'cause I clearly deserve everything that's—"

"That's not true, Mrs. Braxton," I cut her off, knowing full well where she was going with that. "No woman *deserves* to be abused. Physically, emotionally, or otherwise. That kind of sentiment only *keeps* a woman in the vicious cycle of abuse. It has everything to do with what you said earlier. You were young and immature back then. You made a mistake. You used poor judgment. Now you're smarter, wiser, and hopefully a better woman for it."

"Well, thanks for saying that. You're being kind. And thank you for allowing me to vent free of charge."

"I hope talking this out has helped in some way. I wish I could tell you more, but I'm an attorney, and the advice I can give to you is limited to legal matters. However, if you feel that you could benefit from something more, such as counseling, I can certainly recommend—"

"That won't be necessary." Rose got up, gathered her belongings, and prepared to leave my office. "I'm going to look over this an-ancil . . ."

"Ancillary relief."

"Right. I'll read the pamphlet and be in touch shortly."

"Will you still be going through with this divorce?" I asked.

"I think so."

I walked her to the door.

"May I ask you a personal question, Ms. Gentry?" she turned to me and said before exiting my office.

"That depends on how personal it is. I'll try to answer your question as best I can, though."

"Is there a man in your life right now?"

That certainly wasn't a question I expected her to ask. Nevertheless, Tony immediately flashed in my head for a quick second. Though he wasn't *even* what I had in mind, he was the closest thing I had to having a man at the moment.

"No, there isn't at the moment. Why do you ask?"

"Mind if I pass along some free advice to you this time?"

"Um . . . sure, go right ahead."

"I don't know if you're in the market for one or not, but if you are, be careful what you ask for, 'cause you just might get it."

My appointment book was clear for the rest of the afternoon, and menstrual cramps were beginning to kick my butt, a combination that made this the perfect time to leave work early, go home, and curl up on my sofa with a bowl of Häagen Dazs mint chip and a novel I had picked up at Borders bookstore recently: *Devil in a Blue Dress* by Walter Mosley. Listening to Rose's story made me sort of sad. At the same time, it made me very thankful. Thankful that none of my foolish decisions where men were concerned had brought me the kind of turmoil she was currently dealing with. Her words of advice to me hit home more than she knew. I had been asking the good Lord to bring me something for quite some time. My ideal kind of man, to be specific. At the same time, if I was to be as truthful with myself as Rose Braxton had just been with herself, I'd have to admit that thus far—minus the packaging, of course—Tony was exactly the kind of man I had been asking for: handsome, intelligent, personable, employed, *employable*—there is a difference—good sense of humor, take-charge attitude, fashionable. You get the point. Not that I intended to do so, but in so many words, I may have revealed some of that to Tony during our lunch at the Cheesecake Factory. That's when the business about going to Philly came up in the first place. I told him quite a few things that afternoon. Though none of which, I suppose, I *should* have told him.

I checked my e-mail one last time before logging off my computer. Tony's ears must have been burning because I had a new message from him.

> Just thinking 'bout you, B. Hope your day's going well. And hope you're giving lots of thought to next week. Holla at a "brotha" (ha, ha, ha).☺

I laughed at his routine humor, which never seemed to be on hiatus. I didn't e-mail him back, though. Decided to call him later that evening instead. Besides, I had some thinking to do between now and then. The Fourth was just a few days away, and I couldn't leave him hanging. Had to let him know one way or the other what I was going to do. Feeling like I did at the moment, I was much closer to saying yes than no. As I stated, I had run out of alternatives, and like Cyndi Lauper sang, a girl just wanted to have fun—*with somebody*.

I logged off my computer, shut down the power, grabbed my Coach bag and briefcase, and hightailed it to the Metro station.

JULY . . .

14

A Room for Two

The sun was bright, and the A/C felt good in Tony's Volvo as we cruised 95 North en route to Philadelphia. And man, was it *hot!*

Somehow, Tony did it. Managed to talk me in to going to Philly with him. There's more. He even got me to agree to make a mini vacation of it. Got me to agree to stay in the City of Brotherly Love for three whole days with him. Obviously, this all meant I didn't do what I was supposed to do. Remember? Kick him to the curb? Nope, I didn't put the brakes on his moves. Didn't tell him there was zero chance of him and me happening on a romantic level. Didn't do *jack*.

Now, in my defense, I will say I didn't agree to any of it right away. I went along with it strictly by default. (At least, that's my official excuse and I'm sticking to it.) I did try hookin' up with a few brothas from around the way that had been trying to get with me for some time, but that I wasn't feeling for one reason or another. Surely I could land a date to do something with one of them over the biggest holiday weekend of the summer. I could tolerate one of these bruhs for a *day*. Surely one of them would want me on their arm for a barbecue, picnic, or something like that. Well, surely a sista must've waited too late, 'cause I got the same response from every one of those aforementioned brothas when I called: "Sorry, I've already made plans." What is it about men you're *not* interested in? Is it just me, or do they all seem to have this utterly annoying way of circling around you like a bunch of gnats on a hot summer evening, but come the moment you may actually *want* to be in their company, you can't find their asses with a magnifying glass? Exasperating muthafuttas!

Anyway, Tony and I hadn't discussed what the "arrangements" would be for our getaway before we left D.C.—nor did I bring it up. I just opted to sit back and see how he was going to carry it. Kind of exciting, I thought. I simply packed a small suitcase and made sure I was ready when he came by my condo to pick me up.

We made it to Philly in less than two and a half hours. Tony took Exit 14 to Broad Street and headed south toward downtown. Minutes later, we pulled in front of the Marriott in Center City. The hotel looked pretty nice from the outside, and Market Street was bustling with activity.

"This is it. Our home for the next few days," Tony said. "Oh, and don't worry, I booked us separate rooms."

A bellhop welcomed us to Philadelphia and the Marriott and promptly retrieved our luggage from the trunk of the car. I tipped him a buck per bag. Tony gave the valet guys his information and car keys, and the two of us made our way inside the hotel.

Separate rooms?

Hmmm. I knew *Tony* didn't think this was necessary. Naturally, that made it something he did solely for my benefit. So right off the bat I was feeling a little self-conscious that he was incurring an unnecessary expense on my account. At the same time, I was digging the fact that he was behaving like a true gentleman instead of a presumptuous jerk. He got a few Brownie points for that. Despite my earlier reservations about taking the trip with Tony, I was happy to be there, and really looking forward to the next few days. If nothing else, it sure beat staying home and doing nothing.

The Marriot was busy. There were about fifteen people ahead of us waiting in line to check in. Glad I had my Reeboks on.

"Oh, damn!"

"What is it?"

"My watch. I took it off to put lotion on my hands. I think I left it in your car. At least I hope I did. You mind checking?"

"Let me run outside and catch the valet dudes before they park the car," he said.

He hurried back outside while I held our spot in the line. As I did so, I began observing some of the couples who were milling about in the hotel lobby. Looked like a lot of out-of-towners in town for the holiday. That's one of my favorite pastimes by the way—observing couples. I like to analyze how folks look together. See if they've got any visual chemistry going on. Whether the man seems really into his woman and vice versa. Observe if they're holding hands. If he's at her side stride for stride or walking two feet in front or behind her. Little things like that speak volumes about the state of one's relationship, in my book. When the day comes that I'm finally in a *real* relationship, I imagine somebody will be observing me and my man in much the same manner. And even though I won't know this individual from Adam and should therefore probably care less, I hope that person comes away with a good impression of us. I hope he or she walks away thinking, *Those two look good together, and they're definitely in love.*

Anyway, there was one couple in particular that really grabbed my attention. They were standing about five heads or so in front of me in the check-in line. She was slim, with beautiful cocoa-brown skin and a slammin' perm. Tall, too. About five-tennish. If she wasn't already a model, she ought to have been thinking about having a portfolio done. Her companion, a caramel-colored brotha sportin' a Micheal Jordan baldy and a neatly trimmed beard, was quite tall as well. Heck, he might have even been an NBA player for all I knew. Did I mention he was also ridiculously handsome? Those two looked *good* together. Wow. There's nothing more beautiful than the sight of some black-on-black love. It's so . . . so . . . inspirational to me. Makes me want to quote Jesse: *Keep hope alive, girl. Keep hope alive!*

I studied the two of them—him a little more than her. Feel me? I tried not to stare. Didn't want them to *catch* me studying them. I had an urge. I wanted to walk right up and interview them. Ask them things like "How long have y'all been together? Where did y'all meet? Was it love at first sight?" Ask the sista if he was a "good black man." Her ideal package. If so, how long did it take her to find him, and did he have a single cousin who looked anything like him for me?

Tony returned from outside and joined me in the check-in line again. I aborted my surveillance for the moment.

"Too bad this line ain't moving as fast as those valet dudes," he said.

"Did you find my watch?"

"Naw. They had already taken the car to park it. I have to wait for them to bring it back out front."

"I can't believe they've only got two desk clerks working this joint, as crowded as it is in here," I complained mildly.

"I'm gonna run back outside in a second. You cool? Tired? Feet hurt? Want to sit down? Want something to drink—"

"I'm fine, Tony."

"Just checkin'. You are my special guest for the next few days. I want to make sure you're having a good time."

"Well, it's only been a few hours, but I must say you've been a good host thus far. Don't mess it up."

"Never that. I'm gone."

"Take your time, but hurry up."

"Cute."

"Talking about me, right?"

"Word."

"*Word?* Where did you learn that?"

"Watching BET."

"BET?"

"Black Entertainment—"

"I *know* what BET is, Tony."

"You're surprised I watch that channel, huh? What? 'Cause I'm a white boy? Don't sleep on me, girl. I read *Jet* magazine, too."

"Boy, go on outside and see if you can find my watch, please. You silly man."

Tony had a knack for making me laugh. He'd had me cracking up several times on the drive here. Maybe I had been jumping the gun a few days ago. Blowin' him off in entirety was a tad bit gratuitous I would now admit. There was no reason why I couldn't hang on to my fine, sexy, Italian placeholder for a minute. Just because he could never be my Mr. Right didn't mean he couldn't be my *platonic* friend—not my fuckbuddy. (Already told y'all sleeping with a white man would give me the heebie-jeeebies.) Lisa was right. A woman could never have too many quality friends in her life—especially male ones. All I needed to do was make sure the situation didn't get out of hand. Make sure I didn't exceed any of the personal boundaries I set for myself. Keep Tony in the no-contact zone. Meaning no hand-holding or other touchy-feely stuff. That included kissing. Absolutely, positively out of the question! No French, Spanish, German, or any other kind.

Granted, I had already said quite a few things I would and wouldn't do in regard to this man, and if I were being graded on this I'd deserve a big fat "F" for my follow-through thus far. This time, however, I really meant it. I was going to say what I mean and mean what I say.

Separate rooms?

When Tony came back this time, he had my watch in his hand.

"Oh, thank you, thank you for finding it. Where was it?"

"Underneath the front seat."

As we continued our long wait to check in, I pondered the best way to make our sleeping arrangement over the next few days more comfortable—and reasonable—for the both of us.

"Yo, Gianni. What's up with the accommodations?"

"Huh?"

"The separate rooms? What? You 'fraid I'm gonna try to jump your bones or something?"

I flipped the script. Had *him* bustin' a gut this time.

"If that urge hits you at any time over the next three days, I will *not* try to stop you," he said, tongue-in-cheek— I think. "I got separate rooms because I figured you'd be more comfortable with that."

"*I'd* be more comfortable? Care to elaborate?"

"Not right here and now, I don't. Remind me over dinner."

"Suit yourself. But isn't that going to be kind of expensive? You told me your parents' house isn't far from here didn't you? You know, Tony, if you want to stay with them instead and save yourself some money, I won't think you're a cheapskate. I swear. I'll be perfectly okay staying here at the hotel by myself."

"Bailey."

"Yes?"

"I appreciate what you're trying to do. But that's just downright silly! We came up here together; we're going to stay together. Well, sorta."

"Aren't your folks expecting to see you anyway?"

"They don't know I'm in town."

Actually, I was kind of glad to hear him say that. As much as I was looking forward to being in Philly and spending a few days with Tony, I really wasn't trying to meet the parents, too.

"When we get up to the front desk, I want you to cancel one of those rooms." Tony gave me a look like he had just hit the lotto.

"You *sure?*"

"I'm sure. We're adults. I think the two of us can share a room together. Unless of course, you just don't want—"

"Nope, nope, nope. That works for me."

"Uh, Tony, one more thing."

"What's that, B?"

"*Separate beds.*"

We got our weekend under way by hitting South Street soon after we finished unpacking and showering. Got our shop on; ate some famous Philly cheesestakes. We devoted the next morning to doing the cultural thing; visiting the African-American museum, the Free Library of Philadelphia, and the Liberty Bell. Afterward, we even took a joyride around the city on the SEPTA rail system. Which I found totally yuck, by the way. It's got nothing on D.C.'s Metrorail. Anyway, following that, we went back to the hotel to catch forty winks, then changed and went to Zanzibar Blue to hear some great jazz. Why is it that time flies when you're having fun? Before I knew it, our three-day stay in Philly was almost over.

In case you're wondering (and I know you all are) no, we didn't have sex. In fact, our three nights together in a single room were surprisingly uneventful, in part because we wore ourselves out during the day and evening. We didn't get back to our room until after two in the morning each night. By then, we were both so exhausted we were in la-la land as soon as our heads hit our pillows. But we did travel well. I didn't gross Tony out in any way, nor did he display any repellent habits to turn me off. Tony didn't snore—thank goodness—and we were both kind enough to burn incense for the other after making "number two."

Tony went to bed in a T-shirt and silk boxers each night. Mm, mm, mm. Did he look good in those silk boxers. His body was well-toned with sexy definition; almost enough to make a sista . . . never mind, I'm digressing. My evening attire consisted of two plain-jane nightgowns, a T-shirt, and a pair of old Howard University gym shorts. I did pack a sexy camisole or two—mostly out of habit—but they never left my suitcase. (No sense in writing a check my ass wasn't going to be able to cash.)

* * *

"I almost forgot to remind you of what I was supposed to remind you of," I rambled while digging into a heaping plate of scrumptious lasagna at Dante & Luigi's, the restaurant Tony was so eager to take me to.

"Well, remind on, 'cause I don't remember what you were supposed to remind me of," Tony said.

"You promised to elaborate on why you felt I'd be more comfortable in separate rooms."

"Oh, that."

The expression on Tony's face told me he really didn't want to have the discussion. He summoned the waiter over and ordered another glass of wine for himself.

"Bailey?"

"I'm good," I said, declining a second glass.

"How's your lasagna?"

"Excellent. And your chicken parmigiana?"

"All that. All day, every day."

"Great. Now can you quit stalling and answer my question?"

"Was I wrong? Would you not have been more comfortable in your own room?"

"Do you always answer a question with a question?"

"Do I do that?"

"You just did it again. No, Tony. I wouldn't say you were wrong—per se. Actually, I owe you a big thank-you for being considerate enough to even think along those lines. A lot of guys would have just assumed . . . you know . . ."

"I'm not like a lot of guys."

"Hmph. You can say that again. Not the type I'm used to anyway."

"Meaning black guys?"

"I've never gone out of town with a white guy before. In fact, I've never done *anything* with a white guy before."

"I think you've just answered your own question, Bailey. That right there is the reason I booked us separate rooms."

"You've lost me."

"As much fun as we're having, I think you're having some issues with my uh . . . 'Caucasian-ness,' shall we say."

"Did I say I was having trouble with it?"

"Didn't have to. A man can tell when a woman is off balance."

"Off balance? Is that what you think I am?"

"I didn't mean that in a negative way. All I meant was, I don't think you're quite sure what to make of me. Us, for that matter. I bet at some point over the last couple of days you've questioned yourself as to why you're even here in Philly with me."

He was so right.

"Believe me, Tony. I'd question why I was having dinner with you one hundred and twenty miles away in another city, if you were black as the ace of spades."

"All right, I'll shut up then."

"If I seem a bit off balance to you, it's only because we don't really know each other. We met when? The end of May? What's that? Six weeks ago? And yet here we are, already taking a vacation together. We're just beginning to learn about one another. Getting to know a man on any level can bring a woman a certain level of anxiousness."

"You present your argument well, Counselor. You must be a hell of a lawyer. I'd love to see you work a courtroom."

"You trying to be funny, Gianni?"

"No, ma'am."

"Funny you should mention that, though."

"Why's that?"

"Oh, I'm just a little concerned about a client whose

divorce I'm handling . . . but never mind that. No talking shop here. We're on vacation, right?"

"Can I ask you one more question before we drop this subject entirely?"

"If you must," I sighed.

"Are you telling me you wouldn't be just a *little* bit more relaxed if you were in this restaurant having dinner with a black guy instead of me? You know, a lot of people can't deal with this right here. Folks stare, look at you funny. Some black women can't *stand* the sight of a black man with a white woman . . ."

I nearly blurted out to him that I'm a card-carrying member of that club, but caught myself. This definitely wasn't the time to go *there*.

"Derrick, my roommate—"

"The black guy?"

"Mmm-hmm. You know he's dating an Asian woman."

"I didn't know that."

"Yeah. And whenever he's out with Li'l Sushi, he's got some incident to tell me about when he gets back to the apartment. And it almost always involves some encounter he's had with a black woman. Generally him getting the 'look of death' as he calls it."

"Excuse me, Tony. Did I hear you correctly? Did you say *Li'l Sushi?*"

"Yeah. That's Derrick's pet name for his girl."

Brothas, I sighed under my breath.

"Well, let me tell you. I've been getting plenty of looks from the brothas on South Street this week," Tony goes on. "Though, I'm certain they're not for the same reasons Derrick's getting grief from the sistas."

I don't want to, but my curiosity won't let me not ask.

"Oh? What's the reason for the looks *you're* getting?"

"They're not looks of disapproval, I do know that.

They're more like looks of awe. You know, *Day-um, homie. How that white boy pull that?*"

Tony's got me laughing again—hard. I have to put my knife and fork down, and take a timeout from my meal so I don't choke to death. I'm thinking he's a little too funky for a white guy. Says he's Italian, but there's got to be a little chocolate mixed in there somewhere.

"Know what, Bailey G?"

"What, Tony G?"

"I do not care if somebody's got an issue with me being out with a woman who's not an Italian-American. If some bruh's got an issue with me being with a black woman, too bad. If some white girl has an issue with the same, too bad. I find you interesting, Bailey. I think you're attractive, sexy, funny. You're a young, black, female attorney, and though I can't possibly relate, I know enough to get where you are you've probably had to negotiate more than a few obstacles. More than the average white woman in your position would have had to, I'm sure."

"Well, thanks for being cognizant of that. It means a lot."

"You've accomplished a great deal at a young age. I admire that about you. So, before we hit Ninety-Five South and head for home in the morning, let me tell you right here, right now, I'm really glad you decided to take me up on my offer. I've enjoyed your company these past few days. In fact, I'm going to put myself out there and admit something to you."

"What's that?"

"I'm feeling you. Probably a lot more than you're feeling me right now. But that's okay, see. It's still early. Hopefully that might change as you get to know me better."

I was taken off guard by Tony's candor. So much so that I offered no response to what he just said. An awkward silence engulfed our table. I felt sort of embarrassed for him right then. He broke the awkward silence with a change of subject.

"So . . . are you full yet?"

"Stuffed. Kudos, Gianni. This was delicious. You were right on about this restaurant."

"Dessert?"

"Yes, but not here. What's next on the agenda?"

"Why don't we go to Penn's Landing and watch the fireworks?"

"Groovy. But you have to let me stop and get some ice cream on the way there. I'm going to go use the little-girls' room before we leave."

"And I'm'a hit this check while you do that."

Fireworks lit up the black sky over the Delaware River. Our view of them from the Pier at Penn's Landing was awesome. The Fourth of July was upon us and we were checking out in the morning. The city was hype that night. Everyone was out and about: young people, old people, black people, white people, gays, lesbians, freaks, freakettes. I was having my dessert, two scoops of Häagen Dazs mint chip. Tony's arm felt nice wrapped around my shoulder. Look, I know what I said about the "no-contact zone." The night air was a bit chilly by the water, okay?

And that's when it happened. Like a scene out of some old black-and-white movie—no pun intended. Awkward, unrehearsed, and totally spontaneous. In the middle of watching the fireworks, we simultaneously turned to each other. Tony's eyes diverted from mine and focused in on my full, thick lips. My eyes remained focused on his brown eyes and jet-black hair. Hair that always looked as if he just stepped out of the shower and it was still wet. Not a word was spoken between us. We just stared at one another. A stare that seemed to go on indefinitely, though in reality, lasted no more than a few seconds. My head began to have a conversation with me.

No, no, no. Don't do it, girl . . .

My body interrupted; told my head to take a hike.

Please! Go for yours, girl. You're among strangers . . .

While my mind and body duked it out, Tony leaned in, lowered his six-one frame to meet my considerably shorter one, and kissed me. Yes indeed. I let a white man kiss me—in *public* no less! I didn't even try to resist. Didn't do jack—again. My head was too disgusted with me.

Gol-lee and gee effin' whiz, Bailey. What 'chu go and let him do that for?

Seconds elapsed. Tony disengaged his lips from mine and resumed his prior position. I took a deep breath, and sheepishly asked, "What was that for?"

He said nothing. So what did I do? Answered his hush with a kiss of my own, that's what. When our lips met again, I opened my mouth, inviting Tony's tongue to come inside and play with mine. He enthusiastically accepted the invitation. As his tongue traced circles against the roof of my mouth, mine tickled the bottom of his. Tony tasted good. Like Häagen Dazs mint chip.

By the time we got back to D.C., and somehow despite my subconscious denials, my feelings had begun turning in a direction I never thought possible for them to go.

15

Playing My Cards Right

I drove my Audi up into the driveway of Mo's three-level townhouse in Largo. I really dug his townhouse because it had a driveway and a garage. Not to mention a decent-sized lawn out front and yard in the back. Some of those so-called town homes in the area were a complete joke: small, cramped, and stacked one on top of another.

Anyway, that night, Mo was having a few friends over to play Spades and Bid Whist, socialize, and eat chips with dip and other assorted finger foods. He and Lisa threw these types of get-togethers fairly regularly. I packed an overnight bag because Lisa wanted me to ride out to the Rehoboth outlets in Delaware with her first thing in the morning. Tonight would be the first I'd gotten to see those two since they got back from their romantic escape in the Poconos. I was dying to hear all about it. I had been fantasizing about going to the Poconos myself one day—when I landed my Mr. Right, that is. (Being that my love life was so not happening at the moment, I lived vicariously through Mo and Lisa, if you hadn't gathered that already.) At the same time, Lisa was dying to know what I ultimately ended up doing while she was up in the mountains of Pennsylvania sipping champagne, eating strawberries, and watching herself make love in the mirrored headboard of the big, heart-shaped bed she and Mo slept in. I chose to keep her in suspense for a few days after I got back. I really wanted to *see* the look on her face when I told her that I went away with Tony. She was going to flip!

Mo answered the door. After he greeted me with a hug and a "whassup," I handed him a container of my homemade spinach dip that I brought over for the party and waltzed inside his house. Mo had quite the decorative touch for a man. His home didn't at all resemble your typical bachelor's pad. There were no black leather sofa and love seat to be found anywhere. The majority of the house was done up in a color scheme of multiple shades of brown and lime green, with accents of black splattered throughout. A pretty funky scene, and it worked. All his furnishings sat on a foundation of plush, cream-colored carpeting that ran throughout the entire house. It was shoes-off when you stepped in that man's abode—no exceptions. Mo was quite the neat freak, too, as you've probably surmised. Yet one more thing Lisa had to get used to, in addition to his height and skin tone. She was quite the queen of domestic disarray.

Gathered around the round oak kitchen table playing cards were some old faces and a new one I hadn't seen before. Of the old faces was a sista named Franchesca—Frankie, for short—who worked with Lisa at Fannie Mae. Frankie had a gorgeous face, cinnamon-colored with a few freckles around the nose. She was about my height, and very thick in the thighs. To get a true picture of Frankie, I'd say think of an overweight Halle Berry, if you can imagine such a thing. The sista could definitely stand to lose thirty pounds or more. But that was her issue—I had my own, okay? Oh, that new face I mentioned, well, it belonged to this very handsome brotha. Butterscotch complexion, short, wavy, reddish-brown hair, thin nose, narrow lips, and dark brown eyes. He resembled that BET newscaster, Ed Gordon, a little bit. Even seated, I could tell he was pretty tall. And though I no longer had a sweet tooth for butterscotch, I could definitely lick this one from head to toe. *Hello!*

The card game was already in full swing, with Lisa at the head of the table talking her usual shit—how she was going to whup everyone's ass.

"Whassup, girl?" she enthusiastically greeted me when I entered the kitchen.

"Everybody, y'all remember my best friend, Bailey. Bailey, I think you remember everyone here."

"Faces, but I'm terrible with names, so give 'em to me again," I told her. Lisa went around the table and introduced everyone.

"That's Pete over there. His girlfriend, Willow; Greg, his wife, Natalie; and that's Kevin . . ."

(FYI, Kevin was the cutie-pie I hadn't seen before.)

". . . and I know you remember Frankie."

"Oh yeah, I remember Ms. Frankie. How you been, girlfriend? Long time no see."

"Fine, and you? I love what you've done with your hair," she remarked, referring to my cornrow extensions.

"All right already. Enough yakkin', Bailey, grab a chair, sit down, and get in this game so I can whup your ass, too," Lisa bragged.

"In a minute. What you got up in here to drink, Mo?"

"Coronas, Zinfandel, wine coolers, juice, water . . ."

"I'll have a Corona."

"Help yourself, they're in the fridge."

I grabbed a Corona out of the refrigerator, then accidentally on purpose pulled a chair up next to that cute Kevin fellow. Lisa was looking dead at me when I did so and gave me one of her patented looks. I silently mouthed *Mind your business* to her.

Twenty minutes or so into Spades, it was clear, whose night it was going to be—Lisa's. The heifer was on fire. Whuppin' everybody's ass, just as she predicted.

"You go, girl," Mo cheered his woman on. "My baby's the shit, ain't she?"

His sentiment was met with a collective round of "*What-eva*" from all the other players seated around the table.

"You know it, Sweet Daddy," Lisa said, planting a wet sloppy kiss on Mo's lips in front of everyone.

"Ill. You two need to get a room," I sarcastically told them.

"Don't hate," Mo fired back.

"Y'all still must be feeling the love from that week in the Poconos, huh?" Pete remarked.

"We had a bomb-diggity time, Pete," Mo told him.

"Which resort did y'all stay at?" asked Willow, Pete's girl.

"Cove Haven."

"What suite?"

"The Garden of Eden. That's the one with the indoor pool, the heart-shaped whirlpool . . . it was all that and then some. You and Pete should go if you haven't been there yet."

"We've been," said Mo's other friend, Greg. "I took my wife there two years ago."

"Where did you and Natalie stay?" Lisa inquired.

"In the Champagne Towers at Paradise Stream. Man, me and Natty were drinking champagne butt-naked *in* a champagne glass!"

"*Greg!*" Natalie playfully slapped her husband upside his head, embarrassed by his semi-revealing revelation.

"*Heelloo,* can we change the subject up in here please?" I chimed in, breaking up the little love-fest going on. "Greg, that was a TMI violation."

"What's that?" he asked.

"Too much information!"

Everybody at the table burst out laughing.

"Besides, all this talk about champagne this and heart-shaped that is about to make a sista gag up in here."

"Oh, that's okay, 'cause we're all gonna be gaggin' once we taste your spinach dip," Mo jon'd on me.

I couldn't let him get away with that.

"Mo."

"What?"

"Yo' mama! Look," I continued, "y'all need to show a little compassion for the single people here who don't have the luxury of a partner to join them on a romantic escapade to the Poconos. Can I get an amen from all the 'Minus Spouse or Significant Others' in the house tonight?"

Okay. That was just my nosy little way of finding out that Kevin fellow's relationship status. Pretty slick, huh? Anyway, a hearty "Amen" he proclaimed. (Ah, sookie-sookie now.)

"Don't fret, Bailey," Lisa said. "From the looks of things, you may not be a member of that club for too much longer—if you play your cards right. Get it? Cards right? Aw man, my quick wit just slays me at times."

"Say what? What's going on baby? Has Bailey met somebody?" Mo inquired.

"Oh. I haven't told you, Boo. Bailey's got herself a—"

"Shut up, Lisa!"

"Oops. Never mind, Boo."

"I'm sorry, tell me your name again," I turned to Kevin and asked, changing the subject.

"It's Kevin."

"Right, Kevin. Do you work with Maurice?"

"No. I'm Franchesca's cousin. I'm staying with her for a few days."

"Is that right? Where do you live?"

"Minneapolis."

"As in Minnesota?"

"Yep."

"Whoa. I didn't know there were any black people in Minneapolis."

"Prince," Lisa said, putting her two cents into what I had intended to be a private conversation. For that she received a patented look of my own.

"Well, aside from me, there are ten other black people in the state." Kevin said that with such conviction, I didn't immediately catch on that he was being facetious.

"Whew. I could *never* live in Minneapolis."

"Oh yeah? Why not?"

"Because. It's too cold there. You know our people don't like cold weather."

"That's true. Winter can be brutal. But I've found living in Minneapolis to be just like anything else in life. You search to find a positive or two in the situation and work hard to make the adjustment. Over time, you realize that what you may not have liked about it at first was just small stuff in the big scheme of things. I've got a job I love and a nice home in a very nice community. As soon as I moved there, I went out and cleared the shelves of an Eddie Bauer store. So now I've got an impressive collection of gear to brave the elements with. Trust me. Living in Minnesota ain't all that bad. Even with the cold weather."

"My, what an excellent parallel, Kevin," Lisa said, putting her two cents into our conversation again and simultaneously giving me another of her looks.

Didn't have a clue what her last look was about.

The card games went on until about ten o'clock before we called it a night, at which time Mo summoned all the guys down into the basement to check out his Nintendo collection and his new 52-inch big-screen TV. Lisa threw a pot of coffee on the stove for the ladies. I went up to Frankie and playfully punched her in the arm.

"That's for not telling me you had such a handsome cousin, Frankie. C'mon, girlfriend. Let's me and you go into the living room and chat a bit."

We excused ourselves from the rest of the ladies, left the kitchen, and sat on the living room floor. (Mo's living room furniture was for show only. No sitting.)

"My bad, Bailey. Heck, I didn't even mention Kevin to Lisa. I forget about my cousin sometimes. It's not like we see or talk to each other that often, living in different states. In fact, the last time we got together was about three years ago when I went out to Minneapolis to visit him."

"Was he born there?"

"Minneapolis? Oh, no. We're both from Cleveland. Kevin was really into sports back in high school and lucked up and got a basketball scholarship to play for the University of Minnesota. Unfortunately, his game in college didn't live up to the promise it showed in high school. He didn't make the NBA. He did receive a few offers to play in Europe, though. Kevin played pro ball for two years overseas. One year in Turkey and another in . . . Greece, I believe it was. After that, he got homesick and decided to give up basketball, come back to the States, and get a corporate job."

"Impressive. Can I be nosy?"

"Go ahead."

"Okay. So he's not involved with anyone, right? How old is he?"

"Kevin's about two years younger than me, so he's thirty-one. Thirty-one or thirty-two. I forget. Why? You dig?"

"I dig."

"Well, I'll have to let my cousin know that. Although I must correct you about one small thing."

"What's that?"

"Kevin *does* have a girlfriend. At least he did when he arrived at my apartment two days ago. I don't know what he was calling himself 'amen-ing' about earlier when you asked that question at the table."

"Say what?"

"A white girl."

"Uh-uh."

"Mmm-hmm. Named Becky Sue."

Silence.

I punched Frankie in the arm again.

"Tsk, girl, you had me going there for a second."

"I swear I'm not making this up. Kevin's dating a white girl named Becky Sue, from Eden Prairie, Minnesota."

"That beautiful brotha's with a white girl? Named *Becky Sue?* Lawd, have mercy! What is going on in the black community? Are the brothas abandoning us in droves or what?"

Urrgh. With that bit of news, the wind left my sails.

"Hmph. It sure seems that way doesn't it? But you got

to cut my cuz some slack, Bailey. Remember, he does live in Minneapolis. It's not like he's going to be meeting a whole lot of sistas living there."

"This is true."

"Now, I will say this much about Kevin. Growing up in Ohio, that boy loved him some brown sugar. But like the saying goes, 'When in Rome, do like the Romans.' Or something like that. You know what?"

"What?" I answered Frankie, my voice now heavy with dejection.

"I think he might have been digging you a little bit, too."

"Really?"

"Mmm-hmm. I think he misses the taste of brown sugar from time to time. I think you may have reminded him of how much tonight."

"What 'chu talking about, girlfriend?"

"Kevin pinched me on the leg when you walked in the kitchen earlier and whispered in my ear, 'Who's that?'"

I suddenly felt the wind returning to my sails. Frankie glanced at her watch.

"Ooh, it's getting late, I got to get out of here. Why don't I do this—"

Frankie opened her purse and took out a piece of paper and a pen.

"Give me your number, Bailey. I'll feel Kevin out. See what the deal is with him and Becky Sue. If I get the slightest impression that he might be interested in getting to know you or that things aren't exactly copacetic between those two, I'll give him your number. How's that sound?"

"That sounds workable!"

I gave Frankie my number and we hugged. Afterward, we returned to the kitchen so she could say good-bye to Lisa and the other ladies, who were still drinking coffee and chit-chattin'. Right about that time, the guys came back upstairs from the basement. I promptly went over to say good-bye to Kevin.

"Your cousin's about to leave, so I wanted to tell you that it was a pleasure meeting you, Kevin."

"Same here, Bailey."

I was hoping he'd say a little more to me than that, but he didn't. Despite what Frankie had just told me, I didn't get the slightest vibe that he was interested in me at all. Phooey. I wasn't going to sweat it one way or the other.

"Stay warm out there in the cold Midwest."

"No doubt."

When all the guests had gone home, I helped Lisa clear the table and tidy the kitchen. Afterward, the two of us went downstairs into the basement to talk for a bit before retiring for the night. Mo came downstairs a few minutes after us and began playing a video game. Mo's basement, by the way, *was* typical male. Adorning his walls were posters of sports icons like Michael Jordan and Muhammad Ali, and scantily clad, big-booty pin-up chicks from all around the globe. And yes, Lisa was totally cool with the latter.

"Okay, I've waited long enough. Tell me. What did y'all do in the Poconos, Lisa?"

"Made our own X-rated video in the Garden of Eden," Mo interrupted. "Wanna check it out, B?"

"You? Naked? Hell, no!"

"Oh, be quiet, Mo. Don't pay him any mind, Bailey. In his *dreams* we made an X-rated video. Look here; forget about what we did for a minute. Let's talk about you. What did you end up doing while we were away?"

"I went to Philly for a couple of days."

"No you didn't, girl. You went away with Tony?"

"*Who's Tony?*"

"Mind your business, Mo. I'm talking to Bailey."

"Uh, I do believe this is *my* house, Lisa."

"What-eva. Just sit over there, play with your joystick, and stop interrupting us. Go ahead, Bailey."

"Well, I decided to take your advice—at the last minute of course—and only because every other guy I called had already made plans."

"Mmm-hmm. *Right.* C'mon, give me the details."

"Tony and I talked and he asked me if I would stay with him for a couple of days up there. I agreed, packed a bag, and waited for him to come and pick me up. We got to Philly on Saturday afternoon and left Tuesday morning."

"Cool beans! Where did y'all stay?"

"At a Marriot hotel in Center City."

"Uh huh. Tell me more, tell me more."

"Um . . . we stayed in the same hotel room—separate beds of course. At first, Tony booked us separate rooms, but I thought that was a bit ridiculous. Don't you?"

"I concur. How did sharing a room with him for three nights work out?"

"Fine. No problems at all. He didn't snore, have any bad hygiene habits, or anything like that."

Lisa stretched out on the futon she sat on, kicked her legs in the air, raised her hands to the heavens, and began hollering, "OH, MY GOD, I CAN'T BELIEVE IT. I CAN-NOT BELIEVE IT!"

Next, she took a deep breath, lowered her voice, and asked point-blank, "Did you fuck him?"

"*No!* How may times I got to tell you this, Lisa? I ain't sleeping with no white guy."

"You went to bed with a loaf of Wonder Bread, Bailey?" That was Mo, again, finding his way all up into our conversation. Now it was my turn to raise my voice, 'cause like Marvin Gaye said, these two were about to make me wanna holler.

"HELLOOOO, Y'ALL AIN'T LISTENING! I DIDN'T SLEEP WITH ANYBODEEE! Not a white man, brown man, Chinese man, no man! Got that?"

Mo dropped his joystick on the floor, rushed over, and plopped down on the futon next to Lisa.

"Who's this white boy?" he asked. I looked at him incredulously.

"Humor him, Bailey. Please, or he won't go away," Lisa said.

"If you *must* know, Maurice, his name's Tony. Tony Gianni."

"Bailey says he's really good-looking, Mo."

"Gianni . . . Gianni . . . what's he, Jewish?"

"*Italian,*" Lisa and I said in unison.

"Is that a problem?" I asked Mo.

"Not at all. Ain't nothing wrong with you going out with an Italian dude. Not to me. *Y'all* are the ones that be trippin' over that interracial stuff, not us."

A scowl quickly replaced the smile that had been on Lisa's face.

"I beg your pardon?" she said.

Mo quickly deduced that he had probably treaded where he shouldn't have.

"Uh, I think now is a good time for me to see my way out of y'alls conversation and get back to my game."

"Yeah, you do that," Lisa told him. "Now, back to you, Bailey. So what exactly did you and Tony do for three days in Philly?"

"Quite a bit actually. Visited a few museums, did some shopping on South Street, had dinner at a couple of really neat restaurants, watched a fireworks show, went to Dave & Busters and played some arcade games. Oh, and Tony took me to this really nice jazz club called Zanzibar Blue. I really had a great time."

"Sounds like it. See, didn't I tell you that you would have a good time? Aren't you glad you took my advice and went with Tony?"

"I am. It was one of the most enjoyable getaways I've had in a long time."

"Good. So, are you feeling differently at all about him now?"

"Mmm-hmm. I'm feeling *something*."

I shifted my eyes away from Lisa and over in the direction of Mo, who was now entrenched in his video game and finally minding his own business. She knew what I wanted her to do.

"Maurice, darling."

"Yes?"

"It's late. Why don't you give that game a rest and go to bed. I'll be up shortly."

Mo paused and looked over at the two of us. Our expressions said it all.

"Aw'aight, a brotha can take a hint. I'm outta here. Don't stay down here too long."

"I won't, honey. Good night."

Mo strolled over and kissed Lisa goodnight and said the same to me before marching upstairs to bed.

Finally, we had some privacy to talk.

"Okay, I'm all ears, B. Tell me. What's this you're feeling?"

16

Single, Looking, and Hoping

"I don't know what to call this feeling I'm feeling, but I'm not feeling it," I told Lisa and laughed.

"You've got to give me a little more than that to go on."

"Tony's a good guy, he really is. And the more I spend time with him . . ."

"Aaah, I know what this is about. You're catching feelings for this guy, aren't you?"

"Is this insane or what, Lisa? I mean, Tony is *hardly* what I had in mind. I'm not even attracted to white men for crying out loud."

"This is true. But for whatever reason, you're attracted to *this* one."

"What's up with that?"

"Attraction's a baffling phenomenon, Bailey. Just when you think you've got your love blueprint down pat, boom! Cupid throws you a curve ball and gets you all off balance."

"Off balance, huh? That's interesting. That's the exact term Tony used to describe my state of mind as he saw it."

"Listen. When I met Maurice, I thought he was too light and too short. But the afternoon we met, I was in a place that allowed me to be receptive to someone I wouldn't have normally been receptive to. I had to give it to him. The brotha came correct that Wednesday, September fourteenth, on Amtrak Metroliner number 127. And because he did, I couldn't deny him the opportunity to win me over. Now, I'm not going to sit here and lie to you. It *did* help that he wasn't ugly, had command of the English language, and didn't approach me with some bullshit pickup line. I was going to be on that train for the next three hours or so. I was single, looking, and hoping—just like you right now. Reading a book or taking some work out of my bag to do wasn't going to cure my love jones. What did I have to lose? By the time that train pulled into Union Station three hours later, the fact that this brotha wasn't the package I had in mind didn't seem like much of an issue anymore. Cupid tossed me that curve ball, and I was going to try my hardest to knock it out of the ballpark."

"I feel you, girl, but c'mon. At least Mo is *black*. Right about now, I *wish* Tony was a short, light-skinned brotha."

"Well, he's got the light part down pat."

"Fun-ny, Lisa. I'm just saying I could work with *that*."

"No you couldn't."

"Could, too."

"Please. Don't give me that. If Tony were a short, light-skinned brotha you'd be ready to kick him to the curb for being just that—a short, light-skinned brotha. You're only saying this now because that seems like a better alternative to the one you're currently dealing with. I've known you nearly my entire life, Bailey. You're picky. Always have been. Too much for your own good. I'll say it again. Mr. Right doesn't always come in the package—"

"Oh, for cryin' out loud. Are we back on that again? You sound like a broken record, Lisa. I'm out of here."

"You can't leave."

"Why not?"

"You're spending the night, remember?"

"Oh, yeah. In that case, shut up, Lisa! Change the subject. What 'chu think about Frankie's cousin? That right there was some butterscotch eye-candy that even a dark-chocolate-lovin'-sista like me could work with."

"Yeah, Kevin had it going on. I was surprised when Frankie strolled in here with him. She never mentioned to me that she had a cousin in Minneapolis. I peeped you trying to get your mack on. You were about as obvious as Al Sharpton front-and-center at a Klan rally."

"Was I?"

"Yes, you were!"

"Ah, it doesn't matter. Kevin and I had no shot at being a love connection anyway with him living out there in the cold-as-hell state of Minnesota."

"You see, that's part of your problem right there."

"Gol-lee and gee effin' whiz, Lisa. What did I do now?"

"Do you have any idea why I gave you that look when you were talking to Kevin earlier?"

"Uh, no, but I gather you're about to let me know."

"Here's a guy—a nice looking guy—that for all you know might be a hell of a catch. On top of that, he happens to be the cousin of a good friend of your best friend. Which means you've automatically got two people in your corner who could be of great assistance to you in your efforts to get closer to this man. You with me so far?"

"I'm with you."

"He tells you where he lives and what's the *first* thing that comes flyin' out of your big mouth? 'I could *never* live there.'"

"Tsk. Don't you think you're being a wee bit over-dramatic here?"

"Au contraire. I don't think I'm being overdramatic at all. Suppose this Kevin dude was digging you, Bailey. So much so that he was thinking about hollerin' at you because he's single, looking, and hoping, too? Now, suppose he's looking for a woman that's open to relocating because he happens to love living in the cold-as-hell state of Minnesota? You see where I'm going with this? With that ill-timed remark of yours—no matter how innocent you thought it was—you may have given Kevin a reason to cancel your ass as a prospect before he even got a chance to learn anything about you."

"But I was telling him the truth. I *wouldn't* want to live in Minneapolis."

"First thing? *Never* say never, Bailey. Didn't your Grandma Lucy Pearl ever tell you that? Secondly, did this dude even *ask* you if you wanted to live in Minneapolis?"

"Well . . . no."

"*Duh!* Then what are you *volunteering* totally unnecessary and useless information for? Confucius says, 'He no ask, you no tell.'"

"Did he really?"

"No, dummy. I'm just fuckin' with you. My point is: who knows? If you had kept your trap shut, you and Kevin might have really hit it if off tonight. And then who knows? Both of you may have gained a totally new perspective on your geographical preferences. You might have gained a new perspective on living in the Midwest. It's not cold there *all* of the time. He may have come to the conclusion that he'd be a fool not to do whatever was necessary for him to lock up a prize package such as yourself. A package he's damn sure not likely to find living in lily-white Minneapolis. It's like the dude so poignantly stated earlier. You look for a positive in a given situation and go on from there. The small stuff and the important stuff will all sort itself in due time. Look at it this way. At worse, you've met yourself a cool brotha who lives in another state. And you know what I say about having quality male friends. Bottom line, I'm going to tell you something you like to say to me a lot: *Shut up, Bailey! Just let things flow, for crying out loud!*"

"Okay, okay. You've made your point. You sound like Tony now."

"Oh?"

"He says he wants things between us to flow naturally."

"He told you that?"

"Mmm-hmm. He really likes me. He's hoping we can have a relationship with each other. And I'm speaking more than friends. And one other thing. I didn't sleep with him like I said, but I did leave out a li'l som'um."

"What?"

"We swapped spit."

Silence.

"Bailey."

"Yes, Lisa."

"I think it's about time I met this Tony dude."

AUGUST . . .

17

Foursome

I awoke at the crack of dawn Saturday morning. Probably because I had too much on the brain when I went to bed Friday night. Rose Braxton's divorce case, for one. It had been a couple of weeks since her husband was served. So far, I hadn't heard any news from her or from her husband's attorney, if he had indeed retained one. In any event, Mr. Braxton had thirty days to respond to the summons. I was truly hoping—as was Rose—that he would not try to contest the divorce. With alimony and child custody issues also on the table, this wasn't likely to be an easy, quick wrap-up anyway. I knew any additional resistance on Mr. Braxton's part would only drag matters out longer. I was simply going to have to adopt a "no news is good news" attitude for the time being, unless I heard something to the contrary. I did however, feel much better knowing we did get a restraining order for Rose in the event that her husband decided to act the fool.

On a lighter note—I suppose—another reason I had trouble sleeping was because of what I was scheduled to do on a social trip later that evening. Ready for this? Tony and I were going on a double date with Mo and Lisa. I'm sure I don't have to tell you that the prospect of this foursome had a sista one part anxious and one part excited. Excited because I really wanted Mo and Lisa—well, mostly, Lisa—to meet Tony. Besides, she had been buggin' me to make this happen ever since I was over to play cards with them; it was practically all she talked about during the drive out to Delaware the following morning. Now, I know some women will say it really doesn't matter to them if their best friend likes the man . . . I mean, *male friend,* in their life or not. Not me. I care. Which in turn got me thinking about a number of things. Like what if my best friend in the whole wide world didn't like Tony after finally meeting him face to face? What if she thought he was unattractive? A total wuss-ass? Wondered what the hell I saw in him in the first place? How about the opposite extreme? What if she really liked Tony? Found him to be a slice of Caucasian nirvana, and therefore felt I should cease acting like the picky you-know-what she swears that I am, forgo my obsessive, long-standing nothing-but-a-black-man-will-do-for-me mantra, and allow myself to be swept away in the swirl? Either way, I knew one thing was for certain: I'd have a much clearer perspective on me, Tony, and the concept of interracial relationships by this same time tomorrow.

We all decided the forum for our double date ought to be a nice dinner somewhere. The only question was where. Mo and Lisa graciously said they'd leave that up to Tony and me. I was thinking the Cheesecake Factory or Houston's. Or maybe it would be special to dine somewhere all four of us hadn't been before. Perhaps

that Italian restaurant on the corner of Wisconsin and
N Street in Georgetown I recalled seeing the last time I
was passing through that part of town.

I let out a big yawn, stretched, rubbed my eyes, and
peeked at the clock radio facing me on my nightstand.
Its big red numbers said 8:22 AM. Hopefully Tony was up
by now. I wanted to get his input, so I gave him a buzz
to see if he had any thoughts about where we should go
to eat.

"Hello?"

"Good morning, Mr. Gianni. Did I wake you?"

"Good morning to you, too, Ms. Gentry. No, I'm wide
awake."

"What 'chu doing?"

"Putting on a pair of sweat shorts and getting ready for
my morning run. You're not calling to tell me tonight
isn't happening anymore, are you?"

"Nope, nothing like that. We're still on. In fact, my
friends are really looking forward to it."

"Good, 'cause so am I. This should be fun."

"Do you have a preference on where you want go?" I
asked.

"I've got a few ideas. Your friends like ethnic food
at all?"

"Such as?"

"Ethiopian? Thai? There are a couple of nice spots I
know of not far from my place in Adams Morgan."

"Ethnic food, huh? Cool. I hadn't even thought along
those lines. I'm not sure if they like Ethiopian or Thai,
but I'm certainly down to give it a try. Let me call over
there and find out—"

"Wait up, Bailey. Before you do, tell me what you had
in mind."

"Um, I don't know, I was just hoping we could go

somewhere that none of us have eaten before. I had this Italian spot in Georgetown in mind. Paolo's. Heard of it?"

Tony laughed.

"What's so funny?"

"I've eaten there a few times before."

"Damn!"

"But it's cool, B. We can still go if you want to."

"Did you like the food?"

"All day, every day."

"I don't know, Tony. Now that I think about it, I like your idea better."

"You sure? 'Cause I really don't have a problem eating at Paolo's again."

"I'm sure. How's the parking situation?"

"Horrific. It's a total madhouse weekends on Eighteenth Street. My advice is that everyone gets there early to allow sufficient enough time to . . . never mind. Skip it. Let's just go to Georgetown."

"How come?"

"Because you're not even sure if your friends like Ethiopian or Thai, and if they haven't tried it before, tonight may not be the best time for experimenting. Know what I mean? And besides, like I said, it's going to be murder trying to find parking. We won't have that problem in Georgetown. There are plenty of garages and lots all over the place. Since this is our first time going out with your friends, let's just keep it simple, okay? Hopefully, it won't be our last outing together. We can do the ethnic thing another time."

"That makes sense. Listen, I'm going to swing by your apartment and pick you up. Unless your ego won't let you play passenger to a woman driver."

"My ego's got no problem with that. You *can* drive, can't you?"

"You're just going to have to find that out aren't you? Buckle up."

"Since you're picking me up, I have a request to make."

"And what's that?"

"I want you to come by a little early and actually *visit* my home before we meet your friends for dinner. We can have a glass of wine together, and I'll let you listen to a few cuts off my *Weather Report* CD. Uh, that's real jazz, Bailey, unlike that pop-ish, watered-down stuff you like to listen to."

Prior to Tony's request, I had paid no mind to the fact that neither of us had ever set foot in the other's home. We had always arrived for our dates in separate cars. Tony did come to my condo complex that one time to pick me up when we were going to Philly, but I never invited him upstairs.

"I can do that. What time should we meet them at the restaurant?"

"Six is good."

"Six it is, then. I'll call Mo and Lisa, tell them where we're going and what time to be there. I'll give you a call when I'm on my way over to your place."

"Cool. Oh . . ."

"Yes?"

"Dress code?"

"Casual. No tennis shoes."

Tony laughed, and hung up the phone. He knew I was just messin' with him. He wouldn't dare show up in Adidas—unlike a few guys from my past who had the unmitigated audacity to take me to dinner in full athletic attire.

Now, I suppose I could have waited a bit later to call Mo and Lisa, but after getting off the phone with Tony,

I was suddenly feeling kind of hyped about tonight, and not paying attention to the time anymore. In my excitement, I totally forgot that Mo likes to sleep late on the weekends. Too late. The phone was already ringing. I was hoping Lisa would answer, but Mo did on the third ring.

"Good morning, Mo," I said, sounding chirpy as a parakeet. "May I speak to Lisa?"

"You woke me up, Bailey," he said, sounding both dazed and peeved at the same time.

I glanced over at my clock radio again. Its big red numbers now read 8:31 AM. "Oops. Sorry, man. Put your woman on the phone and go back to sleep."

"Wait a second. I've got a question for you."

"What's that?"

"We still hookin' up with you and your new boyfriend later?"

"He's not my boyfriend, and yes, we're still on for dinner."

"Then what is he to you?"

"Just a friend."

Mo started croonin' the old Biz Markie hit.

"Yoouuu, got what I nee-eed, but you say he's just a friend, oh you say he's just a friend. Oh baby—"

"Maurice!"

"What, Bailey?"

"Shhhh. Stop singing. Please. Didn't you just say I woke you up?"

"You did."

"Then you're probably a little incoherent right now. The sooner you put Lisa on the phone, the sooner you can go back to sleep. Right?"

"Uh, right, right. Mmm, I smell bacon. She must be in the kitchen. LEE-SAAH, PICK UP THE PHONE. Later, B."

"Later, M."

"Yo, B."

"What, M?"

"Please don't call my house this early on the weekend anymore."

"Aw'aight. Sorry, dude."

Lisa picked up the line in the kitchen. "I got it, Mo. Hang up. Hello?"

"Hey, girl. What's going on?"

"Nothing. Just making breakfast. You're calling kinda of early."

"I know, I'm sorry. Your man just got finished bustin' me out for that. I just wanted to tell you what the dilly is for this evening."

"So, where are we going?" Lisa asked excitedly.

"To this Italian spot in Georgetown called Paolo's. Heard of it?"

"On Wisconsin and N?"

"Ah, man, don't tell me you've eaten there already, too."

"Naw, I haven't. I've just seen the place before."

"Good. Meet us at the restaurant. Six o'clock. And I don't mean six o'clock *C.P.* time either, Lisa."

"Heifer, please. I know *your* ass ain't talking. Just make sure you and Tony are on time. You better not have us waiting on y'all."

"We'll be there on time. Dress is casual. And please tell Maurice to behave himself tonight."

"Don't worry about him."

"I guess that's it then. I'll see y'all later this evening."

"I'm so excited, Bailey. I can't wait to finally meet this guy!" Lisa's giddiness over our impending foursome had me feeling more anxious than excited all over again.

"Lisa Parker?"

"What, Bailey Gentry?"

"Don't go making a big deal out of this, okay? It's just two friends having a casual meal with more friends."

"Mmm-hmm. My bacon's about to burn. Bye, girl."

Click.

18

Mixed Signals

"Tell me, Bailey. What are you expecting out of tonight?"

I was talking to myself—out loud. Look, it wasn't like I was doing it while meandering along M Street during lunch hour. I was alone in my car on my way to Tony's. Grandma Lucy Pearl used to have conversations with herself in private all of the time. Or so she said. (I mean, it wasn't like I was *there*.) Come to think of it, once that Alzheimer's took hold of her, she became pretty talkative with herself in *public*, too. Anyways, she told me that talking to one's self is perfectly okay—so as long as you don't *answer* yourself. I never quite understood what she meant by the latter.

"Gee, I don't know, Bailey. What *are* you expecting out of tonight?" I answered myself. (Sorry, Grandma.)

"Well, let's see. I'm hungry, so I hope the food is good. Hope the conversation is stimulating. Hope Mo behaves himself and doesn't start jonin' on me in front of Tony.

Hope Lisa doesn't try to instigate a love connection. Most of all, I hope the four of us have a super-fantastic time. This could end up being the first and *only* double date Tony and I have. I could meet my black prince any day now. (Pray for me.)"

As I reached Columbia Road, butterflies begin stirring in my stomach. Why, I don't know. Oh, who was I trying to kid. I knew exactly why I had butterflies in my stomach. I knew this evening was not just another date with Tony. This wasn't just two friends having dinner with more friends, the spiel I tried handing Lisa earlier that morning—which I knew she wasn't buying at all. Truth was, what was about to go down this evening was on a whole 'nother level. Dinner, movies, late-night phone conversation, out-of-town getaways. Then a double date with my best friend? All that and a sista had *never* been the slightest bit interested in white men. Guess it was sorta like Rose Braxton put it when describing her bizarre relationship with her estranged husband, Sydney: "Go figure."

Look. I already have a pretty good idea what y'all are thinking; sounds like the start of romance, right? Bet Tony was thinking the same thing. With good reason, I suppose. Because, despite everything I had been internalizing, I'd outwardly given him every signal to think so. Hell. I *swapped spit* with the man, for cryin' out loud! But therein lies the problem with signals. I mean, how often is our mind, body, and spirit in sync with the signals we're giving off?

Let me throw out a question to you ladies. Have any of you ever found yourselves in my shoes? I don't mean contemplating a hookup with a white guy necessarily, but maybe in some other closely related way? Remember that particular guy who (to your utter bewilderment) somehow managed to find his way into your personal space? On one level he possessed almost everything you've ever wanted in a man, yet on another, was everything you so *did not* want in a man? Now ask yourself, were the signals you were sending that man accurately expressing the uncertainty that was going on inside of you? What's that? Some of you can't relate? Okay then, let me spin the question another way. A way to which most of you probably *can* relate. Do you think the signals *he* was sending *you* were truly expressing what was going on with *him*? Get it now? Mmm-hmm. Thought so.

Though I wished Tony didn't have a thing for me, at least he was being up-front with me. I could respect that. He didn't have me guessing. Didn't have me trying to read his mind. What kind of girl wouldn't be attracted to a man like that—black, white, purple, or green? Tony Gianni was doing all the right things, but I still felt he was all wrong for me. Definitely not the signal(s) I was sending him.

Lucky for me, a car was pulling out of a parking space just as I approached Tony's block. I drove right in, parked, shut off the engine and radio, and took in my surroundings for a second. Didn't see anyone on the block except for two gay guys—one black and one white—walking arm-and-arm. Damn. Even *they're* down with the swirl. I took a glimpse of myself in the rearview mirror. Hoped my face looked okay. My outfit too, for that matter. I had originally planned on rockin' my summertime "casual-but-sexy" look. Something like an eye-grabbin' halter top that exposed one or both of my shoulders and a pair of jeans that fit my ass like a glove. And by the way, though I talk about it a lot, my ass is hardly my only physical ass-set—get it? I've got a great pair of legs, too, so I wanted to show them off again. I decided to go with a snug-fitting, pink mini halter dress with matching fuchsia Steve Madden sandals that my freshly painted toes looked just too cute in. Untied my ponytail, allowing my braids to hang free and loose, coated my thick lips with some Bobbi Brown, and put on a little eyeliner. That's about as far as I went in the makeup department, though. Way I figured it, I'd wear more when I was older and had a bunch of lines, cracks, and crevices to hide. I was twenty-nine, beautiful, and loving it—no need for all of that. I took a deep breath and spoke to myself one final time before getting out of the car.

"Bailey, don't let this evening end up being a big mistake on our part."

I strolled towards the entrance of Tony's apartment building, an eight-story structure called the Wyoming, and pressed the intercom button for his apartment.

"Who is it?" a static-filled voice asked on the other end. Static aside, the voice didn't sound like Tony's, which threw me. Had me wondering if I had pressed the wrong button by accident.

"I'm looking for Tony Gianni. Do I have the right apartment?" No reply from the person on the other end of the intercom, but I was buzzed in just the same. Once inside the lobby, my first decision was whether to take the stairs or the elevator. I opted for the latter.

On a wall facing me as I exited onto the second floor were two signs. One read UNIT NUMBERS 200-205, and the other, UNIT NUMBERS 206-210. I followed the arrows pointing toward the hallway that would lead me to unit number 203. I knocked. Tony came to the door dressed in a black ribbed-knit T-shirt, showing off that well-defined body of his, and a pair of gray pleated khakis. He was looking and smelling real good.

"Whassup, Bailey? Come on in," he said, giving me a hug and a kiss on the cheek. The scent of Tony's cologne lingered on my skin following our embrace. His apartment was an old-style unit, fairly large, with beautiful hardwood floors. Other than a black leather sofa and loveseat, the living room was hardly furnished. Surrounding the kitchen area were three barstools I recognized as ones I saw in an Ikea catalog I'd gotten in the mail. I love that store. Scattered throughout the room were several large CD towers that I would guess must have held at least a thousand CDs or more.

"Have a seat and make yourself comfortable," Tony said. "Can I get you something to drink before that glass of wine?"

"I'm good. I'll wait for the wine if that's cool with you. What kind do you have anyway?" I asked.

"Got some Merlot and some Zinfandel."

"I'll have the Merlot when you get around to it. Hey, was that you who answered the intercom downstairs? Didn't sound like you."

"That was Derrick."

On cue, Derrick emerged and joined us in the living room. Something about his appearance looked different from how I remembered him at the party back in May. Couldn't put my finger on it, though.

"Speaking of the devil, Derrick, you remember Bailey don't you?"

"Sure do. How have you been since we last saw each other?"

"Just fine. And you?"

"Can't complain. Welcome to our humble abode and all that good stuff."

"Thank you."

"Will you two excuse me a moment?" Tony said. "I've got a quick call I need to make. I'll be right back, Bailey."

"Take your time, but hurry up," I told him. That drew a laugh out of Derrick and a "Not that again" out of Tony.

"I like that, Bailey. I might have to borrow it," Derrick said.

The two of us proceeded to make small talk while I waited for Tony to finish with his call.

"So, I hear you two are going to have dinner in George-town."

"Yes. We're going to be joining my girlfriend and her boyfriend there."

"Ah, okay. So you two are going on a double date. Those are fun."

"Let's hope this one is," I mumbled.

Derrick didn't hear me. Good. Just then I had a pass-ing thought. I wondered what Derrick thought about his white roomie keeping company with one of "his" women. I was awfully curious to know. I knew this much: If the shoe were on the other foot, and a brotha was in my apartment getting ready to take my white roomie . . . hold up. Tony did say Derrick was dating an Asian girl, didn't he? Hmph. Never mind. That made him a pseudo brotha in my book.

"You guys have quite the music collection I see."

"Tell me about it. We're going to need a bigger place just for all the CDs pretty soon. There's about a thou-sand of 'em between the two of us. My collection is over in those racks, and Tony's collection is in these over here," Derrick pointed. Wow. My guesstimate was right on the button.

"Mind if I take a look?"

"Go right ahead. But listen, you and Tony aren't the

only ones going out this evening. I've got a date myself, so I'm gonna have to run. But you take care, Bailey, and I hope to see you again real soon. Let Tony know I left, okay?"

"Oh, okay, Derrick. Sure. Um, nice seeing you again. Have fun."

Now it dawned on me what was different about his appearance. He shaved his beard and mustache off.

I knelt down in front of one of Tony's CD racks to check out his music collection. All the artists were filed in alphabetical order. There were a bunch of CDs by artists I had never heard of before. Must've been his jazz stuff. As for the stuff I did recognize, I was quite impressed; Bell Biv DeVoe, Will Downing, Incognito—I absolutely love that group—Teena Marie, Parliament, A Tribe Called Quest.

This has got to be the blackest white boy I have ever met, I thought to myself.

"What do you think?"

Tony startled the living crap out of me. I wasn't aware that he had finished his call and was back in the room.

"Huh?"

"My CD collection. What do you think about it?"

"Oh, your taste in music is more diverse than I thought."

"Told you. Let me guess. You were still expecting KISS, Mötley Crüe, and the Rolling Stones."

"Oh, there goes Mr. Comedian with the white-boy jokes again. You said it, not me. And for your information, *I* happen to like the Rolling Stones. I think Mick Jagger's got some rhythm, for a . . ."

"Go ahead, say it. White boy. Sorta like me, right?"

"Sorta like you." I stood up and took my seat back on the sofa.

"By the way, Bailey, I meant to tell you this when you first came in the door. You're wearing the hell outta that dress. I don't think I've ever seen you in one before. Nice wheels, too, if I may say so."

I blushed.

"Tony."

"Yeeesss?"

"Thanks for the compliment. And you *have* seen me in a dress before. I wore one in Philly."

"Did you?"

"Tsk. I see how much attention you were paying to me."

"Oh, c'mon. We both know that's a bit of an exaggeration, don't we?"

I knew exactly where Tony was going with that and I wasn't trying to meet him there.

"Your place is interesting."

"Is that a polite way of saying you don't like my apartment?"

"It's my way of saying your apartment is very nice. It's just not what I envisioned it to look like."

"That's probably because you envisioned my place being *my* place. Know what I mean? Remember, there are two distinct people living in here."

"This is true. I'm ready for that glass of wine now."

"Okey-doke. Why don't you pick out a CD and put it on while I get that?"

"Sure. But I thought you wanted me to listen to some jazz CD of yours? Weather Vane?"

"Weather *Report*, and we've got a little time for that."

Tony jogged to the kitchen and took down a couple of wine glasses from a cabinet above his head, over the sink. I retrieved Incognito's *Positivity* from his tower, put in on the changer, and forwarded it to track number nine. My favorite cut on the album: "Deep Waters." Wasn't the most upbeat song to play at that moment, but fitting for the moment. I felt as though I was treading in some deep water.

Tony handed me my glass of wine, took a seat next to me on the sofa, and offered up a toast.

"Here's to great company at present and what I'm sure will be more to come over dinner."

"Cheers," we said in unison, then touched glasses and sipped.

"Mmm, this is good, Tony."

"I'm glad you finally made it to my home, Bailey. It's not much, but I'll give you a tour when you finish with that. Would it be inappropriate for me to include a viewing of my bedroom in that tour?"

"So as long as you don't get ideas about spending any time with me in your bedroom," I replied with a smile.

"Ouch!"

"What-eva, Gianni."

"So, tell me a little more about these friends of yours we're about to go out with."

"Well, Lisa and I grew up together in Northwest. We met in third grade and have been inseparable ever since. And Maurice—or Mo, as we call him—that's Lisa's boyfriend. He's cool people. I think you'll like him. Typical dude. He's into video games, sports, music . . ."

"How long have they been going together?"

"They met in eighty-nine, so that's what? Five years now."

"How old is Mo?"

"Thirty-two."

I took another sip of my Merlot and gazed at Tony. *White men look so much better with dark hair.*

"Can I do something to you, Tony?"

"Eeew, I think I like the sound of that."

"Oh, get your mind out the gutter. I want to touch your hair."

"Touch my hair? For what?"

"I just want to see how it feels."

"You're weird, B. You know that?"

"Oh, c'mon. Cooperate with a sista, will ya?"

Tony bowed his head and allowed me to cop a feel of his mane.

"It's very soft. Dry. Not oily or greasy."

"Oily? Greasy?"

"Your hair always looks wet. Like you just stepped out of the shower and whatnot."

"I'm Italian, baby. That's just how we do it. And what's up with *your* hair?"

"*My* hair?" I said, fixin' to catch a 'tude. (Don't talk about a sista's hair, feel me?)

"I know that's not all yours—"

No he didn't.

"Dang, Gianni. Did you invite me over to insult me?"

"I'm not trying to insult you," he said—laughing his head off in the process, mind you. "Extensions, weaves, it's all good. But some of those weaves the sistas be wearing are jacked up!"

I was really trying hard not to laugh at Tony—or *with* him—but I couldn't help it.

"I know that's right."

"Not yours, though. Honest. Those braids really compliment your face. Look. I don't know how we got on the topic of hair, but since we have, I've got a question."

"No, you can't touch my hair."

"Duh! That wasn't my question."

"Don't you be duh-in' me."

"My question *is* . . . how long would your braids be if that was all your natural hair?"

"Uh . . . not very long. Next topic?"

"Oookay. I'm gon' leave that line of questioning alone."

"Good idea, Tony. You know who you remind me of?"

"Who?"

"A young Al Pacino."

Tony instantaneously went into a rendition of Pacino's classic line in the movie *Scarface*:

"*Say hello to my little friend.*"

. . . a real bad imitation.

"You think so? No one's ever told me I look like Al before. Andy Garcia maybe."

"No. Pacino. Definitely Pacino. Is there an actress you think I resemble?"

"Mmm . . . no. You are unique Bailey Gentry. Attractively unique."

"And you're quite the charmer, Mr. Gianni." *Don't know if it's me or the wine, but it's starting to get warm in here.*

"Whoa, look at the time, Tony. We should get a move on."

"Cool. But let me play you a cut from Weather Report and give you a quick tour of the place first."

While a tune called "Birdland" played, Tony gave me a tour of his apartment. Bedroom included.

19

Chatter

Despite my promise to be on time, Tony and I arrived at the restaurant fifteen minutes late. We rolled up to find Mo and Lisa standing outside in front of Paolo's waiting on us.

"Hey, girl," I greeted Lisa with a hug and kiss. "Lisa, this is Tony; Tony, my girlfriend, Lisa."

Lisa looked like a total hottie in denim shorts and a crop top that stopped about an inch above her navel, showing off her flat stomach and belly ring. In her ears were a pair of oversized hoop earrings that really set off her cute face and short boy cut. Mo was wearing a T-shirt that read DEF JAM RECORDS, a pair of cream-colored, three-quarter-length shorts that tied at the waist with a draw-string, and brown sandals. On his head was a Kangol cap turned backwards so that the kangaroo emblem was facing front.

"Nice to meet you, Tony. This is my boyfriend, Maurice."

Mo gave Tony a pound and one of those "brotha" embraces.

"Whassup, my man."

"How ya' doing?"

"Aw'aight. Now that we've got all the pleasantries out of the way, you two are late!" Lisa fussed. "Whose fault is that? Tell me it's not yours, Tony," she said jokingly. Sorta jokingly.

"I'll take the blame for that," Tony said. "Bailey and I got a little wrapped up in something and the time just kinda slipped away from us. Sorry."

"Wrapped up in something? Mmm-hmmm . . ."

"Let's get out of the street and take this inside," Mo said, cutting Lisa off before she could get on one of her rolls.

"Good idea," I said.

"Table for four? Right this way," said our attractive hostess. She was short and petite, with long black hair and an olive complexion. Must've been an Italian, like Tony. She must have also thought she was slick. Not. I noticed her making googly eyes at Tony as soon as we came in the restaurant. She was probably wondering what he was doing in here with a sista. I couldn't get mad at her on that count, though. I was sorta wondering what *I* was doing in here with him. We followed her as she proceeded to corral the perfect table for the four of us; right in the front window of the restaurant, where we could people-watch folks strolling up and down Wisconsin Avenue.

We hadn't been seated more than two minutes before Lisa—a.k.a. Ms. Jabber Jaws—started pouring it on thick.

"I'm so glad to finally meet you, Tony. Bailey's told me *sooo* much about you."

"Good things, I hope."

"But of course. You wouldn't be here with the three of us if that weren't the case, now, would you?" she kidded him.

"Who's eaten here before? What's good?" Mo grunted. It was pretty obvious he wanted Lisa to curb her enthusiasm a notch or two. Obvious to everyone *except* Lisa.

"I have," Tony said, "and I'm partial to almost everything on the menu. Y'all like Italian food, I take it."

"I'll eat almost anything. 'Specially when I'm hungry—like right now! Where's the waiter with our menus?" Mo impatiently wondered while looking around.

"How about you, Lisa?" Tony asked.

"Huh?"

"You like Italian food?"

"I do. It's probably my second favorite type of food."

"What's the first?"

"Soul food. Fried chicken, catfish, candied yams, black-eyed peas, collard greens, potato salad . . ."

Gol-lee.

"Tony *knows* what soul food is, Lisa."

"Well *excuusse me,* Missy," Lisa said, twisting her head around like it was on a swivel.

"You two behave," Mo admonished.

Having just met her, Tony was feeling my best friend, I could already surmise. That and that he was comfortable with the atmosphere. That was good. It helped me to relax, too. I hadn't gotten a good read on what Lisa thought. It was still too early.

"Are you from the South, Lisa?" Tony asked.

"No, I'm actually from right here in D.C. My parents are, though. Memphis, Tennessee."

"How 'bout you, Mo?"

"I'm a Northern boy. NYC."

"Oh yeah? What part?"

"Harlem."

"Get out. How long have you been in this area?"

"Since Eighty-six."

"Was your relocation job-related?"

"Naw, I just needed a change of scenery and a quality of life adjustment."

Lisa cleared her throat—loudly.

"What?"

"That's what he tells everybody when they ask him that question, Tony," she whispered. "I think the real reason my boyfriend moved here was to escape all the honeys he was jugglin' in Harlem. I think they all found out about one another and were about to blow up his spot."

Mo stuck his palm in Lisa's face. "Talk to the hand. As I was saying, Ton', before I was so rudely interrupted . . . I didn't want to move too far from my family. That's why I picked Maryland. Ever been to my hometown?"

"New York? Yeah. Numerous times. Never been to Harlem, though. Not yet, I should say. I really want to see a show at the Apollo and dine at Sylvia's. I hear that restaurant's all that. All day, every day."

Lisa looked at me and raised her eyebrows.

"Sylvia's huh? Then you must like soul food, too," Lisa said.

"I do. Since you're from New York, I take it you've been to both the Apollo and Sylvia's, Mo?" Tony asked.

"Many times. In fact, me and Lisa went up to New York and had dinner there about . . . what was it, Lisa?"

"Two years ago?"

"Yeah, something like that."

"Ever heard of Georgia Brown's on Fifteenth Street? Their cuisine is Southern, too," Lisa informed Tony.

"I've heard of it, but I haven't been there either. Which one do you like better?"

"What do you think, Boo?"

"They're both excellent, but two totally different atmospheres," Mo said. "GB's is more upscale, and Sylvia's is like dining in somebody's living room. It's got a real homey, laid-back feel to it."

"I'd have to agree with Mo."

"Well, cool. Thanks for the tip, y'all. I'll have to try 'em both out."

"Hey, why don't you and Bailey make New York and Harlem your next out-of-town getaway? What do you think about that, Bailey?" Lisa suggested, putting me all on the spot.

Shut up, Lisa!

"We'll see," was the best I could reply.

"I've got some relatives in New York," Tony went on. "A few in Bensonhurst, Brooklyn, and a few more in Howard Beach, Queens."

"*Infamous* Howard Beach, huh?" Mo cracked.

"Yeah, I . . . I guess you could call it that."

I wasn't sure what Mo meant by that, but Tony did, obviously, and it seemed to make him a bit uncomfortable.

"What's so infamous about Howard Beach?" My curiosity beckoned.

"I'll let Tony explain that to you later. Our waiter's finally here."

The waiter introduced himself, handed us our menus, and apologized profusely for the wait. The four of us took a time-out from table talk to peruse our dinner options. After a few moments of deliberation, I decided on the baked ziti with a side salad. Tony ordered a dish called *zuppa toscana,* a contraption of smoked sausage, chopped greens, potatoes, and bacon, among other ingredients. Lisa ordered penne with artichokes and shrimp, and Mo, spaghetti and meatballs. (Gee. Think bruh could have sprung for something a little more creative than S&Ms?) Tony ordered a bottle of wine for the table and two orders of fried calamari as an appetizer, at which point, Lisa looked at me and winked. That was my cue. She was feeling Tony. She resumed the table talk that had been temporarily put on hold.

"Bailey tells me you work downtown, Tony."

"That's correct. I'm at the Federal Reserve."

"What do you do there?"

"I work in human resources."

"Recruitment?"

"I wish. No, I'm on the benefits and policy side. You guys work downtown, too?"

"I do," Lisa said. "I'm a mortgage processor at Fannie Mae."

"I'm an account executive for an ad agency in Bethesda," Mo added. "I've been thinking about finding a job in D.C., though. It would sure make my commute from Largo a lot shorter."

"You're still driving to work every day?" I asked him.

"For the most part. I take the Metro now and then, but I really prefer being on my own schedule and being in the comfort of my own vehicle."

"I bet you do. Especially in that vehicle you're pushing these days."

"What are you driving?" Tony inquired.

Mo pretended like he didn't want to say, but I knew he was frontin'.

"A Lexus SC 400."

"I hear that! What year?"

"Ninety-three."

"Color?"

"Black."

"That's hot, Mo. I love that car."

Tony and Mo seemed to be hitting it off. And this double date thingy, it seemed to be going pretty good. Who would have thunk it?

Our waiter returned with the calamari, and we got busy. I wasn't that hungry when I first walked into the restaurant, but I sure was by that time.

"What's your favorite sport?" Mo asked Tony, changing the topic of discussion over to one of his favorite things.

"Football."

"Redskins fan?"

"Eagles."

"He's a Philly cat, Mo," I butted in. "I hate the Eagles. Sorry, Gianni."

"Don't apologize, Bailey. Mo and I hate the Eagles, too. Hail to the Redskins. Hail to the Redskins," Lisa teased.

"Uh, don't get carried away, baby. I'm with you on that Eagles thing, but I ain't feeling your 'Skins either. Giants rule!" Mo exclaimed, while playfully nibbling on his woman's ear.

Lisa giggled, obviously tickled by her man's PDA. (That's Public Display of Affection, for the acronym-challenged.)

I wish I had somebody to nibble on my ear right about now. My ear and a few other places. Hello!

I needed more wine. That or some Hennessey.

"At least the Redskins won the Super Bowl two years ago," Lisa squabbled.

"And who won it the year before?" Mo fired back, never one to back down from a squabble.

As soon as our entrées arrived, conversation was put on hold again so we could get our eat on. My baked ziti was out of this world. And so was Tony's zuppa toscana—judging by the way he devoured it. He offered to feed me some of it, but I politely declined. (It seemed like too romantic of a gesture to perform in front of Mo and Lisa at the time.) Lisa gave two thumbs up to her penne, and Mo declared his spaghetti and meatballs "on point." Though I couldn't resist the urge to needle him in regard to his choice of an entrée.

"Yo, Maurice. Why you come all the way to George-town to eat something you could've made yourself at home in ten minutes?"

"What are you talking about?"

"Spaghetti and meatballs? What? You couldn't find peanut butter and jelly on the menu?"

I had Tony and Lisa crackin' up, not to mention the couple seated at the table next to ours, who overheard my wisecrack.

"You tryin' to jon', Bailey? I *know* you don't want none of this," Mo said, pointing to himself.

"Oh, chill out, homie. It's only love."

"Mmm-hmm. Mess with me again, ya hear?"

The waiter handed us our dessert menus.

"Who's up for dessert?" Tony inquired.

"I'm going to have to pass on that," Lisa sighed, rub-bing her belly and slouching in her seat.

"Ditto for me," Mo followed.

"I want dessert," I said. "What's this? Y'all gonna make me eat alone?"

"I won't let you eat alone, Bailey," Tony came to my ap-petite rescue.

"Aw, isn't that cute?"

I don't have to tell you who uttered that.

Tony ordered a slice of cheesecake, and I ordered a slice of something called cannoli cake. The waiter described it as yellow sponge cake with ricotta cheese, chocolate chips, and buttercream frosting. Sounded yummy.

"So, does anyone have any vacation plans before the year ends?" I asked, starting a brand-new topic of discussion.

"Good question. Honey?" Lisa turned to ask Mo.

"Where you want to go?"

"I'd like us to take a romantic cruise to the Caribbean."

"And when would you like us to do this?"

"I think the fall would be ideal."

"Cool. Let's put it on the calendar for next fall."

"No, honey, this fall."

I threw my two cents in. "We're already in August, Lisa."

"Thank you, B. We have to *save* for a cruise, Lisa. You know, like maybe a year in advance or something like that. I just can't up and get on a ship with a month or two's notice. Don't let the townhouse and Lexus fool you, baby. Your man ain't got it like that. But if *you* do, that's something you definitely need to let me know."

"All right, all right. Next fall it is. Let's start saving for it now. What about you, Bailey?"

"Well, forget any summer plans, 'cause summer will be over in another month or so. You know what I'd really like to do, even if it's not this year? Take a trip to Europe. Tony told me all about his trip to Italy last spring. Got me all gassed up about going there myself."

"Wow. Was it your first time in Europe?" Lisa asked Tony.

"No, I've been to Italy a couple of times. My folks are what you'd call *true* Italian-Americans. Straight outta Palermo. They came to the states in Fifty-four."

"What are their names, if you don't mind me asking?"

Sheesh, Lisa. Can you be any nosier?

"Don't mind at all. My mother's name is Donna. Donna means 'lady.' My father's name is Primo. *Pree-mo Gi-an-ni*," he said, pronouncing each syllable with emphasis, and doing that thing with his hands Italians sometimes do when they speak. "His name means 'the first one.' He was the first of four children. I'm an only child, so I'm the firstborn of my parents, too. My full name is Primo Anthony Gianni Junior."

"You've never told me that," I told him, surprised to hear this.

"Yeah, I know. I don't tell people that 'cause I don't want people calling me Primo. I like Tony better."

"Primo, huh? That sounds like a 'brotha' name," Mo remarked. "Primo Johnson. I like how that sounds."

We all busted out laughing.

"Enough about me. Somebody else's turn. What's your full name, Mo?" Tony inquired.

"Maurice Tyrell Taylor," he said full of pride.

I nearly spit my wine out.

"*Ty-rell?* What in the world . . . is he serious, Lisa?"

"Girl, that's nothing. His sister's middle name is *Tyronica*. Now, if that don't sound like some prehistoric dinosaur . . . Boo, what was your moms *thinking?*"

"Yo, Lisa. Why you gotta to be talking 'bout my moms in front of folks? And you makin' fun of my name, Bailey?"

I needed a sip of water I was laughing so hard. Poor Tony looked as though he was about to lose a rib.

"Wooo, lawdy! Mm, mm, mm. I'm sorry. I didn't mean to poke fun at your name, Tylenol . . . I mean, Ty-rell."

"Both you *and* Lisa 'bout to get cursed out in a minute," Mo warned.

"Oh stop it, honey," Lisa said playfully slapping him upside his head. "We're just playing with you. My full name is Lisa Beverly Parker, Tony. And I don't know what any of that means."

"Yours, Bailey?" Tony asked.

"Bailey. What the hell kinda name is *Bailey* for a *girl?*" Mo wouldn't let it rest.

"Later for you—*Thy-roid.* My birth name is Bailey Crystal McClendon, Tony."

"McClendon? So where does Gentry come from?"

I was afraid he'd ask that. I told Tony early on that I wasn't too keen on discussing my family life. Never told him why, though. Lisa and Mo knew the deal, however. Anyway, this wasn't the time or the place to rehash the saga of Bailey McClendon.

"Long story, Gianni."

"You still have family over in Italy?" Mo asked Tony, quickly changing the subject. I knew this was his way of coming to my rescue. We would go at it now and then, but Mo was cool people. I was happy Lisa was with someone like him.

"No immediate family to speak of. That wasn't the reason I went to Italy, though. I went—well, the first time that is—because I just thought it was important for me make a trip to the land of my ancestors before I leave this earth. And that my parents were actually born in Italy just made it all the more exciting."

"That's beautiful, Tony. Beautiful," Lisa said. "Forget Italy, Bailey. Your first trip overseas should be to the land of your ancestors. Africa."

"Oh, really? Any particular part?"

"Pick one."

"Okay, I'll find a map and throw a dart at it first thing Monday morning when I get to work."

"You're joking. I'm serious. Forget that cruise to the Caribbean next fall, honey. Let's go to Africa instead."

"Sorry. That's a trip you're going to have to take with Bailey."

"You don't want to go to Africa with me?"

"Nope."

"And why not?"

"I've *never* had a desire to go to Africa, Lisa. Just 'cause I'm black doesn't mean I should want to go, either. Our people kill me with that Africa mess!"

Lisa sucked her teeth. "I'm shocked at you, Maurice."

"And why's that? Not once have I ever heard you mention any desire to go to Africa before this moment."

"Just 'cause I haven't mentioned it doesn't mean going there hasn't been on my mind. C'mon, honey, I think it's important that we do like Tony did and visit the land of our roots."

"See what you've started, Tony?" Mo joked. "Look, I'm'a keep it real for all of y'all. If and when I feel the need to get in touch with my roots, I'm gonna do like I always do: take my black ass—'scuse me, Tony—back to One-Twenty-Fifth and Lennox Avenue. That's where *my* roots are."

Mo had us all laughing hysterically again. (We were just having a good 'ol time, can't you tell?)

"I'ma have to agree with you," Tony said. "What I did isn't something everybody needs to do."

"Right on, Tony Ton'. Me and you are going to have to hang out one day without these two broads," Mo laughed.

Our desserts arrived. Ten minutes and one slice of cheesecake and one of cannoli cake later, it was time to call the foursome a wrap. We requested the check and surveyed the damage. Tony paid for the wine, appetizer, and our two entrées. Mo took care of what he and Lisa ate. After splitting a 15 percent tip, the four of us headed for the door.

"Good night. Please come back again," our attractive hostess said—seemingly to no one else but Tony, with one final peer of her googly eyes. For that she received a healthy roll of *my* eyeballs as I strolled past her on the way out.

As the lingering summer sun had all but given way to the moon, we said our good-nights outside on the corner of Wisconsin and N.

"All right you guys, we gotta bounce. Mo and I had a blast. It was a pleasure meeting you, Tony. Hope to see you again. Come give me a hug."

Tony stepped forward and hugged Lisa. Afterward, he and Mo shook hands and did that "brotha" embrace thing again. Mo gave me a hug next.

"Good night, Ty-rell," I teased him one last time.

"Yeah, okay. I'm'a get you back for that in there, Bailey. Count on it."

"And I'm sure you won't rest until you do."

Lisa and I embraced.

"Where did you guys park?"

"We lucked up and found a spot on P Street. Where are y'all?"

"In the garage at Georgetown Park."

"Okay. Take care, kiddos. Drive safely."

"You, too. See ya."

The four of us departed Wisconsin Avenue in opposite directions. Lisa and Mo towards P Street, and me and Tony toward the parking garage.

20

Sista Interrupted

It was a tad past 9 o'clock when we pulled up in front of Tony's building. Our double date with Mo and Lisa now over, it was time for us to say good-night. Or was it?

"It's still early. How about a nightcap?" Tony said to me, as we sat in my idling car.

"A nightcap? I've had three glasses of wine already. I'm a lawyer, how would I look getting arrested for DUI?"

"You don't appear intoxicated to me."

"I'm not. I'm just being facetious."

"Then come on up. You can have your choice of beverage. It doesn't have to be alcohol, either. I've got sparkling apple cider, O'Doul's, coffee . . ."

"You think of everything don't you, Gianni?"

"Oh, c'mon. Just find a place to park. Like Guy sang, the party ain't over."

"Tsk. What 'chu know about Guy?"

Tony started singing the group's classic.

"*Groove me, baby, tooooiiight . . .*"

He had me crackin' up again.

"Okay, okay. Stop singing. Please! I'll come and join you for a nightcap. But only for a little while. I'm getting tired."

I drove around Tony's neighborhood for fifteen minutes trying to find a parking space. Eventually, I found one—three blocks away. I was pissed! Maybe I should have taken my inability to find a spot closer as a sign—or a good excuse—to take my ass home and call it a night. I really could have used the downtime to clear my head, analyze the events of the evening—which I thought went surprisingly well—and figure out what my next move was going to be. Or perhaps more important, what it wasn't going to be. Furthermore, my hormones were raging. Probably not a good thing given that I had just agreed to go back up to Tony's for a nightcap. Always trust your first instinct, ladies. It usually ends up being the right move.

I parked, and we began the three-block stroll back to his building together. I used the moment to ask Tony to elaborate on Mo's cryptic remark about Howard Beach, Queens, during dinner earlier.

"Back in Eighty-six, I believe it was, around Christmas that year, three black guys were driving through Howard Beach, Queens, when their car broke down," he began to tell the story.

"Some white boys saw them, took exception to their presence, began taunting them with racial insults, and warned them to get out of their neighborhood, pronto. I don't think the black guys took their threat too seriously at first. In any event, they went into a nearby pizza parlor to get something to eat, and to call a tow truck. By the time they were done eating, there were a gang of about ten or so bat-wielding white boys surrounding the pizza shop waiting for them. This mob proceeded to attack the black guys and beat them as they tried to run away. One of the black guys managed to get away from this mob unharmed. The other two were beaten; one of those two eventually managed to escape and hide as well. The third guy wasn't as lucky."

"What happened?" I asked Tony in disbelief.

"They chased him onto a freeway, where he was struck and killed by a passing car."

"Oh, my God. That's horrible!"

"That crime and the trial that followed galvanized New York in some of the worst racial tension that city had ever seen. Shit was out of control for good while. I'm surprised you didn't hear about this."

"Now that I'm listening to you relate this incident, I think I do recall hearing something about it."

"You had to. It got national headlines. I was still living in Philly when I got wind of it."

"Well, I couldn't help notice the look on your face when Mo mentioned Howard Beach. It seemed to make you a bit uncomfortable. Were you?"

"Not because of Mo's comment. He was right, and I'm sure he wasn't trying to *make* me uncomfortable. What bothered me was the fact that it was 'my people,' so to speak, who did this unspeakable shit. A number of the assholes engaged in this were Italians. There's a heavy Italian demographic in that town that just doesn't care too much for black people. Mo's from New York, so I know he knows this. So there I am at the table—the lone Italian guy—dining with three black people, and Howard Beach comes up in conversation."

"*You* brought it up."

"I did. All I'm trying to say is, if the shoe was on the

other foot, and you were with a group of white people, and one of them made reference to some reprehensible deed that a black person committed against white people, wouldn't it make you feel a little uncomfortable?"

"It might. And for the record, that scenario you mention has happened to me on more than a few occasions. So, what was the verdict?"

Tony shook his head from side to side, seemingly in disgust.

"Oh, hell no! Don't tell me those assholes got off like those damn cops who beat Rodney King."

"Three of the attackers were charged with first-degree assault and second-degree manslaughter."

"Assault? Manslaughter? *Second degree*? No *murder* charge?"

"Nope. And worse, a fourth dude was acquitted of *all* charges. Of the three that were convicted, I believe they got an average sentence of something like seven to twenty-one years. I do believe all of them are still in jail as we speak, however."

I shook my head in disgust this time.

"Mm, mm, mm. I don't know why I'm shocked that they weren't convicted of murder. When has *justice* ever been a given for black folks? Hmph. Don't let me get started here. This isn't the time or the place. Well, you've satisfied my curiosity. Now I know why Howard Beach is infamous. I'm almost sorry I asked, though. That story is depressing, Tony."

"I hear ya."

"Gol-lee. Are we there yet?"

"One more block. Suck it up. You can make it."

"Good thing I wore my sandals. If I was in heels right now, you'd be carrying me back to your building."

"Oooh, I think I'd like that."

"Get your mind out the gutter, Gianni."

"You know, there was something you said over dinner that's got me kinda curious, too," Tony said.

"What's that?"

"Your given name. You said it was Bailey Crystal *McClendon?*"

"Long story, Gianni."

"That's what you said over dinner."

"I see your hearing is excellent!"

"Oh, okay. None of my business, huh?"

"We're here! Finally," I groaned as we reached the entrance of Tony's apartment building, ignoring his question.

Tony's phone was ringing when we got inside his apartment. He told me to go ahead and make myself comfortable while he answered it. I did just that, kicked off my sandals and curled up on his sofa.

"Uh-huh . . . yeah . . . that's cool . . . maybe . . . mm-hmm . . . went out to eat . . . something like that . . ."

That was him on the phone with whomever he was on the phone with. Okay, so a sista's been in this situation a time or two or three before, and from where I was sitting, (and eavesdropping,) it sounded to me like Tony was having one of those I've-got-a-female-in-my-crib-so-I-better-not-let-the-one-on-the-phone-know-and-vice-versa conversations. His back was to me as he chatted. I was checking out his ass in those gray khakis he was wearing. It was looking kinda right. Checking out his broad shoulders. They were looking kinda right, too. A sista's hormones were raging. Did I mention that already?

My head and my body began to go at each other in another of their usual clashes. My body got this particular round started:

What 'chu waiting for, Bailey? Go 'head and fuck that white

boy's brains out. It's been months, and you're obviously in need
of some real bad. Maybe you won't come down with a case of
the heebie-jeebies at all. And if you do, so what? Just go home
and sleep it off.

My head:

Yeah, but you'll sure hate yourself in the morning, now, won't
you? Use your head—no pun intended. Have that nightcap
and get your black ass outta his apartment before you do some-
thing stupid.

". . . All right, I'll talk to you later."

Tony hung up the phone and joined me on the sofa.

"Okay, Bailey, enough is enough. It's time for you to
make up your mind. What's it gonna be?"

"Huh? What?"

"Your nightcap? What are you having?"

"Oooh . . ."

Shit! For a second there, I thought Tony was reading
my mind. Asking me whether or not I was ready to knock
boots with him. I was trippin'. That settled it. I was de-
claring my head the winner of this argument and getting
my ass out of his apartment.

"A quick glass of water with a little ice will be fine."

"That's all you want?"

"That'll do it. I really need to get going, Tony."

Tony went into the kitchen, got me a glass of water,
then came back out and sat real close to me on the sofa.

"Where were you a second ago?"

"Huh?"

"You seemed deep in thought."

"Oh. I think I'm just wearing down." *In more ways than*
one. "So, who was that on the phone?"

(It *really* wasn't my intention to be that nosy. I just
opened my mouth and the words sorta spilled out.)

"A friend of mine."

(Okay. I'd already gone this far, why stop now?)

"What's her name?"

Tony laughed. "Did I say it was a she?"

I gave him a "don't even give me that" look.

"Okay, let's say—hypothetically speaking of course—that I was on the phone with a woman. Would you be jealous?" he asked.

Surprisingly, I did feel a twinge of the green-eyed monster a second ago.

"Being that we're speaking in the hypothetical, what if I told you I would be a little jealous?"

Tony inched closer to me.

"Well, in that case, I'd be extremely flattered. But then you must know your sentiment would be totally unwarranted."

"Oh? And how so?"

"Because I know what I want."

"And that is?"

"This."

Tony took the glass of water from my hand and sat it on the floor. Grabbed the back of my head, and pressed his lips against mine. Started tonguing me down. Hard and deep. In no time at all, I had got him out of his shirt and we were engaged in a full-fledged necking session reminiscent of middle- and high-school days, when necking was as far as sexual expression went between a boy and a girl. (For most boys and girls anyway.) When Tony wasn't attacking my lips and tongue with his lips and tongue, he'd take his oral assault to my neck, licking and sucking every inch of it with fervor. Moaning as he did. As if the taste of my cocoa-brown flesh was intoxicating him. When he'd come up for air, I'd attack him in return, with an oral assault of my own to his ears, neck, and chest. All this kissing, licking, and sucking had a sista as moist as a Duncan Hines cake.

All hot and bothered now, I wanted Tony to play with me. Wanted him to *feel* the dampness he had created in me. I spread my legs further apart. Hiked my already short mini dress up even higher, and guided his hand underneath it. Tony knew exactly what to do. Fingered me like a detective. Thrilled me. Made *me* moan.

"Mmm, Tony. That feels good."

Next thing I knew, I was flat on my back, and my dress was somewhere up around my navel. Tony's face covered mine. I closed my eyes and concentrated on only his lips, the smell of his breath, and the scent of his cologne. Time passed—how much I can't tell you. The kisses stopped coming. I couldn't smell his breath anymore. I reopened my eyes. He was gone. I panicked.

What's going on? Where did he go?

Wait. He was still here. I knew because I felt his hands on my hips, tugging at my thong trying to get it off. He wasn't messin' with a toothpick here, so he had to use a little "elbow grease," feel me? A little more effort and I felt the elastic band of my thong down around my ankles. The hair on Tony's head tickled my inner thighs. So did his breath.

This cannot be happening.

All I did was come up for a quick nightcap, and now I was on my back with my legs open and my underwear down around my ankles. Be that as it may, Tony was fixin' to give a sista a special treat—and that had me singing a Rick James song—

"*Give it to me, baby. Just-give-it-to-me, baaa-beee.*"

Out of nowhere—smack-dab in the middle of my euphoria—a wave of trepidation hit me. The kind that comes with letting go and giving in to one's lustful cravings. *What am I doing here? I don't want this. Yes, I do. Oh, I don't know* what *I want. I'm confused.* Confused and horny. A hell of a state of mind to be in at that particular moment, ya think? About the only thing I was certain of was this: If I felt Tony's tongue on my clit—

Snap, click.

What was that?

I heard a key enter the door of Tony's apartment and a lock turn. The metal-to-metal intrusion broke the groove we were in. There was a pause and laughter on the other side of the door. Tony heard it too and jerked his head out from between my thighs. Yours truly jumped off the sofa and tried to run (don't ask where the hell *to*). Forgot Tony left my thong wrapped around my ankles. I lost my balance, fell backward, and hit the hardwood floor ass-first.

Mutha fuck!!

With no time to acknowledge the newfound pain in my ass, I quickly got back to my feet, retrieved my thong from around my ankles, and pulled it back up my thighs, while pulling my dress back down my thighs. Did both in one smooth motion. Actually impressed myself with the maneuver. Tony and I quickly assumed a normal position on the sofa. A second lock turned. The apartment door swung open and in walked Derrick with his Asian chick in tow.

I could only imagine what the two of us must've looked like when Derrick and his Asian chick walked in on us. (Never mind the expressions that must've been on our faces.) Probably like two teenagers just caught doing the nasty by their parents. At least that's exactly how I felt. I was *so* embarrassed—on two fronts. First, for almost getting busted, and second, for my unceremonious plummet to the hardwood. All I wanted at the moment was for Tony's hardwood floor to open up and swallow me!

Knew I should have just taken my ass home.

"I . . . uh . . . did-n't-ex-pect-you-guys-home-so-ear-ly," Derrick said to Tony and me. Slow and *de-li-be-rate-ly*. His eyes moving back and forth between us like he was watching a tennis match. Only a naïve fool would be clueless as to what they had just walked in on. I doubted Derrick was a naïve fool.

"What are *you* guys doing home so early?" Tony countered, sounding one part surprised and one part miffed at their bad timing. Neither bothered to answer his question. They were too busy trying to wipe the smirks off their faces.

"Mylene, this is Tony's friend, Bailey. Bailey, this is my girlfriend, Mylene," Derrick said.

"Pleased to meet you."

"Same here."

Mylene was a bit taller than me; about five-six or five-seven. Thin, dark-colored hair, cut long on the sides and in the back with a short bang in the front. Highlighted streaks ran throughout her hairdo. Couldn't tell if she was Chinese, Japanese, Korean or what. Attractive. I'll give her that. Far from crossover material, though. But then that's just my opinion. Who knows what goes through the mind of a brotha who would leave a sista on the sideline for an Asian chick. Anyways, Mylene had on a cute mini dress, too. Not as cute as the one I was wearing, however. And she was definitely not filling hers out the way I was.

"We're gonna head back to my room and give you two some privacy," Derrick said. "Let y'all get back to *whatever* it is y'all were doing before we interrupted."

I see bruh's a bit of a smartass.

"That won't be necessary, Derrick. I was just about to leave. Nice to see you again, and nice meeting you, Mylene," I said, slipping my fuchsia sandals back on and reaching for my purse. "C'mon, Gianni. You're walking me back to my car."

"Um, give me a second," Tony whispered. "I don't want to stand up just yet."

During the walk to the elevator, the ride down it, out the front door of the Wyoming onto Columbia Road, and the three-block walk back to my automobile, not a single word was spoken between Tony and me. When we reached my car, we just looked at each other and broke out in simultaneous, uncontrollable laughter that seemed to go on a good minute or two before we were able to get it—and ourselves—under control. Thank God for laughter. The ultimate elixir for some of life's most embarrassing moments.

"Look, Bailey, about what just hap—"

I pressed my index finger against Tony's lips. "Ssshh. It's late. Thanks for dinner and for walking me back to my car. Good night."

During the drive home from Tony's, my emotions were all over the place. One moment, I was banging the steering wheel in laughter, the next, almost in tears. It took a while for it all to sink in, but as much as my cat needed to be fed, I was relieved that Derrick and his girl showed up when they did. Tony was ready for intimacy. I was simply horny.

Close to three months had passed since our first date, and I'd been around enough men to know that ninety days is about the maximum one is going to spend around a woman he's interested in without sex being a required part of the equation. And even that's pushing it. A strong case could be made that Tony had been *extremely* patient with me thus far. Maybe it was a "white guy" thing. Nevertheless, if that night's encounter wasn't a sure indication that I needed to shit or get off the pot, I don't know what was.

By the time I reached the driveway of my condominium complex, I had also reached a conclusion. A startling one. Even though doing so was akin to sacrilege for black folks in my book, I was going to attempt the unthinkable. The implausible. The downright *unworkable.* I was going to give the swirl a shot. And though the mere contemplation of that began to make my stomach queasy as I walked up the stairs to my unit, I was determined to forge ahead. Boldly go where a sista hadn't gone before. Step outside my comfort zone for the first time.

I slipped out of my mini dress and put on my favorite Howard University T-shirt that I loved to sleep in. The message light on my phone was blinking, but I didn't bother to see who had called. First things first. I had to satisfy a craving for something that hit me during the drive home: Häagen Dazs mint chip. I went into the kitchen, fixed myself a bowl, crawled into bed, turned on the tube and caught the tail end of the news, then watched a little of *Saturday Night Live.* When I finished eating my ice cream, I checked to see who had called. The automated voice on my answering machine said I had one new message. I hit the PLAY button.

"Whassuuup! It's your girl, Lisa-Lisa. The time is now ten PM. Heifer, where are you? Hmmm, you must still be over at Tony's house. I'm feelin' him, B. He's some fine-ass white chocolate, you hear me? A white boy with an awful lot of black in him. Get it? White Chocolate? Ha, ha, ha.

My quick wit just slays me sometimes. Here's my advice, Ms. Thang. Stop pussyfootin'—no pun intended—and fuck that Italiano's brains out. In fact, I hope the reason you're not home to answer this call is because you're somewhere doing that very thing right now. If so, call me tomorrow. I want all the details! Smooches."

Lisa's message had me laughing hysterically. She's so crazy. I kind of dug the "White Chocolate" moniker. And as far as fuckin' Tony's brains out? Hmph. She had no idea.

I almost did, girl. I almost did.

21

Will You Go With Me?

Monifah, with her new fresh-from-the-beauty-salon finger waves, was looking more ghetto fabulous than usual today. She handed me a couple of message slips as I rushed past the reception desk en route to my office. I had on a brand-new pair of $167 Vigotti slingbacks that were killing my feet like nobody's business. A sista needed to sit and get them off her puppies quick, fast, and in a hurry. I let out an orgasmic "Aaaah" as soon as I was able to do so. That's when this rather disconcerting thought crossed my mind: What if my feet swelled and I couldn't get these puppies back on? Making my foot woes worse: Today of all days, I didn't have my favorite pair of backup flats in the office. I usually kept a pair under my desk in case of an emergency. (Like this very type of an emergency.) I wore them home a few nights ago when I was having a similar foot quandary with a different pair of shoes. I had yet to remember to throw them in a bag and bring them back to the office with me. I was simply going to have to muscle those Vigottis back on, limp over to Nine West at lunchtime, and cop me a new pair of backups. No way was I going to be able to wear those shoes home on the Metro that evening.

After settling in behind my desk, I logged onto my computer, checked my email, and flipped through the phone messages Monifah handed me to see who wanted to talk to me and why. One of the messages was from Tony.

To: Bailey Gentry
From: Tony Gianni
Mssg: Give me a call when you get in this morning. Thanx.

I had been avoiding Tony just a little bit since we went out with Mo and Lisa. I know I said I was ready to embark on a "real" relationship with him. But if I was actually going to be able to pull that mission impossible off without self-destructing in the process, I was going to need a few days of non-contact with him—verbal or physical—in order to get my mind, body, and soul prepared for the task. I flipped through a few more until I came across one from Rose. Monifah had checked the "urgent" box on that one.

To: Bailey Gentry
From: Rose Braxton
Mssg: Ms. Gentry. Please call me at work ASAP. 202-555-4000 x587.

I didn't like the tone of that message. I peeked at my date book. The thirty-day window for Rose's husband to respond to the divorce petition was going to be up shortly. If he didn't, I could move forward with getting my client an absolute divorce and, finally, her freedom. And following that, her other requests for full custody of her son, child support, and alimony.

I got up from my desk, went into the office kitchen, and made myself a cup of java. Starbucks, the heavy-duty stuff. I didn't usually drink coffee. But I had a feeling as strong as that coffee that between my aching feet and that message from Rose, I might be in for a humdinger of a day. I returned to my desk and dialed Rose in order to ascertain her urgency.

"Hello, you've reached the desk of Rose Braxton. I'm not available to take your call . . ."

Darn. Got her voice mail.

"Good morning, Rose. It's your attorney, Bailey Gentry. Got your message and I'm returning your call. Please call me back at your earliest convenience. In the event you get my voice mail, please dial zero for the receptionist and have me paged. Thank you."

I hoped it wouldn't be round two of an annoying bout of phone tag.

Rose called me back five minutes later, sounding panic-stricken, whispering, and talking a hundred miles per hour.

"Sydney came up to my job yesterday acting all uncouth. Scared the shit out of me! What am I going to—"

"Slow down, Mrs. Braxton—"

"Call me, *Rose*, dammit!"

No she didn't just raise her voice at me.

"*Rose!* Take a deep breath and try to relax for a second. Now slowly, tell me, what happened?"

"Look, I thought I could talk, but I can't right now. I got some nosy-ass coworkers who ain't got nothing better to do than be all up in my face. YEAH, I'M TALKING

ABOUT YOU! DO YOUR JOB AND STOP LOOKING AT ME!" I heard her yell at someone in the distance.

"Rose. Are you still there? *Rose*—"

"I'm here, I'm here. Can't stand that nosy bitch! What was I saying?"

"Look, you're obviously very upset right now, and I don't want you to get in any trouble at work. Is it possible for you to stop by my office today? I'll stay as late as necessary to accommodate you." Rose worked in the 1140 building on Connecticut Avenue, which was only a five-minute walk to the offices of JB&H on Nineteenth Street.

"Can't do it this evening. I have to pick up my son after work. I can come during my lunch hour, though."

Damn. I had planned on doing some much-needed shoe shopping at that time. But a good lawyer always puts her client's needs first. Shoe shopping was going to have to wait. That and the agony of my feet!

"What time are we talking about?"

"How's one o'clock? I definitely want to eat lunch before I come by."

"Sounds good. By the way. There's a café downstairs in my building if you want to check that out. They've got sandwiches, salads, and a pay-by-the-ounce buffet. You can get something down there and come straight upstairs when you're done."

"That'll work. See you at one, Ms. Gentry."

Shortly after Rose hung up, my phone rang again.

"Bailey Gentry speaking."

"Hello, stranger."

It was Tony.

"Hey, Tony, how are you? I got your message. I just haven't had a moment to call you back yet. It's been nonstop since I got in. Where are you? What's all that commotion?"

"I'm outside on my cell phone. Look, I'm not going to keep you. I know you're busy. I just wanted to know if you had anything planned at lunchtime."

"Whassup?"

"I'm on my way to a meeting a couple of blocks from your job. Would you like to go to lunch with me when I'm through?"

Seeing Tony wasn't something I'd really planned on doing today. But on second thought, if we did go to lunch, I could use the moment to give him the news; that I was finally ready to elevate him from placeholder to boyfriend status.

"What time is your meeting over? I have a client coming in at one o'clock and it could be a quick session or a long one. I have no idea yet."

"It starts at ten and I figure it'll run at least an hour, hour-fifteen, maybe."

I checked the time on the digital display of my office phone. It was now a quarter to ten.

"If I meet you, it's going to have to be early. Like eleven-thirty, quarter-to-twelve, and I'm definitely not going to be able to take a full hour. Sorry. If you can work with that, I'm game for a quickie—a quickie lunch that is. I forget I have to watch my words around you, Gianni. I know how your gutter-brain thinks," I laughed.

"See? I didn't say a word."

"Anyway . . . if I see you, it'll give me a chance to talk to you about something."

"Well, I doubt I'm going to be hungry enough to eat lunch at that hour. But since I'm going to be in the neighborhood, how 'bout I just stop in and see you for a minute."

"That's cool, too."

"What do you want to talk to me about?"

"Patience, Gianni. Tell you when I see you."

"Okey-doke. I'll be by as soon as I get out of this meeting. Expect me around eleven-thirty-ish. Bye."

Eleven-forty-three, Monifah got me on the intercom.

"Bailey, Tony Gianni is here to see you."

"Thank you. Tell him I'll be right out."

I muscled my shoes back on, gritted my teeth, and walked gingerly out to the reception area to greet Tony. I arrived to find Monifah out from behind her desk, all up in Tony's face flappin' her lips while simultaneously giving him an eyeful of her straight out of *Frederick's of Hollywood*, booty-clinging, cleavage-exposing dress. A dress that was clearly more suited to a D.C. nightclub than a D.C. law office.

Anyway, Tony was looking absolutely *scrumptious*. On his face was a few days worth of shadow. Eee, I find that so sexy on a man! (Did I mention that already?) He was wearing a chocolate brown, double-breasted suit over a tan dress shirt and a solid-orange silk tie. The look was bold, in-your-face, and a sista was feeling it! Definitely a more stylish look than what I was accustomed to seeing from the men in the office: that "lawyerly" navy blue suit, white button-down dress shirt, and burgundy necktie. B-o-r-i-n-g! Oh, and the all-important shoe check: two thumbs up. He was sportin' the right color footwear: *Brown*. There's no greater male fashion faux paus in my book than a man in a brown suit and *black* shoes!

"Ready, Freddy?" I said, putting an end to Monifah's jibber-jabber.

"Ready," he said.

"I'll be back in about twenty minutes or so. Would you send all my calls straight to voice mail?"

"Will do, Bailey. You two have a good lunch. *Bye, Tony.*"

"Bye, Monifah. Nice to see you again," Tony said, cheesin' at her like a happy mouse himself.

Uh-uh.

"Your receptionist—excuse me, admin assistant—is something else," Tony said once we got outside of the office suite.

"That's an understatement. I think she's kind of sweet on you, too."

"Me? Naw, she's just vagarious."

"Mmm-hmm. What did you think of that dress?"

Tony laughed.

"A bit over the top—for the office. But girlfriend's definitely wearing the hell out it. Monifah's built like a brick—"

"Uh, I get it, Tony. I get it. Enough about her."

"Right. Enough about her. It's all about you. And this is for you." Tony took his hand from behind his back and handed me a single pink rose.

"What's this?"

"A *rose.*"

"I can see *that,*" I said, blushing so much I thought my cheeks would crack. "What I meant is, I didn't expect this."

"That's me. Mr. Full of Surprises. All day, every day."

"Thank you. But you shouldn't have."

"I didn't really. I copped it for two bucks from a vagrant outside."

"You silly man, you. Where are we going?"

"I'm not hungry. But you said you wanted to talk, so lead the way. And why are you walking like that?"

"'Cause these friggin' shoes are killing my feet."

Tony looked down and checked out my kicks.

"That's too bad 'cause they sure look good on your feet."

"Thank you. Vigottis."

"Go on with your bad self, you slave to fashion."

"I'm not that hungry either, Tony, but I think I better grab a salad or something to eat at my desk later. There's a pretty nice café downstairs. Why don't we go there? Obviously, I'm not up for any walking."

Once inside the café, Tony grabbed a table while I limped over to the salad bar.

"You better eat that salad now," he said, when I joined him at the table he selected.

"Why is that?"

"The management in this joint might not take too kindly to your occupying space without eating."

"Please. I *paid* for this salad. When I decide to eat it is my business. Besides, it's still early. It's not that crowded in here."

"Well? Just don't sit there and keep me in suspense. What do you want to talk to me about? It doesn't have anything to do with what happened . . . you know."

"What would make you think that?"

"For one thing, we've never discussed *you know what.* And for another, if I didn't know any better, I'd swear you've been avoiding me since that night."

"No, Tony, this has nothing to do with that night. Not directly. Although I suppose maybe *indirectly.* Here's the thing. I've been doing a lot of thinking. You and I have been seeing each other off and on now for the better part of three months and . . ."

"And . . . ?"

"And I asked you a while back where you wanted our relationship to go. Your answer was that you just wanted to let things flow. I took that to mean that perhaps we could take a stab at being in a committed relationship at some point. Am I on point so far?"

"You're on point so far."

"Well, I'd say a lot has flowed since we met Thursday, May fifth, at that Urban League fund-raiser, where you complimented me on my Bobbi Brown lipstick and proceeded to buy me a glass of Hennessey."

Tony folded his arms across his chest.

"Did you write all that down in your journal?"

"How do you know I keep a journal?"

"Every woman keeps a journal."

"Tsk. What-eva. Anyways, what I'm asking you is . . ."

Here it goes. Lawd, please don't let this be a big mistake on my part.

". . . what do you think about me and you taking a stab at it?"

"By 'it,' you mean?"

"Me and you dating for real."

"By 'for real' you mean?"

"Exclusively, Tony. Ex-clu-sive-ly."

"Let me get this straight, B. You asking me to *go* with you?"

Great. This is hard enough for me as it is and he wants to make jokes.

"Tony—"

"Wow," he cut me off, "this is sorta like back in elementary school when I passed a balled-up note to Brandy Scott that read, 'Will you go with me?' with the 'yes,' 'no,' or 'maybe' box for her to check off."

As much as I didn't want to laugh at or with him at that moment, I couldn't help it. What he said brought back a lot of funny memories for me, too.

"So you remember those little love notes, huh? I sure got my share of 'em back in the day. Think I may have even sent one myself to a boy or two. So, which box did little Miss Brandy check off?"

"Girl, I'm Tony Gianni. What box you *think* she checked off?"

"Yeah, okay. Little Miss Brandy probably dumped your ass," I teased him. Silence.

"Actually, she did. One week after putting a big fat 'X' in the yes box. Dumped me for an older boy. A fourth-grader named Montell Haskins."

"Montell Haskins? Was Brandy—"

"Black? Mmm-hmm."

"Oh my goodness."

"Yep. The very first girl I ever fell in love with was a sista, and she broke my heart. You wouldn't do that to me would you?"

"Will you get serious for a minute and answer my question, please?"

"Most definitely. I'm with it, B. Been with it. Though, I have to ask you. Are you *sure* you're with it?"

"Is there some reason I shouldn't be?"

(I could think of a myriad of them, but I wanted to get Tony's take.)

"Nothing that *should* matter," he said. "But then this is an imperfect world we live in, so yes, perhaps there are a few things. You're black. I'm white. It's going to be your first time. This is going to be a whole new experience for you. You might find it awkward at times. It's going to be—"

"Keep talking, Gianni, and you're going to talk me right out of this you know."

Tony made the motion of zipping his lips and throwing away the key.

"It's twelve-fifteen. I have a client coming in at one.

She's high maintenance, so I need to get back to the office and get prepared for her."

"Okey-doke. I'm glad we had this talk, B."

"Me too, Tony."

"So, um, I guess this is like our first official day as boyfriend and girlfriend, huh?"

"How 'bout that? You headed back to work?"

"You know, all this good news has suddenly made me kinda hungry after all. I think I'm going to stay here, grab a sandwich, and do some personal stuff on my laptop before I head back to work."

Tony kissed me on the lips. The second time he'd done so in public. This time around felt no less uncomfortable to me.

"Talk to my girl later," he said.

My girl. Wow. Never in my wildest dreams could I imagine those words being said to me by anyone other than a black man.

22

Angry People

Mrs. Braxton arrived at one o'clock sharp at JB&H. (We lawyers love prompt clients. It makes our jobs so much easier.) I made my way out into the reception area to greet her. Physically speaking, she looked great. She was dressed in a black, pinstriped pantsuit that really accentuated her petite yet very curvy frame. And on her feet were a pair of slammin' black, quarter-strapped pumps with stiletto heels. Her hair, makeup, nails, and toes were also impeccably done, reminding me of that attractive, together sista who walked into my office for the very first time a few months ago.

"Good afternoon, Rose. I love that suit. Those shoes, too."

"Why thank you. I could use a compliment today," she said, sounding somewhat depressed.

"Let's go back to my office."

Inside the four walls of my office, Rose and I assumed

our customary positions: me behind my desk, and she seated in front of it.

"Did you get a chance to have lunch?" I asked.

"Yes, I did. I took your suggestion and had a sandwich in the café downstairs."

Rose was spittin' nails. Sydney had come to her job without warning, angry about being served with divorce papers and a restraining order. Nearly went as far as to airing their personal business out in front of Rose's coworkers. With some quick thinking, Rose had managed to preempt the latter from happening.

"First of all, can he still be doing that kind of crap when I have a restraining order on him?" she questioned me.

"No, he can't. Visiting you at your place of employment is a clear violation of your OFP. But I'm not all that surprised to hear he's done so, given what you've previously told me about him. If you recall, Rose, I told you obtaining an order for protection was a prudent thing to do, but it was no guarantee that your husband would *adhere* to its stipulations. Do you remember that?"

"I dunno, I guess."

"But let's put that on the back burner for a second." I grabbed a legal pad from my desk drawer and began taking notes. "What exactly did he say or do when he came to your office? Did he hurt you in any way?"

"No, no he didn't. Not physically. This time. But he threatened me."

"How?"

"He told me if I didn't tell him where I was staying and let him see his son, he'd be back here—meaning my job—restraining order or not, and things were going to get really ugly then."

"Meaning what, exactly?"

"I don't know, and I really wasn't trying to find out. So I told Sydney he could come by my apartment."

"You did *what?*" I barked, slamming my pen down on my legal pad.

"*Don't* fuss at me, Ms. Gentry," Rose fired back. "I know I shouldn't have agreed to that, but I gotta do what I gotta do. You're not the one that has to deal with this fool, I am. And the truth is, Sydney *hasn't* seen his son in a while."

The physically together woman who stepped into my office ten minutes ago looking like a million bucks was coming apart at the seams once again. Tears flowed from her brown eyes like water from a faucet. In light of her current state, I knew I had to be stern with her, but equally compassionate at the same time.

"Rose," I said, pulling a couple of tissues out of a Kleenex box I kept on my desk, and handing them to her, "I do understand where you're coming from. I truly do. However, given everything you said to me five minutes ago, not to mention all the things you've told me over the past several weeks in regard to your husband's penchant for abuse and his general unpredictability, inviting him into your home is certainly not using sound judgment. Surely you must recognize that. There's a *reason* why you have a restraining order against this man. What's wrong with using the telephone?"

"Sydney can't *see* his son over the telephone, now, can he?" she said to me in between sniffles, and with a hint of 'tude in her voice.

"That's the second time you've brought your son up in this conversation. Is *that* the main reason you're contemplating this action? So your husband can see his son?"

"If you're trying to get at something why don't you just come right out and say it, Ms. Gentry?"

"Okay then I will. It's not at all uncommon for someone in your position to go through a lot of mixed emotions in regard to a spouse they're divorcing. Sometimes, no matter how terrible, traumatic, or otherwise draining the marriage is or was, letting go is not that easy for some. Even in abusive situations such as yours, moving on can simply be more terrifying than staying put. And that's why so many couples stay in miserable marriages year after year after year. Do you know if your husband's retained his own attorney or not?"

"He didn't say. But I doubt it. Sydney's in denial right now."

"Well, in a matter of days, his window of opportunity to respond to your petition will be shut. He'll have blown his chance to contest this matter, if he had any intention of doing so at all. All that'll be left for me to litigate on your behalf then will be custody, spousal, and child support. We're approaching the eleventh hour, so to speak. If you feel that you and your husband still need to talk this out, by all means do. You probably owe it to yourself to do so. Through all the good, the bad, and the ugly, you've still got some time invested in this marriage. As your attorney, however, I must tell you that if you're even remotely thinking about doing this within the confines of your home, I'm going to strongly advise you against doing so."

"Why's that?"

"Your order for protection stipulates that your husband cannot enter your home. There's no gray area there. Therefore, even if you *allow* him to enter your home, there's a strong chance he'll be arrested by the police if he's caught doing so. For example, if one of your neighbors sees him entering or leaving your apartment and calls the police, he's likely to be arrested. If someone, say a girlfriend of yours, finds out he was at your apartment and notifies the authorities, he's likely to be arrested. Bail for such an offense isn't going to come cheap either. Understand?"

"You've gotta be kidding. All that can happen to him *with* my permission?"

"Rose. You have convinced a court-appointed judge that your husband poses a serious threat to your safety. You've asked for the court's help in protecting you from your husband. A judge has reviewed your case very carefully and has granted you the protection you have sought. For you to now turn around and willingly allow this threat— namely, your husband—to enter your home is tantamount to—"

"Okay. I get it. I get it," she said, sounding exasperated at that point.

"Look. If your husband retains an attorney, I'm sure I can work out something whereby the four of us can get together and come up with what will hopefully be an amicable solution for both parties in a safe, controlled setting where you don't have to worry about anything or anyone else."

Rose looked at her watch and sighed.

"Let me think about all this. I really need to get back to work. For the record, I do want to end this marriage, Ms. Gentry. I'm not having second thoughts, either. But I am asking Sydney for alimony, child support, and custody of our son. That's a lot. I *know* him. He's not going to take this lying down. And if there is the slightest possibility that I can do something—anything—to reason with him, and reduce any potential ugliness, I need to give it a shot. And one more thing. Though I want custody of Andre, I am not trying to make an enemy of his father in the process. I would like to leave the door open for Sydney in the event that he still wants to have a relationship with his son, and vice versa. And yes, I know all of what I'm saying comes with some risk to my personal safety. But I do bear some of the blame for this bed I've made, so I'm going to have to lie in it. I just have to hope, pray, and leave it in God's hands from here."

"Whatever you decide to do, please, be careful, Rose. I don't want to read about you in the *Washington Post* or hear about you on the news."

"I will. I promise. You know, Ms. Gentry, on a lighter note, I gotta tell you. When this is all over with, my next man is going to be cut from an entirely different kind of cloth. I swear it. No more thugged-out, bad-boy, womanizing, drug-dealing niggas. Oops. I'm sorry. I know I need to stop referring to our men by that derogatory label racist white folks bestowed upon them—them and the rest of us."

"Do that. Please."

"Let me start over. What I mean to say is, no more thugged-out, bad boy, womanizing, drug-dealing black men. I don't care how exciting or addictive they may be on the surface. In fact, I'm even thinking about giving those average, clean-cut nice guys another chance."

"Excuse me? Did I hear you correctly? You mean the kind of guys your folks told you would make lots of money, take care of all your needs, and always be faithful to you? The same kind of guys you once found too one-dimensional, boring, easy, and predictable?"

"You remember me telling you all that, huh?"

"Of course I do. It's a lawyer's job to remember everything their clients tell them."

"Hmph. After all this drama, a boring man is going to be plenty enough excitement for me! I should've listened to my folks. You don't know this about me, but if my parents were here they'd tell you I could be one stubborn bitch at times."

"*Nooo.*"

That brought a hearty laugh out of both of us. Rose Braxton seemed to be leaving my office with her spirits high again.

SEPTEMBER . . .

23

Me and My Boyfriend

It was still hot as hell outdoors, but the Labor Day weekend had now come and gone, signifying the official end of summer. And what a summer it had been!

Unfortunately, I spent the holiday weekend on my hands and knees praying to the porcelain god. Came down with one of those twenty-four-hour stomach viruses that left me weak, dehydrated, and feeling plain old nasty. Tony offered to come by and bring me some chicken-noodle soup, crackers, and anything else he thought I would be able to keep down. I thought that was so sweet—but I politely declined his offer. Don't get me wrong. It's not that I didn't appreciate the gesture. I did. I just thought it was a little too early in our new boyfriend-girlfriend status for him to see me looking totally busted. I called Lisa instead and had her come by and hook me up with some therapies.

When my head wasn't in the toilet, the remainder of

my time was spent in bed watching episodes of *The Real World*, reading, and reflecting on my summer. I couldn't believe Tony Gianni was the only guy I dated all summer. Frankly, I didn't know whether to be happy or profoundly depressed by that. Guess I shouldn't have viewed it as a total downer. At least I had *somebody* of the opposite sex to go out and have a good time with. Besides, my time spent with Tony was hardly mind-numbing. Quite the contrary. We did some really fun stuff together. And if any one knows that things could have been worse, it's certainly me. I could have spent June, July, and August like scores of sistas in the D.C. area who are single, looking, and hoping did: void of any male companionship whatsoever. No friend, no lover, no fuckbuddy; not even a placeholder. What is it my Grandma Lucy Pearl used to say all the time? Oh yeah. *Don't look a gift horse in the mouth.*

Of course, dating Tony and only Tony meant something else, too. Another summer had come and gone without me finding my particular box of chocolate. But rather than dwell on what did or didn't happen, I decided from that point on to focus my energy on the reality of what is. And the "what is" is that the very man I came so close to kicking to the curb a couple of months ago had somehow managed to become my new boyfriend. My new *white* boyfriend.

I can't believe I just used those three words—"my," "white," and "boyfriend"—in the same sentence. Lawd! Grandma Lucy Pearl must be rolling over in her grave right about now. When I was a little girl she would frequently sit me down on her lap, and expound on the importance of keeping the black family intact. How little black girls like me would one day have to carry the torch of raising future generations of the black family. And how a great deal of this responsibility—the teaching, nurturing and so forth, fair or unfairly—would fall directly on our shoulders. She'd reiterate over and over to me how we should continue to give our undying support—no matter how difficult that may be at times— to our black men, just as she and myriad other black women in her day did. "Bailey," Grandma would say, "this is the *only* way the black family unit is going to survive and stay strong." She would then take my tiny hands in hers, and tell me to lock my ten fingers together as tightly as possible. Then she'd do likewise with her own. "You see this?" she'd go on, "Black folks gotta stick to one another. Tight. Just like our hands are right now. If we do, we'll prosper as a people. And I promise you my little dahlin', these white folks out here will never be able to separate us or turn us against one another."

Looking back on it, I knew this was where my strong, pro-black beliefs began to take hold. Where my steadfast devotion to black men began to take root. As a young, skinny, kinky-haired little girl sitting on my grandma's lap, and listening to her words of wisdom in the living room of our home on Fourteenth and Hamilton Street in the early Seventies.

Anyways, getting back to Tony and me. While the two of us were officially an item now, it remained news I hadn't officially made known to anyone else. I didn't tell Lisa about it, and she's my best friend. (I hate keeping things from her.) As far as she knew, Tony and I were still just messin' around. The only thing I did reveal to her was that we *still* hadn't become intimate yet. Of course, her response to that revelation was classic Lisa: "Girl, your coochie must be like sandpaper!"

Look. I simply wasn't ready to go public about us just yet. I guess in part because I wasn't terribly confident

that this passage of mine over to the "other side" was
going to work out. Sorta like when you meet a particular
guy and don't want to bring him around your family just
yet. Or you're a single mom and don't want to introduce
him to your kid just yet 'cause you're not sure how long
the guy's going to be around. Still, in the back of my
mind as well was the uncomfortable feeling I got when
Tony kissed me inside the café that afternoon. My reaction to it alone made me question if I even *wanted* things
to work out between us. Despite all that, I oddly felt
more than ready for the two of us to go out in public as
a real couple for the first time.

The backdrop for our steppin' out party was of all
things, the Black Family Reunion festival on the Mall in
D.C. My idea. Yeah, I know what you're thinking. Dang,
Bailey, couldn't you have picked a forum a bit more
subtle for y'all's first time out as boyfriend and girlfriend? Perhaps. But let's get this party on and poppin'
was my mindset at the time. There were going to be
thousands of folks at that event and I figured we could
simply blend in with the rest of them. Furthermore, I
wasn't at all concerned with Tony feeling out of place or
anything. If there was one thing I learned about him, it
was that he was no fish out of water around black folks.

Boy, was I right about that! Tony was having a good
time. Maybe *too* much of a good time. Feel me? Oh, he
tried being slick and discreet, but he wasn't that slick
and discreet. His eyeballs were clockin' all the honeys
out and about that afternoon, most of whom were
flaunting tits and ass for days. Heck. I even caught myself
marveling at some of those shapely asses that even put
my shapely ass to shame. But I'd be remiss not to mention that there was plenty of eye-candy for the ladies, too.
Oh, yeah. It was a regular *bro-ais!* Something to suit every

sista's fancy. Fine brothas. Ugly brothas. Dark brothas. Light brothas. Tall brothas. Short brothas. Just-got-out-of-jail-looking brothas. Looking gay-as-all-hell brothas. Jheri-curl-having, no-damn-clue-we're-in-the-Nineties-for-cryin'-out-loud-looking brothas.

Tony and I strolled around Constitution and Fifteenth, soaking up all the ambiance of the scene; the booths selling artwork, clothing, jewelry; the various pavilions with themes on economic empowerment, health, fitness, and more. Later on we planned on taking in the traditional R&B concert in the park. Oh, by the way, we weren't holding hands and acting all lovey-dovey as we strolled around. We were going to have to work our way up to that. (At least I was.) That said, however, I'm sure to any onlookers it was clear that we were an item. Speaking of onlookers, I started observing some of the couples out and about that afternoon. (One of my favorite pastimes, remember?) And what I saw was plenty of black-on-black love that clearly had withstood the test of time. Elderly gray-haired couples who still seemed madly in love after thirty, forty, fifty years of marriage. Being the hopeless romantic I am, I found this spectacle, in a word, awe-inspiring. Conversely, I observed many couples who didn't appear to have *any* chemistry going on. Those duos looked as if their sole purpose for being out that afternoon was to scout some new prospects under the day's hot bright sun.

At one point in the day, Tony stepped away to find a porta-john. As I waited for him to return, this gum-popping hoochie in Daisy Dukes, three-inch press-on nails, and more weave than a drunk driver, rolled up on me like there was something she *had* to let me know. I instantly switched into bitch mode 'cause she looked as though she was about to give me some 'tude about something. Being at the Black Family Reunion with a white guy perhaps? Turns out, I had my defensives up for nothing.

"Guuurl, dat guy you wit has got it goin' on, chile! Is dat cho' man and does he have a twin brother for me?" she said, grinning from ear to ear.

If the Daisy Dukes, press-on nails, and busted weave weren't tacky enough, sista-girl had the audacity to be sportin' a gold front tooth. *D-a-y-u-m!!*

I politely told Hooch-zilla—not that it was any of her business—we were just friends, and no, he didn't have a brother. *If he did, you sure wouldn't be his type,* I thought to myself, but didn't dare say to her face.

"Dat's too bad, gurl. But I like what 'chu doin'."

"What I'm doing?"

"Yeah, gurl. Sistas gotta do what they gotta do. 'Specially when deeze brothas don't be actin' right. Know what I'm saying?" She raised her hand and waited on a high five. I humored her and off she ran hoochily on her way.

Now truth be told, my head did swell just a little bit after that encounter. I was flattered that yet another black woman found Tony attractive. Even if she was a straight up hooch-zilla. Her endorsement of him—no matter how ghettofied—seemed to empower me with a new sense of legitimacy in regard to my new relationship with Tony. I only wished that I was feeling good enough about it a second ago to tell her the truth, that yes, he was my man. For the remainder of the afternoon to follow, I kept my eyes peeled for any other sistas who might be clocking my man.

Caught more than a few rubbernecking.

24

Revisiting the Past

I had made a couple of roasted-turkey-and-Swiss sandwiches and brought along some fruit and chips for Tony
and me to eat. Having attended the Black Family Reunion before, I knew that waiting on long lines for food
was something I simply no longer had the patience for.
That and I knew it could be kind of expensive to get
your eat on at functions like this. The fact that this was
Tony's first time and he might not have minded waiting
in line to sample food from the different vendors, or the
prices, went right over my head. I apologized for my pre-
sumptuousness and told him I wouldn't be offended if
he had an appetite for something other than my roasted-
turkey-and-Swiss sandwiches. One thing I didn't bring
along was anything to drink, so Tony picked up a couple
of Snapples from one of the vendors. Next, the two of us
found a patch of grass on the grounds of the Mall, and
commenced having our own private picnic.

"This is mad cool, B. I'm really feeling this atmosphere," Tony said as he chomped on his sandwich and chips.

I noticed you are, I thought to myself. "Ever heard of the Black Family Reunion before?" I asked.

"Oh yeah. But I'd go to a movie or even to dinner by myself before I'd come out to something like this alone."

"Why's that?"

"This ain't the kind of event that would be much fun to attend by yourself. Especially if you're a white boy," he said laughing. "Would you come here alone?"

"Probably not. I'd probably find it depressing in some respects."

"Depressing?"

"Well, it's sorta like what you were getting at. Most of the folks here are all coupled off and what not. If I didn't have anyone to share this with I'd probably feel left out. I would come with Lisa, though. Or even her and Mo."

"How are those two doing anyway?"

"They're fine."

"Tell them I said whassup."

"Will do. And what about your roommate? Would you come here with him?"

"Derrick? Doubt it. He's not into big crowds unless he's at Camden Yards watching the Orioles or at the CAP center watching the Bullets play."

"He was at the fund-raiser with you the night we met. That was a big crowd."

"True, but that's different. That was a dress-up, mingle, eat, drink, and network kind of function. He's *always* up for that kind of thing."

"How long have he and Mylene been an item?"

"About a year and a half now."

"That long, huh?"

"Why?"

"Just curious."

"They make a cute couple, don't they?"

Hmph. I wish Tony hadn't gone there. I couldn't say what I really wanted to say. That a black man with anyone *other* than a black woman could *never* make a cute couple in my book.

"I don't have an opinion about them one way or another."

"Sure you do," he busted me. "You think Derrick should be with a black woman, don't you?"

"Mmm, next subject."

"Fine. How's work? How's that client of yours? The one you said was high maintenance the other day?"

I wished he hadn't gone there either. I really didn't want to think about work today. Especially not Rose Braxton's drama.

"Oh, she's still high maintenance. I think she may even be a little hardheaded, too. But I'm confident everything's going to work out just fine in the end."

"What's her issue?"

"Um, I'd really rather not get into that."

"Oops. My bad. It's a client-attorney thing."

"Exactly. Let's just say she's going through a divorce that's far from amicable."

"Good enough. Now, how about we talk about something that I'm still curious about?" Tony said, pointing to the corner of my mouth where I left some mayonnaise from my sandwich.

"What's that?"

"I know you've said you don't like talking about this subject, but since I'm not just your friend anymore, but your boyfriend now, I was hoping you'd feel a bit more comfortable—"

Before he could get to where he was going, I had already beaten him there.

"You want to know how I went from being Bailey McClendon to Bailey Gentry."

"Please don't tell me it's a long story again."

"It *is* a long story, Tony."

"Well, the weather's beautiful, and we've got these lip-smacking sandwiches and fruit to eat. Unless you've got a date with another dude later, I'd say we've got nothing but time."

"You're not going to leave this alone are you?"

"No, I'm not," he said, taking a swallow of his peach-flavored Snapple iced tea. Tony had been forthcoming with me in regard to his family and some of his upbringing. Guess it was about time for me to return the favor.

"My mother was only fifteen years old when she got pregnant with me. Sixteen when she gave birth to me. The man who fathered me was twenty-three at the time. With me so far?"

"That's statutory rape."

"Correct. Of course, my mother's pregnancy came not only as a shock to her, but to my grandparents also. They had no idea their daughter was keeping company with a boy, let alone having sex with a grown man.

"Now my mother's lover—Thomas is his name—was a guy from the neighborhood who didn't have a formal job, but earned his money doing odd jobs for all the homeowners on the block. He did quite a bit of work for my grandparents, too. Trimming grass, raking leaves, shoveling snow—that sort of stuff. That's how my parents met. Now from an appearance standpoint, my moms was . . . very developed for a fifteen-year-old, shall we say. Voluptuous ass, shapely legs, large breasts. I only inherited her ass and legs, as you can tell."

"I ain't touchin' that," Tony said.

"You better not! Anyway, our neighborhood was a close-knit one where everyone knew everyone. Which translates to everyone was in everyone's business, too. So despite my mom's womanly appearance, there could have been no way Thomas-the-handyman didn't know he was sleeping with a tenth-grader. My grandparents were simply outraged when they learned that their supposedly wholesome teenage daughter, Savannah—that's my mom's name—was about to make them grandparents, something they were hoping to be one day, but clearly not *that* soon. In anger over the news, they took it upon themselves to take complete control of the situation.

"The first thing they do is tell my mother to make certain she puts Thomas's last name on my birth certificate. That name was McClendon."

"Ah, got it now. What was your grandparent's rationale behind that? You were born out of wedlock, weren't you?"

"Slow down, Tony, I'm getting to that. They—my grandparents—reasoned that this would make it easier for my mother to get child support in the event my father didn't do the right thing. Of course, having the McClendon name wasn't nearly as important as my mother simply establishing paternity. Nevertheless, there was probably an even bigger reason why my grandparents were so adamant about whose last name was on my birth certificate. My mother's pregnancy occurred in the early Sixties, a time when folk's attitudes about out-of-wedlock babies were a lot different than they are today. Today, it's no big deal. Heck, some women *consciously* have kids out of wedlock. Some even go to the sperm bank because they want a child without the requirement of a husband. There was no way, though, my grandparents were going to stand for having an illegitimate granddaughter. So, before I emerged from the womb of my mother, they gave young Mr. McClendon the following ultimatum: Marry Savannah as soon as she turns eighteen or we're turning you over to the authorities for statutory rape. My father did what he had to in order to save his ass. He marries my mother at City Hall exactly one week after she turns eighteen and graduates from high school. For the record, my mother did not want to marry Thomas even though she was having his baby. The whole thing was my grandparents' doing."

"Wow. I'm sorry. I had no idea—"

"I'm just getting started, Tony. You wanted to know the story; I'm going to tell you the *whole* story.

"As a family attorney, I know firsthand that a marriage based solely on the premise of 'legitimizing' a child almost never works out. I mean, let's face it. Most marriages have only a fifty percent chance of being successful—and that's when both parties are *willing* participants. It goes without saying that the odds are much lower when the wife's only eighteen, straight out of high school, the husband's twenty-five, hasn't had a real job in his entire life, and both parties for all intents and purposes have been *forced* into marrying one another. All that and neither has a 'pot to piss in or a window to throw it out of,' as my grandma would say.

That incited a chuckle out of Tony.

"I'm not laughing because anything about this is funny, B. It's anything but. It's just that 'pot to piss in' thing—now that's a metaphor I've never heard before."

"It's a black thing, Gianni. You wouldn't understand," I joked with him.

"So where did your parents live after you were born?"

"I'll give you three guesses."

"Hmmm, let's see. Your mother just graduated from

high school, your father doesn't have a steady job; I'd say they either lived with your grandparents or with his parents."

"The former. His folks had six other kids. Some still living at home, so there was no room over there."

"Okay. I'm gonna cut to the chase 'cause this obviously ain't a marriage made in heaven. When did your parents divorce?"

"Officially? Ten years later. But they gave up on each other—and me—long before that."

"Gave up on you how?"

"My mother got a secretarial job a few weeks after the wedding. It wasn't paying much, but it wasn't half bad for someone fresh out of high school, and it was *something*. My pops on the other hand, he didn't do much with himself after the wedding except grow more and more resentful with each passing day for having been blackmailed into marrying my mother in the first place. Suffice to say my father, mother, and grandparents all living under the same roof was a combustible mixture that could only blow sky-high eventually. By my second birthday, Thomas was gone. Out of the house and out of my mother's life and mine for good."

"Did anyone try to talk him out of leaving?"

"They never got that opportunity. He left under the cover of darkness—literally. They all went to bed one night, and by daylight, my father and everything belonging to him that he could stuff into a suitcase were gone. They did find out seven months later via the neighborhood grapevine that he had escaped to Windsor, North Carolina, where he was shackin' with another woman. Tony, let me tell you. When my grandparents got wind of that they wanted to call the sheriffs down there in tobaccoland and have my father shot on sight.

But that's when my mother stepped in and told them once and for all to leave the situation alone and stay the hell out of her business. Let it *and* him go she told them. Moms didn't want Thomas back. In fact, she didn't want *anything* from him. Not even child-support money."

"So what are you telling me? Your mother just let your father waltz off, obligation-free?"

"That about sums it up. According to her, Thomas wasn't worth shit anyway, and she didn't need him to help raise me. You know, a classic case of the 'I can do bad all by myself' blues.

"My mother's decision would prove critical in so many ways, too. For starters, her stance was the complete opposite of what my grandparents wanted her to do. Never mind that she was a grown woman and able to make that decision for herself. Like I told you, from the beginning, she never wanted to marry my father any more than he wanted to marry her. My mother resented what she felt was my grandparent's interference in the situation from the time they found out she was pregnant. In turn, my grandparents resented what they felt was my mother's lack of appreciation for all their support. And so marked the beginning of the end of *their* relationship as well.

"Now, to my mother's credit, I believe her intentions were good at the beginning. She did make an attempt to make a life for the two of us. She moved out of my grandparents' house and got herself a rent-subsidized apartment in Northeast D.C. But in little time, I guess the strain of raising a young daughter as a single parent got the best of her. I think she realized that she bit off more than she could chew. That maybe she did need a man's help or that child-support check after all. Maybe as much as she resented her parent's meddling—and rightfully so—she did need their assistance, too. I guess my mother came to the realization that a lot of young mothers in her position come to even today: She wanted to enjoy her youth to the fullest. She wanted to date. Go clubbin'. Hang out with her girlfriends. Do all the things women her age without kids were doing. Having a five-year-old was weighing her down. Cramping her style. How's that sandwich, Tony?" I asked, interrupting my train of thought for a moment.

"Pretty good. But then again, it's turkey and Swiss. It's not like you *cooked* something for me," he chuckled.

"Fun-ny, Tony. Don't choke on it or you're gonna be SOL. Anyway, I can remember being in our little cramped apartment where it seemed like every other week my moms would be entertaining a different man. If it wasn't that, then it was always someone coming over to watch me while she partied. She would spend hours in front of the mirror getting dolled up, and as soon as she'd finish there would be a knock at the door. Some woman would enter our apartment and my mother would say, "Bailey, this is your Auntie Blah-blah-blah. She's going to watch you for a few hours while Mommy goes out, okay?" I swear I'd want to cry every time I saw her primpin' because I knew it meant she was about to leave me home with some stranger. Know the worst thing about it? Each and every time it would be somebody *different*. I hardly ever saw the same face twice. Yet, the person would always be one of my aunts. After a while, I began to wonder how it was that I had so many 'aunts' I had never seen or heard of before."

Tony shook his head as he finished off his sandwich. This was definitely not the story he was expecting. Nevertheless, I was on a roll now and couldn't stop talking about it. Guess I needed to, because doing so was beginning to feel oddly therapeutic.

"On some occasions after my mother would leave, a man would show up to visit with whichever aunt of mine was baby-sitting me at the time. In my young naivete, I assumed this person must've been my 'Uncle' Blah-blah-blah. Anyways, the two of them would end up going at it on our living-room sofa like I wasn't even in the house."

"Sex?"

"Buck wild!"

"Are you kidding me? You *saw* them having sex?"

"Hmph. Sure did. Of course I was too young at the time to *understand* what I was watching, but yes. I watched my many 'aunts' and 'uncles' having sex on many occasions."

"That's totally jacked. Did you ever tell your mother what you saw?"

"Mmm-hmm. I'd tell her stuff like, 'A man came over when you were gone, took off his clothes, and got on top of Aunt Blah-blah-blah.' You know what she'd say to me, Tony?'

"I'm afraid to ask."

"She'd say, 'Bailey, if a man comes over to visit your aunt while I'm out, just go in your room, close the door, play with your dolls, and don't come out unless you're told to.'"

"Damn. I don't know what to say to you, B. Except that I'm sorry to hear that your childhood was like that. I do appreciate you opening up and sharing this with me, though."

"Well, that's what folks in a relationship do: open up and share things, right?"

"Right."

Tony leaned in and kissed me on the forehead. I didn't feel awkward that he kissed me in public this time. Maybe because he didn't kiss me on the mouth. In any event, the gesture was welcomed. I needed some affection. Therapeutic as this was, reliving my dysfunctional upbringing still left me feeling a bit low.

"So what kind of relationship do you and your mother have now?" he asked.

"None. Haven't since I was seven. That's when she decided she no longer could or wanted to take care of me and decided to turn me over to foster care."

"Oh no."

"It's cool, Tony. I didn't have to go into the foster-care system, thank God. My grandparents came to the rescue. They took me back in with them, and a few years later, I became the adopted daughter of Milton and Lucy Pearl Gentry."

"Happy ending?"

"Happier. My granddad could be a pain in the ass more often than not, but he made a good father figure for me. And my grandma, well, she simply turned out to be a godsend."

"And they've both passed on?"

"Yes. My granddad first. He died in Seventy-nine, and my grandma, she passed three years ago. I'm really happy she at least lived long enough to see me graduate from college. She's the one who really pushed me to finish, go to law school, and fulfill my dream of becoming a lawyer."

"So the fact that you chose family law as your area of practice is no coincidence, I assume."

"Correct. Given what I went through, it was the logical choice."

"You know, I was proud of you to begin with, and that was before I knew any of this. I'm even prouder of you now, Bailey. This just makes your accomplishments all the more amazing."

His praise made me blush.

"Thank you, Tony."

"Hey. Whadda you say we get up and go carve out a good spot for us to watch the concert in a little bit?"

"Sounds like a marvelous idea. Let's go."

25

Decisions, Decisions

Lisa nearly fainted when I gave her the news: that I was taking a leap of faith over to the "other side." Despite her numerous insistences that I do that very thing, she still couldn't believe I had actually decided to go for it. Given her fondness for Tony, this was sweet music to her ears, as you might imagine.

"Wouldn't it be ironic if that Italian Stallion turns out to be your Mr. Right? Especially with *your* issues?" she said to me as we sat in the food court of Columbia Mall having lunch, taking a load off our feet from a full morning of shopping. "That would be some kinda poetic justice for yo' racist ass," she went on, damn near laughing herself into a convulsion.

"I'm glad to see you're getting such a big kick out of this."

"Oh trust me, I *am.*"

"Time will tell if Tony's my Mr. Right or not. In the

meanwhile, I'm just going to take this thing one day at a time. And I don't appreciate your calling me a racist either, Lisa. Being *pro-black* does not make me a racist."

"Oh, get your thong outta your booty crack. I'm only playin' with ya. You're just loyal to the 'cause.' I know."

"Is that a crime?"

"If it were we'd have to arrest ninety-five percent of the sistahood."

"I know that's right." We giggled and gave each other high fives.

"All joking aside, though. I'm proud of you, B."

"Proud of me?"

"Yeah. I know how difficult dating—let alone sexin'—someone other than a black man must be for you. Speaking of which, gimme details. Is Tony well hung, or is his thing-a-ma-jig all pink and—"

"Shut up, Lisa! And lower your voice for cryin' out loud."

"Tsk. Ain't nobody listening to us. So?"

"So what?"

"How was it?"

"I'm not telling you!"

"Why not?"

I rolled my eyes at Lisa and kept right on eating. She peered at me as if she was searching my inner soul.

"Oh my God. You *still* haven't slept with Tony, have you?"

"Dang. If you *must* know, no, I haven't."

"What the hell are you waiting for? *Christmas?*"

I placed my plastic knife and fork down on my Styrofoam plate and wiped my mouth with my napkin. "What's the rush?"

"*Rush?* How long has it been since you met Tony?"

"Three mon—"

"*THREE MONTHS?*"

"Ssshh, Lisa!"

"Aw'aight, aw'aight. I'll lower my voice."

"Thank you!"

"Bailey. You've *never* taken this long to—"

"I've never been involved with a *white guy* before either. This is all very new to me. I'm going to have to take this thing slowly. Besides, maybe I've slept with guys *too* fast in the past. Ever think about that? A little self-control is good for the soul."

Silence.

"You're full of shit!"

"Am not."

"Are too."

"I'm not discussing my sex life with you, Lisa."

"Don't you mean your lack of?"

"What-eva. It's still mine."

"What is it with you? You 'fraid you're gonna catch the hoochie-coochies if you sleep with a white guy?"

"The heebie-jeebies."

We both looked at each other and burst out laughing.

"Girl, you're sick, you know that? I'll tell you this much, though. If it were me, I'd fuck Tony's white—"

"Hey, hey. Watch your mouth, Missy. That's my man you're talking about."

"I'm just saying, lay some of that brown sugar on him, girl, 'cause once he gets a taste of black—"

"He'll never go back."

"Word to the mutha!"

Lisa's always had a way of putting things in perspective for me. Albeit in an eccentric manner, most times.

"Anyhow, I'm really glad you're finally giving Tony a chance. Even though the poor guy's gonna have blue balls foolin' with your ass," she mumbled under her breath.

"I heard that."

"Just remember what I always say about Mr. Right. He doesn't always come in the box we expect him to."

"Are you done?"

"I'm done. Finish eating."

"You've made me lose my appetite."

"Then pass some of that beef and broccoli over here, 'cause I'm still hungry. What's the deal with Chinese food anyway? You can eat loads of it and an hour later you're hungry all over again. Can I ask you something, Bailey?"

"If I say no, will it stop you from asking me?"

"Please. You know better than that. You *are* giving this thing with Tony a chance, aren't you?"

"Meaning?"

"Meaning you're not stringing him along until something or someone better comes along are you? Like someone black, perhaps?"

"Lisa. I have strong feelings for Tony. Don't ask me how those came to be, but they're here. And I would like to think that I'm not the type of woman to string a truly nice guy along. Still and all, I'm not going to lie to you and tell you that I'm no longer hoping that a good brotha comes along and sweeps me off my feet. Although that doesn't seem anywhere close to happening."

"Well, you know how it goes. Nobody wants you, till somebody wants you."

"Ain't that the truth? Is that some irritating shit or is that some irritating shit?"

"Girl, as soon as I hooked up with Maurice dudes started coming out of the woodwork like roaches when the kitchen light goes off in the projects. But then again, dudes have always been beating down my door, haven't they?"

"What-eva!"

"You don't think it has anything to do with these thirty-four Cs do you?" Lisa said as she cupped both her breasts in her hands, and massaged herself.

"I cannot believe you just did that in public."

She looked around to see if anyone was watching. Two young bruhs sitting a few tables away must've been 'cause their eyes were as wide as saucers as they checked Lisa out. She smiled and waved to them.

"How y'all doing?" she flirted.

"Fine and you?" the young bucks responded, looking as though they might have an accident in their pants at any moment.

I looked at Lisa like she was crazy—which she no doubt was.

"Stop flirting with those guys, Lisa! Next thing they're gonna wanna come over here and sit with us."

"Let 'em."

"I don't think so. They look all of seventeen."

Lisa turned around to get a second glimpse of them. "I think you're right. Okay, what was I saying?"

"How nobody wants you till you have somebody."

"Right, right. Here's what I think, B. When a woman's involved she gives off some sort of glow that other men have radar for. Then it becomes some sort of sick challenge for some men to see if they can take you from your man."

"Yeah, and as soon as you give in, your glow disappears, and they dump you in order to search for another woman with that glow."

"Men are such dogs."

"True. But they're all we got."

"Unless you go the lesbian route."

"*Negative!*" we chanted in unison.

"So I take it you, me, Mo, and Tony will be getting together more regularly now?" Lisa asked.

"Definitely. I know Tony would like that."

"Let's make some plans then. How 'bout we all go to dinner after work one day this week? Mo and I will pick the restaurant this time."

"Sounds like a plan."

"Man. I can't wait to get home and tell Mo the news. He's just tickled pink that you're seeing a white guy, you know."

"Oh? And that's because?"

"Who knows? I think he just sees it as something else to tease you about. You ready to roll? I've still got some money to spend before we get out of here."

Lisa and I got up from the table, emptied our trays, and got back to doing one of the things we do best as a team—shop till we drop.

Tony and I had been going out with Mo and Lisa nearly every other night. And while he really enjoyed their company, I also knew he was growing a bit tired of the constant foursomes. All that double-dating, well, that had been my idea. And not because the four of us were having so much fun together, either. No, there was another explanation for it. One-on-ones with Tony were becoming increasingly difficult for me.

You'd probably think that now that I was in an interracial relationship, it would cause me to change some of the previous viewpoints I held concerning them. Perhaps seeing brothas traipsing around in public with blonde, blue-eyed, silicone-enhanced Barbie dolls on their arms wouldn't annoy me quite as much as it used to. That maybe my disdain for the "crossover brotha" would have dissipated just a bit. Think again. Not a damn thing changed. And since I was still feeling the way I always had, being with Tony left me feeling something else, too: like a total hypocrite every time the two of us were out together. Now, for whatever reason, I didn't feel nearly as hypercritical when it was the *four* of us out together. Got it? Good. Let's move on.

The interesting thing is I've always considered myself to be a "conscious" sista. A firm believer in the premise that black men and women need to stick together for the prosperity of our race, our children, and to better effectively combat this oppressive, white, racist society we live in. Just like my Grandma Lucy Pearl taught me years ago as a young girl. Call me a skeptic, but being a double minority—black *and* female—there was never any convincing me that I could unload my burdens on a white male, of all people. How could he *remotely* understand my challenges? My struggles? How could he ever serve as a positive role model to the son or daughter I hoped to give birth to one day?

What's wrong with this picture? Here I was, an attractive, intelligent, educated, black woman living in Metropolitan Washington D.C., a.k.a. "Chocolate City," for crying out loud. So I sit back playing the patient sista role, waiting for my box of chocolate to arrive. Except the only ones knocking on my door or buzzing my intercom of late were hustlers, ruff-necks, young'uns, old farts, and the kinds of bruhs that don't know wearing black shoes with a brown suit is a major fashion faux pas. So for all the city had to offer someone such as myself what did I end up with? A *white boy* from Philadelphia. Mm, mm, mm. I may as well have been living in cold-as-hell Minnesota, ya think?

Those three-and-a-half months since I'd met Tony had

been one part euphoria and one part confusion. Who knows? Maybe that kind of thing was just par for the course when a girl finds most of what she's looking for—and everything she's so *not* looking for—in the same man. I wouldn't admit to it at the time, but Tony was right in his assessment of me while we were in Philly. He did have me off balance. And I was getting more and more frustrated with trying to gain my balance. Granted it had only been a short time, but there were just some things that didn't take a woman long to ascertain. Like if she's working with a keeper or not. Tony was a keeper—not the keeper I had in mind—but a keeper nonetheless. Furthermore, he was becoming more and more important to me. More like my ideal man every day. He had an uncanny knack for doing all the right things at the right time. He made me laugh. (Very, very important.) He was neat, responsible, ambitious. He had a good job, good manners, he was drug-free. Heck, he even had good credit. He was handsome. (Make that *foin!!!*) I didn't have to dress him; he did that quite nicely all by himself. He was intelligent, thoughtful, opinionated. His conversation stimulated me. He was no pushover, either. He never tried to kiss my ass in order to get along with me. In other words, the man had some backbone. (Very, very important.) And unlike most of the mixed sets I had observed in the city, the two of us actually looked *good* together!

I couldn't deny it. Black, white, yellow, or green, Tony was this sista's dream from a vertical standpoint. Horizontally? Now there lay the great unknown. Thus far, intimacy between the two of us had been restricted to hand-holding, hugging, snuggling, some occasional tongue rasslin', and one aborted attempt at "circling the bases" due to an ill-timed appearance by Derrick and his

Asian chick. Which, in addition to all the double-dating, was one more thing Tony was losing patience with—our lack of sexual intimacy to date. Something that also only made things more confusing for me. Translation: I'm feeling all this and he hasn't even fed the cat yet?

Rose Braxton put it best: *Be careful what you ask for.* Was she right about that! Because now that I apparently had most of what I had been asking for, I hadn't a clue what I was going to do with it.

26

Manipulation

Fuck you and that black bitch lawyer of yours, read the opening sentence on a barely legible one-page letter I grabbed off the fax machine in my office. *You want a divorce, you got it.*

I had just petitioned the court to grant Rose Braxton her divorce. Our summons had now gone unanswered for over thirty days, indicating that her husband had no desire to contest it. All that was left now was the stroke of a judge's pen to extract my client from her five hellish years of matrimony. Rose could exhale soon. This was good news indeed. But I wasn't ready to do cartwheels on her behalf just yet. Something wasn't making a lot of sense to me. One and one wasn't adding up to two. That's a red flag in any practice of law.

The facts as I knew them were that my client and her husband had a volatile, abusive, and controlling relationship. So why was Sydney Braxton giving in so easily?

Wasn't Rose just in my office a few short weeks ago telling me how she knew he wasn't the type to take this matter lying down?

I guess I should use this moment to step back and let y'all in on something. Despite what I thought to be very sound advice on my part, Rose went ahead and did just the opposite of what I had advised her to do. In clear violation of the very restraining order she had requested, she allowed her husband back into her home so that, in her words, "they could hash things out in some privacy once and for all." Of course when she informed me of this ill-advised maneuver of hers, I nearly broke a blood vessel in my head. I was furious with her. Had I been speaking Chinese to her that day? What part of "Your order for protection particularly stipulates that your husband cannot enter your home" didn't she understand?

If there was anything positive to come out of my client's foolhardiness it was that she survived the encounter without any bodily harm to herself—or worse. Thankfully, Sydney didn't go postal on her as we both feared he might. In fact, his reaction was quite the opposite, according to Rose. He remained inexplicably cool, calm, and collected as she told him why she was divorcing him and seeking alimony, child support, and full custody of their young son. The bad news? Despite taking this enormous risk to her personal safety, her husband's unanticipated calm left Rose with no more of a sense of what she was up against than she'd had before deciding to tempt fate and violate the terms of her own restraining order.

Now, this supposed calm she said Sydney was exuding during their encounter—well, I wasn't buying it. I assumed it might be nothing more than the proverbial calm before the storm. And judging by the tone of the letter in my hand, I was certain my instincts were dead-on.

I continued reading the letter in its entirety. Though not without putting on my eyeglasses, 'cause it was written in some straight-up chicken scratch if I ever saw it.

> *If you think your muthafuckin' ass is gonna get a dime out of me you got another thing coming. And don't even think you gonna have somebody else playing daddy to my son. You don't want to be with me, fine. But you ain't gonna be with nobody else either. This ain't over until it's over, Rose.*
> —*Syd*
>
> *P.S. I'll be paying that bitch-ass lawyer of yours a little visit, too.*

I snatched my glasses off and squinted to make sure I'd read that last line correctly.

I'll be paying that bitch-ass lawyer of yours a little visit too.

I placed the letter down on my desk, took a deep breath, and thought about what I had just read. My heart was beginning to thump like a 1970s disco song. Several things went racing through my head at once. None of which involved nonviolence, I might add. I immediately picked up the phone and dialed Rose at her job. She answered on the first ring.

"Rose Brax—"

"It's Bailey Gentry," I said, cutting her off before she could finish her greeting.

"Oh, hi. Did you get the fax I sent?"

"Yes, Rose, I got it. That's why I'm calling. When did *you* get this letter?"

"It came in the mail about three days ago."

"*Three da*—three days ago? Why are you just now bringing this to my attention?"

"Is something wrong?"

"Maybe. Did you happen to read your husband's comment at the end of it?"

"Hold on." Rose put me on hold and came back on the line a few seconds later. "Okay, I'm back. I had to pull out my copy of it. The last sentence you said? Let's see . . . um . . . this ain't over until it's over . . . P.S. I'll be paying . . . oooh . . ."

Oh?

"I'm sorry, Ms. Gentry. That part went totally over my head. Oh my God. Don't tell me Sydney's come by your office—"

"Not yet anyway. Do you have any idea what he wants to see me about?"

"I don't know. When I met with him he asked me who my lawyer was. He thought 'Bailey Gentry' was a man. I told him you were a woman. A black woman, in fact. If you ask me, I think he's just looking for somebody to blame for my decision. As if someone's put me up to divorcing him. I think he might be blaming you because you're representing me. It's nothing personal, Ms. Gentry. Sydney would be upset with anybody who was representing me."

Unfortunately, her line of reasoning wasn't easing my angst any. "Look, Mrs. Braxton . . . uh, Rose. We're in the middle of a divorce proceeding—"

"I thought that was a done deal since Sydney didn't respond to the summons in time?"

"The divorce, yes. However, there are still custody and alimony issues yet to be resolved that are totally separate matters from the dissolution of your marriage. We've gone over this." I was getting a little hot under the collar with my hardheaded client.

"I'm sorry. I guess in all the excitement of learning the divorce wouldn't be contested, I got a little sidetracked on those other issues."

"Look, you've got to help me to help you. And the best way you can do this is by staying focused in this matter in its *totality*. It's not over until every detail has been settled. I cannot stress that to you enough. How long after the meeting with your husband did he send you this letter?"

"We got together on a Saturday night, and I got it in the mail the following Wednesday. I know Sydney sounds real angry in that letter, but I swear I didn't hear or see any of this anger when he was over at my house. We talked, and the only thing he said was that he didn't reply to the summons because he had no intention of standing in my way. He said he wanted me to move on with my life if that's what I wanted to do. In fact, he said he thought it was time for him to do the same. And as far as giving me full custody of Andre, child support, and alimony goes, he said he needed some time to think about those things. It was like he was mulling over a way he *could* do all of that. There was no yelling, threatening or anything like that. I felt really good after we talked. Like meeting with him in the privacy of my home was worth the risk. Sydney even spent some quality time with Andre. Took him to Baskin Robbins for some ice cream. Just the two of them. For the first time in years, Sydney was actually behaving like a dad. I went to bed that night feeling pretty good about us, Ms. Gentry. It got me to thinking that maybe after all the drama we could end our marriage *without* a bunch of drama. That maybe he and I going our separate ways wasn't going to be that bad after all, and that our son could still have some semblance of a family in spite of it. So you can imagine when I got this letter from him it just blew me away. Sydney did a complete one-eighty on me."

"All the more reason you should have brought this to my attention immediately." I knew Rose felt bad enough by now and to belabor the issue any further wouldn't have served any worthwhile purpose. "I'm not sure what your husband thinks he's going to accomplish by paying me a visit," I went on. "I'm not representing him in this divorce, so it would be unethical on my part to discuss anything with him."

"Would it help if I called him and told him not to—"

"Hold on a moment, Mrs. Braxton."

My intercom was ringing. I put Rose on hold and hit the button for line two. It was Monifah.

"Yes, Monifah."

"There's a gentlemen by the name of Sydney Braxton here to see you."

Shit!

"Did you tell him I was in the office?"

"No. He didn't have an appointment and didn't say what the purpose of his visit was, so I just told him to have a seat."

"Good. Just let him wait."

All right, Bailey. How are you going to handle this?

"Bailey."

"Yes, Monifah."

"Whoever this guy is, he seems kinda aggregated?"

"I think you mean 'agitated,' Monifah."

"That's what I said."

Sheesh! "He's the husband of one of my clients, Monifah. She's divorcing him."

"Oooh."

"I'll tell you this. He has absolutely no business being here."

"You want me to call one of the sec—"

"No! He'd probably only come back again. I'm going to have to deal with this. I'll be out in a minute."

"You sure you don't want me to call security?" Monifah asked once more.

"I don't think that'll be necessary. If it does become necessary, I'll buzz you, okay?"

"Okay."

I hung up and reconnected with Rose, who was still holding.

"Sorry about that, Mrs. Braxton. You were saying?"

"I was asking you should I call Sydney and tell him—"

"It's too late. He's waiting for me in the receptionist area as we speak."

"Dammit! He is such an asshole! What is he coming to your job for?"

"Don't know, but I'm about to find out, huh? I've got to go."

"All right, but be careful, Ms. Gentry."

I left my office and made my way out into the reception area. The closer I got to it, the harder my heart began to beat, yet strangely, the bolder I began to feel. By the time I reached my destination my fear of the unexpected was totally gone and replaced with a whole lot of 'tude, and a little bit of bravado.

I identified Sydney Braxton immediately. Wasn't hard. He was the only black male seated in the reception area. As I walked past the front desk, I made eye contact with Monifah.

"That's him in the jeans," she whispered.

I approached and stood before him as he remained

seated, flipping through a *Black Enterprise* magazine, unaware of my presence.

"Mr. Braxton?"

"Yes?"

"I'm Bailey Gentry. I'm told you're here to see me."

My eyes watched his as they examined me from top to bottom. I'm not sure what he pictured seeing, but judging by his reaction, I was far from what he was expecting.

"*You're* Bailey Gentry?" he asked.

I looked hot that day. Came in to work in a lime-green and white-polka-dot knit blouse over a booty-huggin' white-cotton pleated skirt that fell just above my knee, with matching asymmetrical belt and lime-green pointed-toe pumps that emphasized the definition of my shapely legs. I must've been on the receiving end of a half dozen pickup lines before I reached the office that morning. A few of which I couldn't help but laugh at. *Were you arrested earlier? It's got to be illegal to look that good. Do you know karate, 'cuz damn, yo' body is kickin'.*

"Yes, I am. What can I do for you, Mr. Braxton?" I asked, not smiling, not being rude, but not being particularly cordial either.

Sydney rose from his seat. He was dark-skinned, about five-ten with a stocky build, and wore his hair in braids. Looked a bit Wesley Snipes-ish in the mug.

"I was hoping you and I could discuss a few things. You know, about this divorce my wife wants."

"Mr. Braxton, I am your *wife's* attorney. I am not at liberty to discuss anything pertaining to the dissolution of your marriage with you. Have you retained an attorney of your own? He or she would be the appropriate person for you to confer with."

"Naw, I haven't. Look, this'll only take a few minutes.

Do you have an office or something we can go in and talk in private? *Please.*"

Against my better judgment, I walked Sydney back to my office to hear him out.

"You've got five minutes, Mr. Braxton."

"Dang, my sista. Are you this rushed with everyone who pays you a visit?"

"If they're not on retainer, yes. And you now have four and a half minutes left."

"Aw'aight, aw'aight. Let me hurry on up and get to the purpose of my visit. As you are my wife's lawyer, I want you to know that I'm not going to contest this divorce. If this is what Rose wants, so be it. But this child support and alimony she's talking, well, that's a whole 'nother story. We're gonna have a little prob—"

"I don't mean to interrupt you, but with all due respect, I must reiterate what I said to you in the reception area. I am not your attorney. I am not at liberty to discuss this divorce or anything related to it with you. Nor, might I add, should you be in here discussing any of this with me. If you've got an issue with any of the things your wife has requested in her summons, I strongly urge you to seek out your own legal representation. It's in your best interest to do so. That said, if this is what you came here to discuss with me, I'm afraid this conversation is over, and you really ought to leave now." I rose from behind my desk to escort Mr. Braxton back to the reception area and out the door.

"Rose ain't getting no alimony or child support from me. I quit my job." That stopped me dead in my tracks.

"So, Rose is wasting your time as well as her time and money. And time is money, right?" he went on. "I know she must be paying you a pretty penny an hour. Money I know she ain't got a lot of."

I sat back down. "You quit your job."

"No money, no payments," he said—arrogantly, as if he no longer had a care in the world.

Right then and there I wanted to jump across my desk and smack the smug look off his face. I was beginning to see for myself why my client wanted to rid herself of this reprobate. "And what prompted you to do that?" I asked, as if I didn't already have some clue.

"Actually, I've been thinking about doing it for some time. You know, I never really liked working for the U. S. Postal Service, to be quite honest with you. I think it's time for me to blaze a new career path. I'm gonna take some time off and mull over what I want to do next."

Yeah, right, muthafutta. Your timing couldn't be more obvious.

"Well, your wife and child aside for a moment, how do you intend to support *yourself* in the meantime?"

"I dunno. Guess I'm'a have to figure something out, huh?"

"Sell drugs *full-time,* maybe?"

That salvo took him completely off guard. Staggered him. Sort of like a boxer who didn't see the left hook coming 'cause he was too busy looking for the straight right. The smugness in his demeanor disappeared immediately.

"Is . . . is that what Rose told you?" he said, trying his best to mask his irritation and recover quickly. "Mm, mm, mm. Rose is such a drama queen. She really needs to stop kidding around with folks like that. You never know when someone's gonna actually believe that nonsense."

"*Is* it nonsense, Mr. Braxton?"

"Utter bullshit is more like it. Man, wait till I see her—"

"You're not going anywhere near her."

"*Excuse me?*"

"My client has a restraining order against you. You've already violated it once when you showed up at her apartment a few days ago. You could do some jail time right now for that offense."

"I didn't violate nothing," he said. "She *invited* me to come over, so get your facts straight. Counselor."

"Maybe. But a court of law just might find my client's bad judgment irrelevant. Of course, if you don't believe me, I could notify the police right now about your visit and see whether or not they agree with me."

The gloves were off now. Mr. Braxton wasn't finding his visit to JB&H so amusing anymore.

"We'll see you in court, Mr. Braxton."

He sucked his teeth.

"Go 'head. Knock yourself out. But it's like I already told you. Rose ain't getting nothing—other than her maiden name back."

"Your five minutes are up. Good-bye, Mr. Braxton."

He bent over, placed his arms down on my desk, and leaned in towards me.

"All you black bitches are the same. You, Rose—"

"GOOD-BYE, MR. BRAXTON!"

"DON'T RUSH ME! And don't raise your voice at me again. Who the fuck do you think you are anyway? You designer-clothes-wearing saddidy-actin' bitch! You might be a big shot up in this office, but you wouldn't get away with talkin' to me like that on the street."

At that point, I had used up every bit of the bravado I had brought into the meeting. Sydney Braxton was truly beginning to unnerve me now. I didn't think I was going to have to do this, but I was wrong. I reached for the phone to dial Monifah and have her call security. At that precise moment, someone knocked on my door. I shouted to whomever it was to come in. I didn't care *who* it was. I was just thankful *someone* was right outside my door. Would you believe it? Like a guardian angel sent to rescue a damsel in distress, it was Mike Harrison, one of the building's security guards. A big burly bruh who goes about six-three, 250 and change. He stuck his head in my door.

"Hey, Ms. Gentry. I was just on our routine security sweep of the premises. Everything all right?"

"Actually, Mike, I'm glad you're here. Would you—"

"Wow, look at the time. I gotta run," Mr. Braxton quipped.

"Mike, would you see to it that this gentleman makes it out of the building safely."

"I can do that."

Sydney bopped his way past Mike who was standing in the doorway waiting for him.

"Wassup, bruh? You a big boy. You play football or som'um?" he said to Mike. He was ignored.

"Thanks, Mike," I said to him as he followed Sydney out. As soon as the two of them disappeared, I dialed Monifah.

"Yes, Bailey?"

"In about fifteen minutes or so, would you call down to the security station and give Mike Harrison a message for me, please?"

"Sure. What's the message?"

"Tell Mike I'd like to take him to lunch at his convenience. Any restaurant in this city. His choice."

The next call I made was to Tony. I really needed to hear his voice.

27

Grinding It Out

"Ah, not again, Bailey," Tony sighed, as the two of us stood in the middle of my living room, slow-dancing to Brenda Russell's "If Only for One Night." After waiting so long to finally have him over to my place, I really enjoyed it when Tony came by and we shared private moments like this.

"I like Mo and Lisa, too, I really do," he went on, "but all this double-dating is getting a bit ridiculous don't you think? I got a better idea. How about you and I going to dinner *alone* for a change. Remember? Like we used to *before* we became boyfriend and girlfriend."

"Oh, it's not that bad."

"Bad? No. But I'm sure you wouldn't want to double-date with Derrick and Mylene two, three times a week."

He had a point there.

"How 'bout this? Let's have dinner with them one more time. End of next week. And I'm only asking you this because I sort of committed us to joining them already. They want to go to Copeland's on Rockville Pike. Cajun food. You like Cajun?"

He ignored me.

"C'mon. Don't be like that. This'll be our last double date with them for a good long while. After next week, you can have me, I promise," I said, playfully kissing him all over his face and neck as we continued to slow dance.

"I can finally *have* you?"

"Oh, gol-lee, Gianni. Is your dirty little mind in the gutter again?"

"Can you blame me if it is? I'm a man, B, I got needs. I *want* you."

"I want you, too, Tony."

Okay, let's pause here a second 'cause I know what y'all are probably thinking. That I'm just bullshitin' Tony, right? Wrong. I did want him. Believe me, my reluctance to get it on with Tony was more principle than personal at that point in time. The aversion I had to "sleeping with the enemy," well, it didn't develop over night. It took some twenty-nine years to be precise. So, cut me some slack, okay? You couldn't very well expect me to get rid of it in a couple of months. Heck. If I could have—but I couldn't—I would've gotten it on with Tony right there and right then. The mood was right; we had Brenda Russell on the CD player; we were slow dancing. All I needed was a little Hennessey to help me forget all about that aversion. Lawd knows I needed the love pipe like a crackhead needs his crack pipe. I couldn't even *remember* the last time I had any. And ladies, you know when it's been that long things have gotten woefully out of hand, feel me? Thought so. Let's move on.

"Look, Tony, I know we haven't become intimate since we decided to do the committed relationship thing and

I'm sorry for that. I'm just not the kind of woman who's quick about jumping into bed."

(Okay. That was a small white lie. I'd done that very thing a time or two or three.)

"I wasn't implying anything of the sort, Bailey."

"I know you weren't."

"What's with you? You old-fashioned or something? You want us to wait until we're married?"

Now that was funny. "*I* can't wait that long, Tony. And who says we're getting married anyway?"

"I'm kidding."

"Better be."

"Personally, I think now is a perfect time for us to . . . you know," Tony said, then fed me his tongue before I could respond. (If this man sexed anything like he kissed, once I went white, *I* might not ever come back!)

Our slow dance turned into more of a slow grind. Tony reached around my waist and helped himself to two heaping handfuls of my bodacious ass. Whew, Lawd! I momentarily fantasized him grippin' my ass that way when we . . . anyway . . .

"Tony . . . honey . . ." I said, freeing his tongue from inside my mouth.

"You talk too much, Bailey. Shut up and kiss—"

"My visitor's in town."

Just like that our slow dance came to a grinding halt. Tony let go of my ass and collapsed on my sofa.

"This is freakin' unbelievable," he exclaimed in utter frustration. "When is she *leaving*?"

"In a few more days. Sorry. So, you're cool with next week, right? Dinner with Mo and Lisa?" I asked, quickly changing the subject, and no doubt irritating Tony further.

"The last supper, Bailey."

"Not forever, Tony."

"For a mighty long time then."

"Okay, fine. They're probably getting sick of us, too. Hey, on an unrelated topic, I want to thank you again for being there for me the other day."

"Everything back to normal?"

"Not sure. But I am sure that I won't be having anymore unwelcome visitors of that nature again."

"You never did say who this guy was that came to see you. You can tell me if it was an old flame. I won't be jealous."

"Hardly! It was the husband of one of my clients."

"That sounds scandalous. Not that high-maintenance one, I hope."

"Mmm-hmm."

"Get out of here. What's the deal with that chick? I know you'll be glad when you wrap up her case."

"You can say that again."

"Look, B, I'm'a get going. Tomorrow's a workday."

(It's amazing how quick a man's mood changes when he knows he ain't getting any.)

"Just 'cause I can't give you no booty doesn't mean you have to leave, Tony. Let's go see a movie. My treat. There's a theater five minutes from here off Powder Mill Road. We can catch the last showing."

"I don't know . . ."

"Please?" I said, then sat in his lap and batted my brown ones at him.

"What's playing?"

"Let's go see *The Shawshank Redemption*. Morgan Freeman's in it."

"Yeah, I hear that's gotten great reviews. And he's a very good actor. Aw'aight."

"Groovy. Give me a minute to put on some lipstick and grab my purse."

* * *

    It was nearly one in the morning when Tony dropped me home. The movie was all that. A first-rate prison drama. Moving, difficult to watch at times, but nothing short of brilliant. I stayed up until Tony called to let me know that he had made it home okay. Passed the time by catching up on my latest issue of *Essence*. While I did so, I noticed the "new call" indicator was flashing on my phone. I didn't have any messages, though, so I checked my caller ID. There was a number on it I didn't recognize. Had a 612 area code. Whoever called must've dialed the wrong number. As soon as Tony gave me the signal that he had reached home safely—two rings and a hang-up—I went straight off to la-la land as soon as my head hit the pillow. Good thing too, since I would only be getting about three hours of sleep before having to get up in the morning for work.

28

Timing Is Everything

Still dragging after our late date at the movies the previous night, I took off work early and came home to get an early jump on dinner. While I was in the kitchen getting it ready, I got another call from that number with the 612 area code. Normally, I let my answering machine take calls I didn't recognize. But whoever this was didn't bother to leave a message yesterday, and here they were calling again.

"Who is this?" I answered.

"May I speak to Bailey, please?" a male voice asked on the other end.

"Speaking."

"Hi, Bailey, this is Kevin. Kevin Wayne. We met a few months ago over at Maurice and Lisa's place. Francesca's cousin."

"From cold-as-hell Minnesota, Kevin?"

"That's the one. And I'll have you know it's a balmy seventy-three degrees in the city of Minneapolis today."

"You don't say?"

Was this a surprise or was this a surprise? I had forgotten all about Kevin. Man, what was it with guys I had been meeting lately? They all seemed to have a knack for getting in touch with me long after they had faded from memory. Tony had done the same thing.

"Wow. I can't believe it's you. How are you? How did you get my number?" I rambled on.

"I got it from Francesca. I hope you don't mind. She thought you'd be all right with that."

Good looking out, Frankie. Good looking out.

"Not at all," I said, trying to sound sexy as I want to be.

"You're probably wondering why I'm calling."

"Uh, yeah. I am. Surely you must know I wasn't expecting to speak with you again."

"That's probably my fault. You've been on my mind, Bailey. I'm sorry I didn't talk with you more that night."

So am I, Kevin. So am I.

"You could have at least asked me for my number," I said flirtatiously.

"Perhaps I should've."

"Why didn't you?"

"Why don't I explain that when I see you."

"When you see me?"

"Yeah. I'm in a cab headed to the airport as we speak. I'm catching a flight to BWI."

"Get outta here. What's bringing you to these parts?" Part of me was hoping he'd say *me*.

"Oh, I've got some business I need to take care of in Maryland. I'm going to be staying at my cousin's."

"For how long?"

"Two, three days perhaps. Why don't we have dinner while I'm there?"

Hmmm, let's see, Kevin. You're a tall, handsome, butterscotch brotha with pretty brown eyes who, as I remember, I was definitely feeling me that night. So much so that five minutes after we met, I already knew I wanted to sex your brains out someday. All that said, however, your timing really sucks, dude. I'm involved with someone now, and I don't think my new man would understand us going out to dinner together. Nah. It's not a good idea.

"That's a *great* idea, Kevin."

"Cool. Well, look, my cab's going to be pulling up to the terminal shortly. I'll give you a call when I land. Can't wait to see you, Bailey."

29

After the Rain

Kevin called me shortly after his flight landed at BWI. I wasn't expecting to hear from him so soon. He asked if I could pick him up from the airport. Said Frankie was supposed to do it, but that she couldn't get her car started. I suppose Kevin could have taken a cab, but a cab from the airport to Frankie's place in College Park would have cost him about forty dollars. Furthermore, he sounded real tired from his flight. I'm sure the last thing he wanted to do after being cooped up in an airplane for three hours was spend the next twenty-five minutes in the back seat of a musty cab trying to give directions to a driver who probably didn't speak English too well. Anyway, I threw on a pair of form-fitting jeans and an old blouse, jumped in my Audi, and headed up to BWI to get him. I will tell you that my plan was to simply pick Kevin up and drive him over to Frankie's. But you know what they say about the best-laid plans.

Kevin was standing outside the USAir terminal looking as good as I remembered him. His tall, basketball-player physique looked great in a white linen shirt and black jeans. As soon as he saw me at the passenger pickup, he hugged and squeezed me as if the two of us were long-lost lovers. I got to tell you. Being held tightly in his strong arms like that gave me a refreshing tingle. He threw his luggage in the trunk, hopped in the front seat, and off we were. Shortly into our trip to Frankie's, the sky—seemingly without warning—opened up and it began to pour. I'm talking *buckets*. My windshield wipers were going full-speed and still I could barely see the road in front of me. It was scary. I for one do not like driving in inclement weather—rain or snow. We were much closer to my place than Frankie's at the time, so I decided to pull off the road and make a pit stop at my place until the deluge subsided a bit and the roads were safer to navigate.

It was a few minutes past ten when I pulled into the parking lot of my condo complex. The choice spaces closest to my building were all gone by then. Neither Kevin nor I had an umbrella handy, and we got absolutely drenched.

"This bites!" I lamented as we stumbled through the front door of my condo literally dripping wet.

"You ain't kidding, Bailey. I haven't seen a storm like this in a long time. They mentioned the threat of rain in the Washington area on the flight in, but this is like a damn *monsoon*," he chuckled.

"Let me get some towels so we can dry off," I said. I retrieved two towels from my linen closet and handed one to Kevin.

"I'm soaked through to my underwear," he proclaimed. "Listen, you go ahead and get out of your wet clothes. Don't worry about me."

I couldn't let Kevin stand around in wet clothes. Not to mention I didn't want him sitting on my furniture in that condition.

"Let me get out of my clothes then I'll get you out of yours," I told him. (That didn't come out quite the way I meant it.)

I went into my bedroom and changed into a cutoff T-shirt and a dry pair of jeans, then searched my closet for something to give Kevin to wear.

"I don't have a thing I can give you other than some sweatsocks to put on your feet," I shouted to him. "What are you, six-five? None of my T-shirts will even fit you."

"If it's okay with you, I'm just going to take off my shirt, and wrap this towel around my shoulders," he shouted back.

"What about your, um . . . bottom half?" I emerged from my bedroom and asked. "You did say you were soaked down there, too."

Kevin grinned at me. A slightly devilish grin. "Well, if you give me another towel, I could take off my pants, too. Of course that would leave me naked, but I can deal with a little nakedness if it doesn't make you too uncomfortable."

"Hey, whatever floats your boat. Let me grab you another towel. The bathroom's that way."

Kevin came out of the bathroom shortly with a towel draped across his shoulders and another wrapped around his waist. Three words came to mind: *Mm, mm, mm.*

"This feels so much better. You mind if I throw these in your dryer?" he said, referring to the wet clothes he had taken off. "That way I won't have to be naked too long."

Bruh, you can stay naked as long as you . . .

"Sure. Give 'em to me."

I tossed Kevin's clothes in the dryer and timed the cycle for twenty minutes.

"Would you like a beer, wine? I know it's been a long evening for you already."

"Wine sounds good."

"Hope you don't mind it cold. The bottle's been in my fridge a while."

"That's fine. Hey, may I use your phone? I should call Francesca and let her know where I am."

"Sure."

I motioned for Kevin to follow me into the kitchen and use the wall phone next to my refrigerator. As he got Frankie on the line, I did a bit of tidying up in there before getting the wine bottle out of the fridge.

"Hey, it's me. You'll never believe where I am. At Bailey's house. I called her and she was kind enough to pick me up from the airport. We were pretty close to her house when it started pouring, so we decided to pull off the road. It's a mess out there. I'm going to stay at her crib until the rain lets up. She'll bring me over your place when it does. I'm no mechanic, but I'll take a look at your car in the morning. See you soon. Huh? Oh, okay. I will."

As Kevin hung up the phone and turned to exit the kitchen, I was simultaneously backing away from the fridge with the wine bottle. We bumped into one another, nearly causing me to drop the bottle. Kevin caught the wine bottle, and me, in his big, strong arms.

"Oops. Me and my clumsy self. You okay?" I asked.

"I'm fine, but we almost lost the . . . Berringer," he said, reading the label on the wine bottle. That unforced moment of contact was all it took to get the sparks flying between us. Right then and there, I wanted to sit that bottle of wine on the countertop, jump on him, wrap my legs around him, and slob him down.

"Would you mind reaching up in that cabinet over there and handing me two glasses, please?"

Kevin took the glasses down for me.

"Here, let me pour those for you," he said. "Francesca says to tell you hello and thanks."

"Tell her I said hi, too."

Next, we made our way into my living room to drink, chat, and wait for the rain to subside, or even better, stop altogether.

"This is too funny, Kevin," I said, staring at him as we sat on my sofa.

"What is?"

"You. Sitting in my living room, dressed in nothing but two bath towels, sipping wine. I can't believe you're here."

"Well, it isn't the scenario I pictured being in at this hour of the day when I boarded that plane earlier in Minneapolis, that's for sure. Nevertheless, being in your lovely condo, which you've hooked up quite nicely, sharing a glass of wine with you, and staring at your fine brown person, well, let me say I don't think I could have picked a better way to unwind after a day of travel."

"You keep talking like that and it can rain all night," I said flirtatiously.

"So what have you been up to since we last saw each other?"

"Do you realize that's the third time you've asked me that since I picked you up from the airport?"

"Is it? Well then, let me ask you—"

"Why didn't you ask me for my number that night at Mo's?" I cut Kevin off before he could finish saying whatever it was he was about to say.

"Would you have liked me to?"

"What do you think?"

"I think we were supposed to discuss this over dinner, remember?"

"What's wrong with right now?"

"If I tell you now, I'm afraid you won't have any incentive to have dinner with me."

"You don't have to worry about that."

"Okay. I'm kind of shy, Bailey."

"That's it? That's the weak excuse you're going to give me, Kevin Wayne? You're shy? Sorry. You're going to have to do better than that," I exclaimed, while subtly inching closer to him on the sofa. That man was turning me on like nobody's business.

"That's it. There is no other reason. Well, maybe that and I didn't want to chump myself in the event you had a man or something."

"That's your story, and you're sticking to it?"

"That's my story, and I'm sticking to it."

"Okay. If you say so."

"What did you think the reason was?"

"That maybe I didn't make a good enough impression on you."

Kevin laughed at that. "I assure you, that was not the case," he said, giving me another of his sexy grins in the process. "I wonder if the rain's let up any?"

"You in a hurry to leave?" I asked with mock seriousness. So convincing he didn't know how to respond. "Relax. I'm kidding, Kevin. Let me take a look." I made my way over to the window again and took a look outside. Indeed, the rain had slacked up now, which left me feeling a bit disappointed. I wasn't ready to drive Kevin over to Frankie's just yet. I was enjoying this. Maybe more than I had any business doing. Not once had I even thought about Tony since picking Kevin up from the airport.

"Well, it looks like the rain has subsided. I guess we can hit the road as soon as your clothes finish drying."

"Okay," he said, and took the last sip of his wine and sat his empty glass down on my coffee table.

Kevin's face seemed to exhibit what I was feeling. He wasn't ready to leave either.

"So, when are we going to have dinner?" I asked.

"How's tomorrow evening sound?"

"Works for me," I told him, without even thinking about any previous plans I may have already made with Tony. "You sure Becky Sue's not going to get bent out of shape?"

I completely took him by surprise with that question.

"B-Becky Sue?" he stuttered. "How do you know about . . . never mind. I already know."

"Don't be upset. You know us women talk. I asked Frankie if you were involved with anyone."

"Mmm-hmm. Well you know, I really wasn't going to ask you yet, but since you've chosen to break the ice on that tip, I guess I ought to know likewise. Are you involved with anyone, Bailey?"

For a millisecond, I thought of telling Kevin no. But I had denied my relationship with Tony once before to a total stranger, and I wasn't about to do it yet again.

"I am."

"Who's the lucky guy?"

"You first. Is she your girlfriend?"

"I don't know how to answer that."

"Sounds like a pretty straightforward question to me."

"Things haven't been right with us for a while. In fact, part of the reason for this trip to Maryland is to give me a chance to get away and clear my head. Figure out whether she's someone I still want to have a relationship with. If I had to take a guess, I'd say the odds of me and Becky Sue staying together are slim. *Real* slim. Your turn."

"It's a very new and different kind of relationship for me. Beyond that I don't want to say much more about it at this time."

"Say no more."

Kevin inched a little closer to me this time. Stared me straight in the eyes. His tone turning a bit more serious.

"It's all good. No sense making something out of nothing. We're just having a meal together. It's not like we're gonna have wild, passionate sex or anything. Right?"

"R-r-right, Kevin."

(Gulp.)

My horny meter began to surge. The room began to spin. And it had nothing to do with the wine, either.

"Let me take these glasses into the kitchen," I said nervously.

I needed to get up and away from Kevin for my own good—his, too. I grabbed our empty wine glasses, excused myself, and made my way over to the kitchen sink. En route, the clothes dryer buzzed.

"Perfect timing, your clothes are all dry," I said as I stood over the sink rinsing out the wine glasses.

Kevin got up and came into the kitchen. Without saying a word, he walked up behind me and pressed himself against me. I felt his penis firmly against my ass through the towel wrapped around his waist. It was rock hard. I gasped. Dropped the wine glasses in the sink and left the faucet running. Stood there motionless unable to move. Kevin's hardness had me paralyzed. He took his hands and moved my braids out of the way, allowing himself access to my neck, which he began to slowly lick and suck on.

"W-w-what are you doing, K-Kevin?" I asked, barely above a whisper.

"You're so beautiful, Bailey," he moaned.

"W-w-what about . . . Becky Sue?" I said, nearly breathless at this point.

"Who?"

Kevin turned off the faucet I had left running. Spun me around, lifted me off my feet like a rag doll, and set me down on top of the sink. Shed the towel wrapped around his shoulders, and unloosed the one wrapped around his waist. Exposed himself to me in all his glory.

Glory Hallelujah!

I took his face in my hands and forced my tongue deep into his mouth. Began tonguing him down like a sista possessed. After several wild and passionate minutes of kissing—only kissing—Kevin lifted me off of the sink and set me back down on my feet. Unbuttoned my jeans, slid them down my legs and off my body. While he did that I pulled my T-shirt over my head and flung it away, offering my small, perky breasts to Kevin. He immediately went to work on 'em. Sucking each one like he was an infant again and I was his mama. Right one, left one. Left one, right one. Once he satisfied his appetite for the taste of my breasts, he spun me around again so that my back was to him and bent me over. My face was now literally in the kitchen sink. Kevin grabbed onto my shoulders, and eased himself into me from behind, causing me to wail in pleasure.

Next I remember lying naked on my Sealy Posturepedic, wrapped in Kevin's naked body, feeling totally relaxed and satisfied. He was first to break the calm we lay in.

"You okay?" he asked, stroking my braids gently.

"Mmm-hmm, I purred, sounding as if he had just slipped me some love dope. "How about you?"

"I'm great. And you're incredible. Just so you know, I didn't plan for any of this to—"

"Ssssh. Neither did I. It just happened. Right?"

"Right."

"What time is it, anyway?" My eyes were closed and I didn't want to open them.

"Midnight."

"Midnight?" I broke out of Kevin's embrace and opened my eyes.

"Oh my goodness. I've got to get you over to Frank—"

"You hear that?" he interrupted me.

"What?"

"The rain. Sounds like it's coming down hard again."

The storm that brought us together like this seemed intent on keeping us like that a while longer.

"As good as you're making me feel—and you're making me feel *good*—I've really got to get you over to your cousin's house. What's she going to think?"

"She's not going to think anything, 'cause she's sleep. Trust me. Look, I'll catch a cab to her place sometime tomorrow. All right, baby?" he said, caressing my relaxed and uncovered body slowly and methodically. I liked the way he called me "baby." The way he was caressing me even more.

"I've got to leave pretty early for work in the morning."

"Call in sick. We can spend the entire morning like this." That sounded like a marvelous idea. "I . . . I guess I could do that."

"Now that's what I'm taking about."

"Okay. I'll call in. But what about Frankie?"

"Girl, will you stop with Frankie? I'm a grown man.

She's my *cousin*, not my guardian. You let me handle her, okay?"

"Okay." Needless to say, after the long drought I had experienced, I was feeling a bit insatiable. I crawled on top of Kevin and began rubbing my hands over his smooth, hairless chest.

"I could get used to this," I told him.

"Me, too. Let's talk about it over dinner tomorrow."

"I'd like that. You know what else I'd like?"

"What?" he grinned, as if he knew exactly what I was about to say.

"To feel you inside of me again."

30

Hero Worship

It was 12:30 in the afternoon a week later, and I was sitting inside of McCormick & Schmidt's restaurant having lunch with Big Mike, the security guard from my building. Taking Mike to lunch was just my small way of saying thank-you for saving me from the clutches of Sydney Braxton a few days ago. Who knows what that jackass would have resorted to if Mike hadn't shown up when he did.

Physically, I was there with him. Mentally, well, that was a whole 'nother story. Following some thought-out deliberation, I decided not to go into Sydney Braxton's behavior in detail with Rose. I simply told her that he came by to discuss the divorce; I told him I couldn't due to ethical reasons, insisted he seek his own legal representation, and sent him on his way.

Alimony, now that was going to be an iffy proposition. I did tell Rose the part about him quitting his job. Of course she was none too thrilled to hear that. She drew the same conclusion I did: that it was hardly career-motivated as he claimed, but rather something done simply to spite her in her efforts to get support money. Like I did, she figured Sydney must've been bringing in a sufficient amount of cash from his illegal enterprises to sustain himself. A revenue stream he knew she wouldn't be able to tap into.

Lastly, I told her I informed Sydney not to go anywhere near her again, and all but let him know a subsequent violation of his restraining order would prompt a call to the authorities. I also made it perfectly clear to Rose that she wasn't to allow Sydney back into her home under *any* circumstances. She swore up and down she was going to follow my advice. I believed her this time around.

"There's something I've been meaning to ask you, Mike," I said, trying to focus my attention back on my lunch date and off my current issues. "It's about that day you showed up at my office. You did say the reason you were there was because you were on your routine security sweep of the premise. Correct?"

"Uh-huh."

"Since when do you guys do routine security sweeps of the premises that include stopping by the personal offices of attorneys?"

Mike started crackin' up. "Pretty smooth, huh?"

"You made that up?"

"Mmm-hmm."

"Then what really brought you by my office when you did?"

"Um . . . I think I'm going to plead the fifth on that, as you lawyers like to say."

"You're not going to tell me?"

"Let me think about it," he said.

"Okay. I won't pry. All that really matters is that you got me out of a jam that day. Folks back in the office building are always jonin' on our security staff, but you guys do a great job. Especially you, Mike."

"They be jonin' on us, huh? Well, forget them suckas," he laughed. "As long as you appreciate us, that's all that matters. This lunch is much appreciated, Ms. Gentry."

"Please. You and I are on a first-name basis now. Besides, you're making me sound old," I teased him.

"You know, it's not often I get to have lunch at a fancy downtown restaurant with an attractive woman such as yourself. Shoot. Who am I kidding? This *never* happens," he laughed. "I kinda wish I was dressed differently for the occasion, though."

"What are you talking about?"

"You're sitting over there looking all cute in that outfit and I'm sitting over here in my security uniform."

"And you look darn handsome in that uniform, Mike Harrison. Like a big, sexy, security teddy bear."

(If you've never seen a six-foot-three, 250-pound guy blush, it's quite a sight.)

"So, you like your job?" I asked.

"It's not bad. Somebody's got to look out for the safety of the building's tenants."

"I heard that."

"But I don't plan on being a security guard forever, if that's what you're wondering. This gig's just a means to an end. I got big plans, Bailey."

"Oh? You mind sharing them with me? Unless I'm being too nosy of course."

"Not at all. If things go according to plan, I'll be working for myself pretty soon."

"Really?"

"Yep. I plan on opening a bodyguard service for athletes, entertainers, and anyone else in need of personal security."

"Good for you, Mike!" His good news was beginning to perk me up. "How far are you along?"

"I hope to get the business off the ground in another year or two at the most. I'm in the process of recruiting some talent for my company as we speak. Some quality individuals with the skills and background needed to be personal bodyguards."

"I'm just too impressed with you, Mike. I love seeing brothas being productive. Making plans. Thinking about their futures. Doing something other than hanging out at the club, mackin' honeys, and washing and waxin' their car rims." I had Mike crackin' up.

"C'mon, Bailey, don't you think you're being a bit harsh on the brothas?"

"Pu-leeze! If anything, I don't think sistas are harsh enough on y'all half the time. Present company excluded, there's just too many of you out there that aren't doing a *goddamn* thing with yourselves."

"I hear that. Well look, that's why I'm working hard not to fall into that dubious category. But you gotta do me a favor, Bailey."

"Anything."

"You let those fools back in the office building keep on poking fun at the security staff. Let 'em go on thinking we're just a bunch of guys and gals content with having 'chill' jobs and whatnot. When my business is off the ground and my company's handling the security detail for the likes of Jordan, Oprah, and Denzel, that's when those suckas'll know that at least Mike Harrison wasn't simply chillin' his way through life."

"Your secret's safe with me."

"Damn. This red snapper is all that and then some! I'm feeling this place, Bailey. Would you mind if I ordered another drink?"

"Mmm . . . I don't know about that, Mike. I can't have you going back to your post this afternoon intoxicated. You might have to rescue me again."

"Oh, c'mon. I'm a big boy. I can handle my liquor."

"Okay. One more, but that's it," I said jokingly.

"Thanks, Bailey. Say, I couldn't help but notice you seemed a bit down on the walk over here."

"I am, a little."

"Anything you want to talk about?"

"I'll give you the *Reader's Digest* version. I was a bit of a badass the other day. Did something that felt real good at the time, but now I regret doing it."

Mike took another bite of his snapper and wiped his mouth. "Life's too short for regrets, Bailey."

"Hmmm. I'll have to take that under advisement, Mike. Now, let me get you that second drink, 'cause I'm suddenly in the mood for another Hennessey myself.

"Waiter . . ."

31

Meeting in the Ladies' Room

It was all I could do to suck it up while me, Tony, Lisa, and Mo dined at Copeland's—our "Last Supper," as it were. Suddenly, I was so *not* in the mood for this double date anymore. Thank goodness no one else at the table knew how hard I was working to fake the funk. Except Lisa that is. I confessed to her all about my rainy-night romp with Frankie's cousin, Kevin. Halfway through dinner, I felt as though I couldn't grin any longer. That's when I gave Lisa the signal and we made a trip to the ladies' room.

Once inside, she was admiring how her low-cut top accentuated her ample cleavage in the bathroom mirror. I was busy admiring how bangin' my backyard looked in my Burberry miniskirt.

"Bailey," Lisa said, dabbing a drop of Fendi perfume in the crease between her thirty-four Cs, "I know you've got issues with white folks—particularly white women raiding our already diminishing pool of eligible black men. But maybe the answer is that more of us in the sistahood need to start dating Italian Stallions like Tony. Maybe we need to start pushing up on all of 'em. The Jewish guys, German guys, Irish guys—"

"What are you talking about, Lisa?"

"Payback."

"Payback?"

"What's good for the goose is good for the gander. Sista's gotta start flippin' the script. We gotta start raiding *their* pool of eligible men. Give them white women something to lose sleep over for a change."

We burst out laughing.

"That's a great idea—in principle. But it'll never fly in practice."

"Tsk. Don't be such a pessimist."

"I'm not. There simply aren't enough of us willing to go that route. You know doggone well nine out of ten sistas would rather scratch each other's eyes out over that one available Tyrone than cross over to the other side."

"Sad but true. Well, I hope you're now part of that ten percent who've decided to skip the catfight. Tony seems to treat you better than any guy I can recall you dating in a long time. I'm far more impressed with him than your previous choices in men. Most of which have been losers with a capital L. He certainly looks better than most of your—"

"Oh shut up, Lisa!"

"What?"

"You and your big titties came up to bat umpteen times and struck out before you met Mo and hit a homer. So don't go acting like *you've* had some kind of history of picking blue chips."

"Whateva, heifer. All I'm saying is, Tony seems to really care about you."

"And I care about him, Lisa. That's why I feel like such

a Judas for sleeping with Kevin—in *my* bed. A bed I haven't even been able to bring myself to sleep with Tony in yet."

"Don't forget the kitchen sink. I know, I know. *Shut up, Lisa.*"

"I can't believe I've been in a supposedly committed relationship for less than a month and I've already cheated. What is wrong me?"

"I dunno, girl. But on a scale of one to ten on the dumbest-things-you've-ever-done-with-men-meter goes, sleeping with Kevin—raw-doggin' it at that—has got to be about a twelve."

"Gee, thanks, Lisa."

"Don't shoot the messenger."

"Like you've never been caught up in the moment and didn't use protection."

"Mmm, maybe once or twice. You sure you ain't . . . ?"

"Pretty sure. It was a non-fertile week. God, this has been such a challenge," I mumbled.

"What has?"

"Dating a white guy. True, there have been moments when it hasn't been an issue, in part because of the *type* of white guy Tony is, but there have been several situations when it's just been downright awkward."

"Explain."

"Like for instance when we had dinner at Paolo's and your boyfriend brought up the Howard Beach thing. That made Tony uncomfortable."

"What the heck was Mo talking about anyway? He never did say and I forgot to ask him."

"He was referring to a racial incident that took place in New York a few years ago when a group of white guys, mostly Italian, attacked and murdered a black guy."

"Oooh, okay. I can see where that would make an Italian white boy a little tight in the company of black folks."

"And another thing, Lisa. I remember an incident when Tony and I were out together and found ourselves in earshot of a conversation taking place between a couple of brothas. Every other sentence out of their mouths was, 'a nigga did this' or 'a nigga did that.' You already know how much I hate hearing that ignorant-ass kind of talk to begin with. Even so, had I been out with a brotha at that moment, I could have easily just let it roll off my back. Being with Tony however, I couldn't do that. In the back of my mind, I just kept wondering what *he* must've been thinking."

"Did you ask him?"

"Of course not!"

"Look, B. Dude lives in *Adams Morgan* for cryin' out loud. I'm sure he's used to hearing that and much worse out of the mouths of not just black folks, but *all kinds* of folks."

"I guess you're right. There are other little minor things, too," I chuckled. "Like when I used the phrase 'a pot to piss in or a window to throw it out.' Tony had never heard that before. Anyway, tell me this. What happens later down the road when I start hanging out with Tony and his white friends?"

"Does he have any white friends?"

"He's white, Lisa, I'm sure has one or two or three. We've both been there, done that, and got the T-shirts. You know how white people can get in social settings. They get a little too much alcohol in 'em, get a little too loosey-goosey next thing you know, any and all kind of shit comes flyin' out their mouths. That worries me, Lisa. I'm not sure I want to put myself into a position of having to deal with such a thing."

We thought we were all alone in the restroom as we where having our conversation, but were startled when a redheaded white woman exited one of the stalls and stepped in between us to use the sink. No "excuse me" or anything on her part. I could tell by the look she gave us that she had been eavesdropping on our conversation. I gave Lisa the "quiet" signal. Wanted to wait until Red got lost before continuing our conversation. Meanwhile, Red was taking her sweet time washing her hands. Like I said. I wasn't in a particularly good mood to begin with, and her rude, slow-handwashing ass was only working my nerves all the more.

"I don't think you're going to get your hands any cleaner, Miss," I said to her.

"You talking to me?" she snapped back, with a bit of 'tude in her dialect.

I took a panoramic glance of the ladies' room. "Well, seeing as though *you're* the only one in here scrubbing like a damn surgeon, I *must* be talking to—"

"Uh, ignore my friend, ma'am," Lisa jumped in. "She's just having a bad day."

Red quickly toweled off and rolled her sky-blue eye-balls at me on her way out.

"You see that, Lisa? She don't know. I'll whup her—"

"Forget that heifer, Bailey! You've got bigger issues to be concerned with right now."

"You're right," I said regaining my composure.

"Getting back to this thing with Kevin for a moment. I know you're feeling hurt, guilty, confused and who knows what else. But what's done is done. You need to pull yourself together before Tony picks up on something."

"Maybe I should just tell him about Kevin?"

"Oh, sure. Go ahead. Absolutely—if you want to break his heart and end y'all's relationship in the process," Lisa sarcastically said.

"Wouldn't you want to know if Mo cheated on you?"

Lisa paused to contemplate that question. "Mo and I

have been an item for five years, Bailey. You and Tony, less
than thirty days. We're talking apples and oranges here.
That said, however, I would never endorse you being delib-
erately dishonest with anyone. But ask yourself something.
What if you did tell him? What then? Would it make him
feel better? Would his knowing strengthen y'all's relationship? Or would it destroy every bit of the progress you two
have been making? I'm a firm believer in the premise that
there are just some things in life we're better off not knowing. But this is your call. Has Kevin taken his pretty, butterscotch ass back to Minnesota yet?"

"Mmm-hmm."

"Good. Leave him there. Don't call him. And if he
calls you, hang up on him."

"That's not nice."

"Fuck nice, Bailey! *Nice* is what got you ass up and
facedown in the kitchen sink."

"See. This is what I get for telling you stuff."

"Your *man* is out there in the dining room with my man.
That's the *only* man you need to be *nice* to right now."

"I'm not disputing anything you're telling me, Lisa. But
can you step out of your practical-thinking mode for just
a second, please? Sleeping with Kevin was wrong. I know
that. But what if our . . . what if it was more than just a
sexual fling? What if our rainy-night tryst was the beginning of something special between us? We didn't plan it.
It just sort of happened. And sometimes things like that
happen for a reason. I felt a connection with Kevin. And
I don't mean just horizontally either. I sense the feeling
may have been mutual, too."

"What about the white chick? What's her name?"

"Becky Sue?"

"Yeah. What's up with that? And did that chile's parents really name her *Becky Sue?*"

"She's not an issue. Things are all but over between them."

"And you know this how?"

"Kevin told me so."

"Did he now? And did he tell you this *before* or *after* he tapped that ass?"

"Tsk. What-eva!"

"Whateva me all you want, Bailey. Newsflash: Ain't no black man leaving his white woman for a black woman. That kinda shit only happens the other way around."

"And I got a newsflash for you. If I was truly into Tony the way I ought to be, maybe I wouldn't have allowed myself to sleep with Kevin in the first place."

"This is true. All the more reason for you to resolve any and all issues you have with this relationship before one or both of you ends up getting hurt. Look at me, Bailey. I said *look at me!*"

Lisa's whole mood turned serious all of a sudden.

"I love you, girl. We've been best friends since we were eight years old. I don't want that somebody getting hurt to be you. As for Tony, I like him. I think he's a great guy. I really think he might be your Mr. Right. The only problem here as I see it is that Tony came to you in a package you were hardly expecting. *Shit happens.* I can relate. But I couldn't be happier with my unanticipated package. Besides, it ain't like you're dating some plain Joe white boy. *Hello!* He's Italian. He's fine. He's white chocolate, a brotha in every sense *but* skin color. If you can't see yourself with Tony simply because he's white, then you need to break it off with him. Now! Before things possibly turn ugly between you two. That's it. I'm done. I've said all I'm going to say. Let's get out of here. We've been in this bathroom way too long. Mo and Tony are probably wondering what happened to us."

32

The Inevitable

Tony was relaxing on my sofa, bobbin' his head to a Brand New Heavies CD playing in random mode. Following dinner with Mo and Lisa, I asked him to come over and chill with me for a while, hoping some alone time would bring me out of my doldrums. In case you're wondering, I played my role well that night. Tony hadn't picked up on any change in my disposition. As far as he could tell, everything was everything. Of course that couldn't be further from the truth. Everything *had* changed. I'd cheated on him. Something I'd never done to any of my previous boyfriends. Furthermore, I'd disappointed myself in the process. On one level, that hurt me more than cheating on Tony. On another, wrong as it was, being with Kevin only whetted my appetite for what I knew deep-down I was still longing for at the end of each day spent with Tony: a good *black* man.

On the ride home from Copeland's, I decided I was

going to keep my secret a secret. Lisa was right; some things in life we're better off not knowing. Anyway, tonight marked the first time Tony had been over to my my place since Kevin had been there. I wondered if Kevin had accidentally on purpose left any incriminating "evidence" behind from our night together. Of course, I was just being paranoid. I had cleaned, vacuumed, and deodorized the scent of our sexual encounter from the air days ago. Nevertheless, these are the kinds of thoughts that permeate one's mind when one's conscience is whipping her. And right about now, mine was administering a royal beat-down.

I grabbed Tony a Heineken out of the fridge and sat next to him on the sofa. I couldn't have been any more ill-prepared for what happened next. Tony took a sip of his beer, placed the bottle down on the coffee table, took my hand, turned to me, and said, "I think I'm falling in love with you, Bailey."

He gazed at me with white-hot passion.

I damn near passed out.

"I'm so glad we've both been mature enough not to let a stupid thing like racial differences get in the way of our relationship," he continued.

If you only knew, Tony, I internalized.

"I don't wanna wait any longer, Bailey. In fact, *I won't.* I gotta make love to you. Right now."

When those words left Tony's mouth, I had hoped it was the Heineken talking. But he had only taken a sip thus far, so that was wishful thinking. Then I hoped he was just being his old comedic self again. But as much as Tony liked to joke around, I knew even he wouldn't joke around like *this*. He was serious. *Dead serious.*

How ironic can love and life be? I cannot begin to tell you how many times I had fantasized about the time, place, and setting in which I would hear a man tell me what I had just heard. Except in my fantasies, those words would always be spoken to me by a man six-foot-two with dreamy brown eyes and skin the color of dark, Godiva chocolate. This wasn't even close.

Tony began to kiss me. Between his kisses to my lips came kisses to my forehead, my neck, my ears. He skillfully undid my top. No bra tonight. I closed my eyes. He laid me the length of my sofa. His lips abandoned mine and sought out my small, perky breasts. Felt my nipples swell between his lips when he found them. His hand methodically worked its way down my stomach and came to rest between my legs. He slowly raised my Burberry miniskirt, reached under it, and maneuvered my panties so as to allow his fingers access to my suddenly moist joy spot. While his fingers probed, his tongue entered my belly button. I kept my eyes shut. Held my breath for a moment in an attempt to dislodge the confusion swirling about in my head. Confusion I had allowed to fester since the day we met. Once again, Tony Gianni was doing all the right things. *Damn him!*

My body began to converse with me.

Chill, Bailey. Let it go. It's inevitable.

My head entered the conversation.

Guuurll, have you done lost your cotton-pickin' mind?

Before I could address either my head or body, every last stitch of my clothing was off. I finally opened my eyes. Watched Tony remove his shirt. His upper torso seemed to beckon for the touch of my hands; my lips. Love, lust, *insanity*—not sure which—came over me. No chance of an interruption from a roommate this go-round. Tony quickly shed the remainder of his clothing, allowing me a glimpse of his world for the first time. A world unlike any other to inhabit mine before. He suited up for the occasion as I lay before him primed, poised, perched on the threshold of the unthinkable. My brown flesh on the brink of fusing with the pallid flesh of my Italian Stallion. My brown soul a moment away from being swept up in the swirl—

33

Ugly

THUD!

And just like that I was startled back into reality, as when the phone rings in the middle of a good dream. The heebie-jeebies surfaced in full affect. I jerked away from Tony just as he was on the doorstep of nirvana. So fast that I rolled right off the sofa and hit the floor face-first. I think I knocked myself out.

I rolled over on my back and stared up at the ceiling of my condo, trying to clear the cobwebs. I swear I saw Sylvester the cat chasing Tweety-Bird around the room. Meanwhile, Tony was standing over me, naked, stunned, his gizmo dangling, all dressed up with no place to go.

"I-I can't do this, Tony. I-I just can't do this."

"What the hell is going on, Bailey?"

"This just isn't going to work for me."

"What the *fuck* are you talking about?" Tony screamed.

It was the first time he had ever raised his voice at me. The first time I'd seen him lose his temper.

"What are you telling me?" he went on.

My God. What have I done?

"Let it go, Tony. *Please!*"

I staggered back to my feet, taking the mandatory standing eight-count. Felt like I had just been hit by Mike Tyson *and* his mama. I touched my face to see if it was still attached to my head. Felt a small knot forming over my right eye and tasted blood in my mouth. I scooped my skirt and top up off the floor. Had no idea where my panties were nor the presence of mind to try and find them. I raced toward the door in all my glory, skirt and top in hand. My only thought was to get the hell out of the apartment quick, fast, and in a hurry before what was going on inside of it got any uglier. I reached the door, opened it, stepped into the hallway, then stopped in my tracks when it dawned on me that a) I was butt-naked, and b) the apartment I was trying to flee was *my own*. Still woozy from introducing my face to the floor, I stumbled back inside my condo in tears.

Allow me to digress a moment. I am now of the conviction that sudden trauma may momentarily cause the brain to go back to more appealing thoughts. I say this because despite being naked, in tears, with a bloody lip and a knot over my eye, and having an angry, befuddled, naked white man in my living room, I inexplicably caught a craving for some Häagen Dazs mint chip. With that, I made a beeline for the kitchen, but Tony intercepted me, spun me around forcefully, and started shaking the living shit out of me.

"*WHY ARE YOU DOING THIS, BAILEY?!!*"

As I said, I had never seen him that angry before. Who could blame him?

"Is there somebody else?" Tony begged for a logical explanation.

"*No.* I mean, yes."

"Who?"

"I don't know. Not yet anyway."

"You're making no fuckin' sense, Bailey!" Tony was on the verge of going ballistic on a sista. His white skin had turned the color of Pink Champale. My crying had advanced to full-fledged bawling. In between that bawling, I managed to get it out. Tell Tony what I should have a long time ago. Long before we arrived at that ugly moment.

"I want a black man. I *need* a black man!"

34

Morning Sickness

The rhythmic pitter-pat of rain woke me early the following morning. My head hurt like a muthafutta. I rubbed the knot over my right eye courtesy of the night before, then got out of bed, and made my way into the bathroom to satisfy my urinary urge. The mirror greeted me with two bloodshot eyes and a slightly swollen lip. In other words, a face I didn't recognize. I must have cried myself to sleep. Last night was the *worst*.

I relieved myself then got back in bed and pulled the covers over my head. Replayed the events of the night before in my mind. Recalled the look of anguish on Tony's face when I told him I needed a black man. Had no recollection of what happened after I told him that; what, if anything, he said in response; or even when he left my apartment. I popped my head out from under the covers and peeked at my alarm clock; 7:47 AM, its big red numerals screamed at me. I needed to talk to somebody. Lisa. I dialed over there hoping Mo wouldn't pick up, but he did, groggy and *very* annoyed.

"Good morning, Mo. May I speak with Lisa, please?"

"Dammit, Bailey! Haven't I told you before about calling here so early in the morning on weekends?"

"Yes, Mo, you did, and I'm *sorry* I've done it again. Can you just put Lisa on the phone please and not give me a hard time? I *really* need to speak with her." I heard Lisa ask Mo who was on the phone as she lay next to him in bed. He handed her the phone while mumbling something about how he better not have to tell me to chill with the break-of-dawn phone calls again.

"Lemme guess," Lisa said, without even saying hello. "You finally put that brown sugar on Tony, didn't you? I knew it. Hot damn. The Ho is back!" she hollered. "Gimme details."

"It's over between us," I said, ignoring her premature enthusiasm. Then I began bawling all over again.

I recounted the events of the night before to her. Told her the sweet, beautiful things Tony said to me and how we got a tad freaky thereafter. Told her how I got all hot and bothered, then played Tony like Moses and stopped him short of the Promised Land.

"Let me get this straight," Lisa said. "You let Tony suck on your titties, tickle your coochie, and get his manhood dressed for battle, *then* showed him a stop sign? Girl, *are you crazy?*"

If things weren't already stressful enough for me, Mo, who was eavesdropping on our conversation, decided to put in his two cents.

"That's jacked up. Why Bailey want to go and do something like that to a brotha?" I overheard him say to Lisa.

"Dang, Mo. Mind your business. And Tony ain't a *brotha,*" Lisa shot back.

"Oh. Let me get this straight," Mo jabbered on. "You've been walking around here calling Tony 'White Chocolate' for weeks now. Now all of a sudden he ain't a *brotha* no more? You know what? Both you *and* Bailey are ridiculous! And by the way, don't be telling me to mind *my* business when *your* friends are calling *my* house waking *my* ass up at seven forty-something in the morning."

"Good grief. Bailey, hold on," Lisa sighed. "Mo's trippin' this morning." Lisa changed locations in the house then got back on the line with me.

"Sorry about that. Must be that time of the month again. Living with Maurice is like living with another woman sometimes."

I went on to give Lisa a blow-by-blow on how it all went down that night.

"I am so upset with you right now I don't know what to do," she said to me. "But I'm not going to fuss at you. Not right now, anyway. I'm just glad you're okay. Things could have *really* gotten out of hand last night. As long as you've had Tony in a holding pattern, he could have spazzed out and . . . n-never mind. I don't even want to think about that possibility."

"What were you going to say? He could have *taken* it? Go ahead and say it. You're not thinking anything I haven't thought of myself."

"I feel bad for you, Bailey—Tony, too for that matter. I *warned* you somebody was going to get hurt if you didn't figure out where your head was. Didn't think it would happen this fast, though. Still, everything's going to be okay. And so are you. You hear me?"

By the time I got off the phone with Lisa, it had stopped raining and the cloudy sky had given way to some much-needed sunshine. It was still unseasonably warm for late September. I showered; threw on a Bebe

T-shirt, jeans, and my Reeboks; tied a bandana over my braids; skipped even the slightest bit of makeup; got in my car; and headed to D.C. Decided to treat myself to brunch at Georgia Brown's, a place where a sista could always find some good-looking brothas getting their eat on. Why that even mattered this morning, I can't tell you. I was looking totally busted.

35

Telling It Like It Is

Following my meal, it looked as though it was going to be a pleasant day after all. From a weather standpoint at least. I wasn't quite ready to return to my empty home just yet, so I walked a few blocks over to Farragut Park and took a seat on an empty bench. I needed to be alone with my thoughts for a little longer. Needless to say, they were all on Tony. I thought about the times over our four months together. The breakfasts, lunches, dinners. Our weekend in Philadelphia. The numerous double dates with Mo and Lisa. As uncomfortable as I often found myself with Tony, I realized that I had also achieved a level of comfort with him I hadn't with any guy preceding him. Furthermore, things being as they were, a weird sense of emptiness had engulfed me.

My thoughts and I only had about a good five minutes together before we were interrupted by a lanky, fair-skinned, dread-locked brotha in full cycling regalia, towing a bike. He asked if I'd mind sharing my bench with him. Before I could answer, he had already placed his bike on its kickstand and sat down. He sat silently next to me for a few moments drinking his Evian water and reading the *Washington City Paper* before breaking the tranquil, meditative silence I happened to be enjoying.

"Penny for your thoughts?"

"What?" I replied, perturbed by his verbal intrusion into my peace and quiet.

"I said penny for your thoughts?"

"I doubt you could *afford* my thoughts today."

"Ah, okay. I see you have a sense of humor, Ms. . . . ?"

"Gentry," I said reluctantly.

"I'm Rex. How are you doing this afternoon, Ms. Gentry?"

Well, I was really enjoying my solitude until you came along and disrupted it.

"I'm fine."

He chuckled.

"I can *see* you're fine. What I asked is *how are you doing?*"

As corny a line as that was, it elicited a laugh out of me, and began to loosen the foul funk I had been swimming in since getting out of bed that morning.

"Don't you know it's dangerous for a sista as fine as you to be sitting in this park alone without her man?" he went on.

"Uh, not that it's any of your business . . ."

"Rex."

"Rex. I don't have a man. Not anymore, anyway. I broke up with him last night." (TMI violation.)

"Let me guess. You caught him cheatin' on you."

"Wrong, Sherlock."

"You want to get married, but he's shucking and jivin'."

"Columbo you ain't."

"Mmm, oh, I got it. He couldn't satisfy you—"

"Mr. Rex. Excuse me, but we hardly know each other."

"Hey look, I'm just making conversation with you. You look kind of depressed. I didn't mean any offense."

I accepted Rex's apology in silence.

"It's not anything like that. Tony was handsome, smart, and he treated me good. Real good. Like a woman's supposed to be treated. I really think he loved me." (TMI violation number two.)

Why I was engaging in conversation with this stranger was beyond me. Doing so however, was beginning to feel therapeutic.

"Sounds to me like this Tony guy was the quintessential Mr. Right. Curious. What *did* he do to make you not want to be with him, if you don't mind me asking?"

I had to think about that. And think some more, in order to come up with an honest answer to Rex's question.

"When it comes right down to it, I broke up with him because he's white," I feebly confessed.

Silence.

Rex took a swig of his Evian and rubbed his chin.

"I'm not sure I'm following you, Ms. Gentry. You were seeing a man, a man you describe as quite a catch, and you broke up with him because he's white? Now, the way I see it, drug abuse, physical abuse, homosexuality; those are the kinda things a man can conceal from a woman in a relationship—if he's crafty enough. But skin color? That's not the kinda thing a man can just *spring* on a woman out of the blue. So forgive me for asking what must sound like a dumb question, but wasn't this Tony fellow white when you *met* him?"

(Just like a man. Always trying to assess everything *logically*.)

"Let me ask you a question, Rex. Do you like black women?"

"I love black women. Ain't nothin' finer on God's green earth."

Hearing him say that made me smile for the first time all day.

"Wow. It's so nice to hear a brotha express that sentiment. Now having said that, Rex, would you date a white woman?"

"Damn straight I would."

Wrong answer, Rex. Wrong answer.

"I'd date a white woman, a Puerto Rican woman, an Asian woman. I'd date a damn alien from outer space if she looked good to me," he said expressing no shame in his game. "Brothas don't be trippin' over race and skin color. We *exercise* our options. We *have* to. I believe y'all are partly the blame for that."

No this knee-grow did not take it there.

I spontaneously slipped into bitch mode for the bitch moment about to commence.

"Excuse me?" I said, spewing 'tude and spit simultaneously in Rex's direction. "I know you're not blaming black women for the black man's inability to—"

"Whoa. Hold on a minute, sweetness. Don't bite my head off. Let a brotha explain what he meant by that."

I glared at Rex with scrunched eyebrows. *Better make this good bruh, or you're getting the hell up off my bench.*

"What I mean is, despite what you claim, I don't think black women are really looking for *good* brothas. What most of y'all are looking for in my opinion is a certain kinda *package* instead. Now, I ain't saying there's anything wrong with this per se, but some of y'all just take that shit too far. Too many of y'all have got got-to-be-itis."

I cut my eyes sharper than a Ginsu knife at Rex.

"Got-to-be *what?*"

"Got-to-be-itis."

"And what is that?" I asked incredulously.

"An epidemic that afflicts single black women in alarming numbers. A disease that *keeps* them in their single-black-woman status. I got three sisters ages twenty-seven to forty-two, and all of 'em are still single with advanced stages of it."

He's joking. Right?

"And what exactly is the diagnosis for a sista with 'got-to-be-itis'?"

"You know she's got it when her girlfriends are trying to hook her lonely ass up with a good brotha and all she can say to them is, he's got-to-be over six feet. He's got-to-be chocolate brown, bald, with at least a mustache. He's got-to-be one hundred eighty-five pounds or more. He's got-to-be a college graduate of a major university. He's got-to-be white-collar. He's got-to-be earning a six-figure income or close to it. He's got-to-be a homeowner. *Shyyyttt!* Y'all ain't the *only* act in town. Let a brotha come up short in just one of those areas and half of y'all wouldn't form your lips to speak to him if he said good morning to you on a crowded street. Then y'all got the *nerve* to look at us all cockeyed, swiveling your heads around on your necks like *we* got a problem when we pass you by with a Caucasian, Latino, or Asian honey on our arm."

He's not joking.

"Take me for example. I consider myself a handsome, articulate brotha," he continued. "I didn't go to Yale, but I do have a high-school diploma. I'm a bike messenger. True, that in itself ain't saying much, but I like what I do. And no, I don't own my own home or condo. I still live with my parents."

That revelation nearly knocked me off the bench we were sitting on. I had to interrupt.

"Excuse me, Rex, but how old are you may I ask?"

"I'm thirty-three. Why?"

"Um . . . never mind. Go on."

Thirty-three? Gol-lee and gee effin' whiz.

"Like I was saying. I still live with my parents. But understand I'm there 'cause I'm comfortable—not 'cause I *can't* get my own place. I've built a small home recording studio in the basement of the house. Took me three years to get it right the way I want it, and I paid for the entire thing from my earnings as a bike messenger. I'm trying to get into the music industry as a hip-hop producer. When I'm not in the lab—a.k.a. my studio—I'm riding this bike and delivering packages. This gig gives me the time and flexibly to pursue my music. So, you see, what I want to do doesn't require any college degree, just a creative mind and the ability to create dope beats—all of which I happen to do very well, thank you very much. I ain't down with corporate America. I don't wanna spend my days sitting behind a desk working for 'The Man.' And I definitely don't want The Man telling me how to dress for work or how I can wear my hair. So, when I meet sistas and they ask me the proverbial 'What do you do for a living?' or that other question that almost always follows next, '*What are your career aspirations, Rex*?', I keep it real. And when I do, how many of 'em do you think wanna get with me?"

If he hadn't already said a mouthful, Mr. Rex was far from finished. Like Ving Rhames's character in the movie *Pulp Fiction*, bruh was about to get medieval on my ass.

"Now, let me ask *you* something, Ms. Gentry," he said, flinging a mouthful of his own 'tude and spit back in my direction. "If *all* black women really desire is that one good black man, then what's wrong with the 'good' brotha who drives the school bus? What's wrong with the 'good' brotha who collects tolls on the Interstate? Aren't these occupations more dignified than knocking elderly, blue-haired white ladies in the head for their Social Security checks? Why isn't it enough if the 'good' brotha only has a high-school diploma? Why can't y'all compromise and leave your high heels in the closet if that 'good' brotha happens to be a little on the short side? And what is it with y'all's fascination with these darker-than-midnight bruhs all of a sudden? I remember a time not too long ago when sistas couldn't drop their drawers fast enough for light-skinned, pretty-boy brothas with 'good' hair. So you know what I say, Ms. Gentry? Go 'head and hold out for that six-four, 220-pound, bald-headed, Hershey-chocolate-colored, six-figure-earning, Mercedes-Benz-driving, MBA-having, four-bedroom-house-owning black man if you want to. But let me assure you, *if* he exists, trust me—he's *not* gonna be holding out for a *black* woman."

When Rex finally finished with his "sermon on the bench," he winked, and shot me a big ear-to-ear smile exposing the gap between his two front teeth. Truth be told, I thought his whole "got-to-be-itis" hypothesis was pretty funny. I also found him to be kind of cute and personable. (Though I wasn't giving him the satisfaction of knowing either of these things.) I didn't agree with all of what he said. Thought much of it was utter gibberish. Nevertheless, I had to give him kudos for his ability to articulate his gibberish.

"Go 'head and laugh at me if you want to," Rex said, "but you know I'm speaking the truth. I sure hope you haven't come down with a case of the 'itis.' That would be a *real* shame."

Rex took me by surprise when he leaned in and gave

me a peck on the cheek. I started blushing and giggling like a silly schoolgirl.

"What was that for?" I asked.

"That was for sharing your bench with me and for being so damn fine."

"Yeah, right. I've go no makeup on, I've got a scarf tied—"

"That's all right. You still look good to me. You know what? Maybe that white boy you were seeing wasn't Mr. Right after all. Maybe he was. Hell if I know. Either way, though, just remember something."

"What's that, Rex?"

"A woman—even one as attractive as you—is only going to get but so many opportunities to snag The One, so don't sleep."

"You sound like my girlfriend Lisa now."

"Say what?"

"Nothing. Just thinking out loud. Hey, if I didn't know any better, I'd think I've just been 'psychologized' by a total stranger on a bench in Farragut Park."

Rex laughed.

"Call it whatever you want. I'm just keeping it real with you, my Nubian sista, 'cause that's what I do. Tell it like it is. Look here, sweetness, I'm fittin' to roll up outta here. I got things to do, people to see, places to be," Rex said, rolling his *City Paper* up under his arm and reaching for his bicycle. "I never did catch your first name."

"Didn't toss it to you."

"Oh, okay. It's like that. So . . . can a brotha get your number, *Ms. Gentry?*"

"Mmm, no. But you can give me yours."

36

Panic Button

The hearing to determine alimony, if any, and the custody of five-year-old Andre Braxton was scheduled for a week from today. As taxing as this case had been for me at times, and as frustrated as I had gotten with my client's actions once or twice, I was truly going to miss representing Rose Braxton when this was all wrapped up. Having the case to focus on meant I didn't have to overly focus on the sad, sad state of my love life. Something I welcomed more than ever now that things with Tony had gone kaput. Anyways, I'm happy to say my client stuck to her word as promised this time. She didn't let Sydney back into her apartment or have any other kind of contact with him. As for that nutcase, well, since his preposterous visit to my office that day, he hadn't written any more threatening letters or made any more harassing visits to his wife's place of employment. He even retained an attorney of his own to represent him in the hearing next week. Great. I still didn't trust that fool as far as I could throw him, though.

In the midst of a slow day at JB&H, slow enough that I decided to knock off early if nothing pressing came my way in the next few hours, I called Rose to touch base and see how she was making out a week before our big date with the judge. She answered her phone at work sounding surprisingly chipper.

"Hi, Rose. It's Bailey Gentry."

"Hey, how are you?"

"I'm good. And you?"

"Getting better every day. It's almost over, Ms. Gentry."

"I know that's right. So, tell me. How does it feel to be on the doorstep of becoming a single woman again?"

"Like I've got a brand-new lease on life. I'm ready to move on in every way, too."

"Meaning?"

"I'm ready for a new relationship."

"My gosh, Rose. The ink's still—"

"Don't misunderstand me, Ms. Gentry. I'm not rushing into anything. But I'm not going to be one of those women who gets divorced, then waits years before she'll even entertain the idea of being in another relationship. Don't feel like I have to do that. I may have been married, but I haven't been in a *relationship* in years. I haven't even turned thirty yet. I'm still young, vibrant, ready to go," she laughed. "I promise I won't jump at the first guy who comes my way. But, if he does come my way say . . . tomorrow, I'm not going to be too quick to blow him off either."

"I'll say this much, you sound good. Your attitude sounds even better."

"Thanks, Ms. Gentry. And thank you for being such a good lawyer. I really feel like my money's been well spent."

"I appreciate hearing that."

"Hey, I got some more good news to tell you."

"What's that?"

"I got a new job."

"Get out! I didn't know you were even looking for a new job."

"Yeah, I kind of kept that to myself. Didn't want to jinx anything. But I had a second interview with this company a few weeks ago and they just made me an offer of employment this morning. It's a great company, too. Awesome benefits, and they have branch offices in New York, Chicago, and Philadelphia with liberal transfer policies for employees who want to relocate. Something I can see my son and I doing in the near future. The best part, though, I'm going to be making ten grand a year more than I am now. Is that incredible or what?"

"That's more than incredible, Rose. That's fantastic." I said, nearly leaping out of my chair in excitement. "The timing couldn't be better, either."

"You can say that again. God is good, Ms. Gentry. Listen, I hope you won't take what I'm about to say the wrong way given all your hard work on my behalf, but I really don't care anymore what happens at that hearing next week—as far as me getting alimony, I mean. I probably wasn't going to get much of anything anyway from that manipulative SOB. All I want is custody of Andre. Everything else'll take care of itself. There are a whole lot of women raising kids as single parents on far less than what I'll be earning. I'll be just fine."

"Listen, with the good news you've just got, we're going to go into that hearing with some positive momentum. Let's just see how it unfolds, okay? You're going to get custody of your son. That much I'm certain of. Let's touch base early next week."

"Sounds good, Ms. Gentry. Take care, and thanks again for all your help. Bye."

I hung up the phone and leaned back in my chair cheesin' so hard I thought my cheeks would crack. Good things happen to good people. And Rose was good people. Finally, I had something to smile about. The way my personal life had been going, Lawd knows I hadn't done much of that over the past few days.

Things were still pretty slow in the office by the time the clock struck four. The only action going on seemed to be outside on the street. For the past hour or so I could hear police sirens blaring like crazy. Not that that type of thing is an anomaly to hear working in downtown D.C., but the ruckus that afternoon was relentless. I logged off the network, turned off my computer, and straightened up my desk while thoughts of two men ran through my brain. The first being Tony, of course, and how quickly things had deteriorated between us. Since our first date, we had never gone several days like this without speaking to one another.

Chill, Bailey. He just needs some space right now. You did drop a bomb on him.

The second was Kevin Wayne. In the midst of everything that had transpired between Tony and me, it suddenly dawned on me that I hadn't heard a peep out of my rainy-night lover since . . . well, that rainy night we made love. I hadn't tried to get in touch with Kevin because of Lisa's recommendation that I back off. Be that as it may, I wondered what was stopping him from getting in touch with me. What was up with that?

Let me find out . . . no. I'm not even going there.

I was sure there was a logical explanation why I hadn't heard from him yet. I grabbed my belongings—jacket, pocketbook, and briefcase—and headed out.

"I'm leaving for the day, so please take a message if anyone calls or is looking for me," I told Monifah, as I passed the reception desk where she was yuckin' it up with Christian Pierre, a new young paralegal who joined the firm about three months ago from Teaneck, New Jersey. Christian was a cutie-pie. Nice bod, too. And he was sweet. Sweet as *Tinkerbell*. I swear that brotha's feet didn't touch the ground when he was running around the office.

"You taking Metro home?" Monifah asked. "It's crazy outside right now. The police have got Connecticut Avenue on lockdown between L and M."

"Is that what all that racket outside is about?"

"Mmm-hmm. I hear there's some kind of hostage situation going on in an office building in the area. You didn't hear about it?"

"Uh, uh."

"Where you been all day, Missy?"

That was Christian.

"Held up in that office of yours again? You need to get out. Get some fresh air. See what's going on in the world outside your office window," he joked in his lispy voice.

"Tomorrow, Christian. I promise," I joked back.

"I bet 'chu somebody got fired and now they've taken the whole dern company hostage," Monifah said, as if someone doing such a thing was mildly amusing to her.

"Well, none of this sounds good to me, so let me get out of here and see if I can navigate my way to the Metro. I'm trying to get home early this evening, y'all feel me?"

As I made my way out of the building onto M Street and headed in the direction of the Metro, there were police cruisers everywhere. Even a SWAT van. Vehicle and pedestrian traffic was being diverted away from Connecticut Avenue. I overheard someone on the street mention that the Farragut North station had been temporarily sealed off.

Why does stuff like this always happen whenever I'm trying to get home early?

I walked briskly alongside a growing mass of other workers occupying the sidewalk, some visibly annoyed by the drama going on, others visibly intrigued by it. I found myself walking stride for stride with a middle-aged man who seemed to be on a mission to get home early, just like me. I asked him if he had any inkling as to what all the commotion was about.

"Some kind of domestic situation I hear. Some wacko's holding his estranged wife at gunpoint in the 1140 building."

And *that's* when it hit me. Froze me in my tracks as if the sidewalk had suddenly turned into quick-drying cement.

My God. Rose works in the 1140 building.

"Ma'am, you okay?" the gentleman turned and asked when he noticed I was no longer walking beside him.

"I-I'm fine, sir. Just remembered I left something in my office," I lied. "You have a nice evening."

I walked to the entrance of the nearest office building. My legs felt wobbly. Like they could no longer carry my weight. Reached in my pocketbook in search of my cell phone. Couldn't find it.

I've got entirely too much shit in this bag.

I was going to stay cool, calm, and collected.

"A guy's holding his wife at gunpoint in the 1140 building."

Just an eerie coincidence—nothing more, I told myself. As soon as I found my cell phone, I was going to call Rose, and she was going to answer sounding as bubbly as she had a few hours ago, when we last spoke. Ah, found it. I pulled out my cell phone, toggled to the

phone book, located Rose's work number, and hit the
SEND button. Her line rang once. Twice. Three times. No
answer. Got her voice mail.

"Hello. You've reached . . ."

I disconnected the call, placed my cell phone back in
my pocketbook, and resumed my walk to the next-
closest Metro station, which was Farragut West. Once I
reached it, I stopped at the entrance of the station and
tried Rose's number again. Again her line rang three
times, unanswered. This time I left a message. Not wanting her to hear the sudden concern in my voice, I kept
my message routine and my tone matter-of-fact.

"Hi, Rose. It's your attorney again. I have a question
for you regarding next week's hearing. I've left the office
for the day, so please call me on my cell phone when you
get this message. The number's . . ."

Whatever my question to her was going to be, I'd have
it all figured out by the time she called me back. I entered the station. An hour and fifteen minutes later, I
was home.

My cell phone never rang.

OCTOBER . . .

37

Resolution

I grabbed the Kleenex box perched on the edge of my desk and tossed it in the trash. Didn't need it anymore. I had cried and snotted the darn thing empty. Finished the last few chews of the jerk-chicken salad I bought for lunch, then glanced at the open page in my appointment book. October. Day six. It had been a couple of weeks since I'd told Tony I needed a black man and left him hanging—literally and figuratively. There'd been no communication between us since. He hadn't called me at my home or office. Hadn't come by to see me at my home or office. Was he still alive? Dead? So hurt he left town? Or worse, was he somewhere plotting the mother of all revenge against me?

Listen. I already know what some of y'all are thinking. Why hadn't I made the first move? Why hadn't I tried to reach out to him? Would you believe me if I said I really wanted to? I wanted to pick up the phone and

hear Tony's sexy voice in the worst way. I knew I owed
him a big explanation. Just couldn't bring my fingers to
do the walking and punch his seven digits. Probably because I didn't know what to say. Where to start. I mean,
what could I possibly tell Tony that would make him understand my behavior over the past few months? Wasn't
sure *I* even understood it.

I got home from work around eight, hungry as all
hell. Checked my mailbox and headed upstairs to my
apartment. Got inside, kicked off the Etienne Aigners,
and checked my caller ID hoping to discover that Tony
had called. I was quite disappointed to see he hadn't,
and equally surprised to see that Kevin had. It was about
time. I'd check his message later. I needed to unwind
first. I collapsed on my sofa and tossed the mail on the
coffee table. In between a BGE electric bill and a credit
card solicitation from Citibank, a handwritten, ad-
dressed envelope caught my attention. There was no
return address in the upper left-hand corner. I flipped it
over and didn't find one on the back of it either. Then I
noticed the postmark: Washington, D.C. I quickly ripped
open the envelope.

> *Dear Bailey,*
>
> *I wanted to call you, but I couldn't. Wanted to come by
> your place, but I couldn't seem to bring myself to do that
> either. Now, I did make it as far as the café downstairs in
> your office building. Well, I'll just say something prevented
> me from riding the elevator up to your floor and leave it
> at that. As much as I want to understand the reason for
> the 180 you pulled on me, I think it's better, for me at least,
> if I don't see you again. Still, there still are some things I
> need to get off my chest and say to you. Hence the reason
> for this letter.*

I've been thinking a lot about a conversation we had over lunch at the Cheesecake Factory shortly after we met. I know we've had many lunch and dinner conversations, so I'll be specific. It's the one where I asked you to describe your ideal man. Remember? I believe your answer was something along the lines of someone who was attentive to your needs, a good listener, compassionate, the potential to be a good provider . . . oh, and you said being handsome and sexy wouldn't hurt either. I guess with all you did say that evening over a plate of chicken scaloppini, it's what you didn't say that speaks volumes now. Never during that entire conversation did you mention that the ideal man for you had to be a black man.

I don't know. Maybe the signs were there all along, but I simply chose to ignore them. Or maybe the reason you never bothered to mention this crucial necessity of yours during that conversation, or at any other time, was because you never factored on me, of all people, emerging as a contender to be your Mr. Right.

I walked out of your place a few weeks ago with my feelings unbelievably hurt. You had my head spinning, B. I'm just glad I didn't end up killing myself or someone else on the road that night. It's funny, but Derrick tells me all the time that black women wouldn't know a good man if one fell from heaven and landed in their lap. Again, his words, not mine. I never subscribed to his assumption that this was a "black woman thing." I could say likewise about more than a few white women I've been with in the past. Plus, I know my roommate's got a few "issues" of his own he needs to address. Nevertheless, his hypothesis has certainly hit home this time.

He saw the kind of shape I was in when I got back to the apartment that night. Naturally I confided in him. That's right. I told Derrick everything. To my surprise, he wasn't surprised in the least. In fact, the only thing that seemed to surprise him was that it took you so long to come clean with me. No matter who or what comes along, black women have been, and probably always will be, extremely loyal to black men, he told me. Then he said something else to me. Tony, fuck it. Whether she's black, white, purple or green, all a man can do when he steps to a woman is come with his best. His "A" game. And hope that it'll be good enough for him to clear the bar. Good enough for him to reach her heart and soul. Derrick couldn't have been more right.

I brought my best when I met you, Bailey. My "A" game, as it were. And I suspect it must have been pretty good. Better than you could have imagined. You must have had some kind of tug-of-war going on with yourself. I sense you found most of what you were really looking for in a man, but regrettably found it in the kind of man you hardly had in mind. The kind a man you would never allow yourself to be with. Pretty ironic, wouldn't you say?

Yes, I'm a white boy, Bailey. All day, every day. Therefore I can't be your good black man. And it's apparent to me now that just being your "good man" would never have been good enough. So I give up. I'm waving my white flag (no pun intended).

At any rate, this letter has gotten much lengthier than I intended it to be, so let me say this one last thing. We don't always get what we want, Bailey. Yet, if we're fortunate enough, someone will come along who gives us everything we need. And maybe if we just let things flow, we'll discover we couldn't want anything more.

I'll always believe that someone for you could have been me.

Ciao, Bella,

Tony

(a.k.a. "White Chocolate")

I carefully folded the three-page letter, placed it back in the envelope, and wiped away the tears that had begun welling in my eyes. Tony was right. I *did* and *didn't* say all of those things to him. Now what months ago seemed like great company and conversation made me ache inside and out. I had deeply hurt a guy who had never been anything but good to me, an action that no longer seemed commensurate with the reason. My mouth had finally written that check my ass couldn't cash. Though not in the way I imagined it would.

I lay on the sofa with my eyes closed. I no longer had an appetite. All I wanted to do was go to sleep now. Maybe slumber would reveal to me how I could be so frank and honest with Tony in one sense, while in another, be less than the same with myself.

DOMESTIC DISPUTE TURNS DEADLY IN DOWNTOWN OFFICE BUILDING, had been the first-page headline in the Metro section of the *Washington Post*. The story had been the talk of D.C. for several days. It even got mentioned in the Nationline section of the *USA Today* newspaper. And in a back-door sort of way, the story brought some publicity to the law firm of Jefferson, Bates, and Hankerson. Some for me as well. As legal counsel to one of the participants in the tragedy, I was interviewed by several news stations in the area. Clips of those interviews ran on all the local TV channels. Any young attorney trying to make a name for himself or herself looks forward to a little free publicity—especially of the television variety. I was no different. Believe me, though. I would have gladly given back my fifteen seconds of airtime for a different ending.

It didn't take long for me to learn why Rose never

returned my call that afternoon. I got my answer as soon
as I arrived home, turned on the evening news, and
heard a reporter give the breaking news:

"*The man currently holding his estranged wife at gunpoint
in a downtown office building has been identified as Sydney
Braxton of Baltimore, Maryland . . .*"

The calm was over and the storm had returned. My
worst nightmare had become reality.

Shortly after Rose and I got off the phone that day,
Sydney showed up at her job unannounced, itching for
a confrontation. Brought his dark cloud of gloom to cast
over her exceptionally sunny day. Rose was off collating
in the copier room when he arrived, so Sydney decided
to pull up a chair and wait—at her cubicle no less. Keep
in mind, none of Rose's coworkers were aware of what
was going on between those two. Sure, some had an
inkling she'd been going through "something" but had
no idea exactly what that something may have been. As
a consequence, Sydney's presence wasn't setting off any
alarms. My client was determined to keep her personal
business private. Maybe she had done too good a job.

Rose returned from the copy machine to find Sydney
lounging in her chair, at her cubicle, as if he didn't have
a care in the world. As if he wasn't *blatantly* violating the
restraining order she placed on him. In the instant she
saw him, all the effort she previously expended to keep
her personal business private went right out the window.
As my grandma Lucy Pearl used to say, "Enough is
enough, and too much stinks!"

Rose went ballistic. Screamed at Sydney to get out of
her chair and the fuck out of her office. She picked up
her phone and dialed 911. But didn't get to complete
that call because Sydney snatched the base of the phone
from the wall outlet. Sydney was out of control.

They were at each other's throats. Curse words and name-calling saturated the air. She pushed. He shoved. She slapped. He slapped back. They were *both* out of control. An alert coworker recognized this wasn't normal behavior for a married couple inside the privacy of their own home, much less a downtown office suite. She picked up her phone and completed that call to 911 Rose was unable to. The police were on their way. Meanwhile, stunned coworkers looked on in disbelief at the surreal spectacle taking place before their eyes. Not one of them attempted to intervene. Not even the men in the office. A damn shame. Or was it? What would you have done if you were one of Rose's coworkers at that moment? Male or female?

. . . I ain't getting in the middle of that and getting myself hurt up. I've got a wife and two small kids at home . . .

. . . Well, don't look at me. You know I'm on medication for my asthma . . .

. . . Look man, all I want to do is finish up these budget reports and get them on Mr. Bossman's desk so I can get outta here at five today . . .

The clock was winding down on Sydney's tyrannical reign. Perhaps the very motive for his rampage. His wife was divorcing him. There was a strong chance he was going to lose his son next. Moreover, he was losing his grip on the very thing manipulative and controlling men value most: their power of intimidation. Sydney had no choice. He had to *really* flex his machismo now. *Make* Rose recognize who she had been fuckin' with once and for all. *Nobody* fucked with Sydney Braxton. He'd only told Rose that about a half million times during the course of their tumultuous marriage. It wasn't his fault that she had been a hardheaded bitch. Right? So he did the unthinkable. Pulled a nine-millimeter from his waistband, grabbed

Rose in a chokehold, and pointed the barrel of it at her temple. Seconds later the police arrived on the scene.

Allow me to digress a moment. This is strictly conjecture; I'm not a mindreader. However, I believe that had to be Sydney's signal moment of clairvoyance in all that madness. The moment where he—even with his macho, I-don't-give-a-fuck-posture—had to have grasped that he had gone too far this time. Pulling a gun on Rose, in front of a room full of eyewitnesses, in plain view of the police—not to mention doing all of this while in violation of his court-ordered restraining order—Sydney had all but guaranteed himself the next several years of his sorry life in a United States correctional facility. The only question: which one and for how long?

Officers on the scene had to proceed extra cautiously, given there was a room full of innocent bystanders trapped in this unfolding drama through no fault of their own. First things first. They sealed off all possible escape routes to the perpetrator—elevators, stairwells, even some of the streets outside. The smartest thing Sydney could do was surrender and hope he could convince the police that the scene they arrived on was just a big misunderstanding. Something like a bad joke gone *terribly* bad. But, lest we forget who we're talking about here. Surrender was not an alternative.

Cops surrounded the hostage and hostage taker. Drew their weapons, and instructed the latter to lay down his. He refused. A standoff ensued. Two hours into this standoff, and following some textbook hostage negotiation, officers were able to convince Sydney Braxton that he had no issues with Rose's *coworkers*. He agreed and allowed those coworkers to go home to their husbands, wives, and kids. With the risk of harm to innocent people out of the way, D.C.'s finest could really get down to business. All they needed was the go-ahead and a clear shot to take the perpetrator out, so they could go home to their husbands, wives, and kids, too.

My copy of the police report stated that at approximately 7:14 PM, nearly four hours after the standoff began, it ended when Sydney Braxton—trapped, with no viable outlet from the quandary he created—pulled the trigger of his nine-millimeter and took a life. His own.

My client always feared her husband would be the death of her one day. She came this close to getting it right.

Now I suppose this tragedy could have ended a lot worse. Sydney could have taken Rose along with him. Why he chose not to is something I guess we'll never know. But Rose was right. God is good. And I guess there are some other things we'll never know as well. For one, if Rose and Sydney, though divorced, could have put aside their hostilities in order to provide their young son with the support of two parents for his ascension into adulthood, instead of adding another young black boy to the growing list of those who'd have to grow up without a father. And given the legacy left to him by his dad, only time would tell what kind of man Andre Braxton would grow up to be.

I paid Rose a visit at Howard University Hospital the day after the incident. She was kept there overnight for routine observation. Whatever that means. Other than the obvious psychological trauma, she seemed okay physically. I offered to put her in touch with some contacts of mine who could help her with her ordeal through professional counseling. She declined my offer. I hadn't seen or spoken to Rose since. She told me at the hospital that she was going to need some time to herself. Time to absorb all that had taken place, and even more time to

absorb all that was likely to now follow. She asked me not
to try and contact her. Said she'd be in touch with me
and everybody else when she felt ready to do so. I understood. Whenever she felt the need to talk again, I'd be
there for her. But as her sista-friend this time. Not her attorney. Our professional relationship was over. There was
nothing left for me to litigate on her behalf. Sydney was
dead. And dead men can't pay alimony or fight you for
child custody.

38

Quick Recovery

When I got in my Audi and pulled out the parking lot of my complex, I had only intended to drive as far as the Safeway less than a mile away. I drove right past it. And kept right on driving. Maybe my subconscious was on autopilot or something, because before I knew it, I was all the way in D.C., on Columbia Road, a few blocks from Tony's apartment building.

I badly needed to get rid of the dull ache moving to and fro in the pit of my being. You ladies know what I'm talking about. That feeling that takes over your body when things aren't quite right between you and your man. Your appetite hasn't been quite the same, your skin's beginning to break out, your sleep . . . hmph . . . what sleep? In essence, you just feel like shit! Visiting the doctor is a waste of time—and a copayment—because you know the problem's not physical. It's all in your head, and there's only one way to rid yourself of the shittiness you've been lugging around for way too long: You've got to confront him.

I circled Tony's block so many times I got dizzy. Felt like I was on an amusement-park ride or something. Part of me knew I was about to make a fool of myself, rolling up on him impromptu like that, but I didn't care. Pride was inconsequential at this juncture. Sure, I had hoped that he would have paid me a visit up close and personal by now, but maybe Tony's three-page letter was as good as I was going to get from him. That wasn't going to be workable. I needed more.

My circling came to an end when I finally found a parking space. I turned off the engine, and gave myself the once-over in the vanity mirror inside my sunshade. I looked okay. Just okay. No makeup, my braids hung loose, and I had on an old terry-cloth sweatsuit and my Reeboks. (I was only going to the supermarket. Not to win back my boyfriend, remember?) I got out of the car and began a deliberate walk towards Tony's building. At the same time, I completely stopped thinking about what I was getting ready to do. I knew if I didn't, I'd come to my senses, turn around, get back in my car, and drive back home. I rang the intercom. I was immediately buzzed in without being asked to identify myself. Got off at the second floor and embarked on a slow march down the hallway towards door number 203. That hallway seemed twice as long as I remembered it. I'm sure it was just my frayed nerves making it seem that way.

I knocked. My heart felt like it was lodged in the middle of my throat. Heard the clicks of multiple locks being unlocked on the other side of the door. A sound that reminded me of the time Derrick and his Asian chick walked in on us. That made me momentarily chuckle to myself. The door swung open. I braced myself to be face-to-face with Tony for the first time in weeks, but instead, I was greeted by Derrick. He looked puzzled to see that it was me, as if he was expecting someone else.

"Hi, Derrick."

"Oh. Hey, Bailey, what are you doing here?" he said. "I'm sorry. That was rude of me. Come on in."

"Thank you."

I stepped inside the apartment and stood in the foyer while Derrick locked the door behind me. I noticed he'd grown back his beard and mustache. Good. He looked much better with both.

"I assume you're looking for Tony?"

"Yes. Is he around?"

"Actually, he's out of town. He went home to Philly for a couple of days. He didn't tell you?"

"We haven't exactly spoken in a few days," I lied. It was more like a few weeks.

"I wonder why?" Derrick said, with what sounded like a twinge of sarcasm to me. I didn't appreciate his tone, but then I hadn't gone there to fight with anybody. I'd gone to make things right with somebody.

"Have a seat. Can I get you something to drink?"

Yeah. A glass of hemlock. No ice, I wanted to say. "Water's fine."

Derrick returned from the kitchen with two ice-cold bottles of water and sat next to me on the sofa.

"Long time no see. You look good, Bailey." Didn't know if he was being sincere or still on his sarcasm trip.

"Yeah, it's been a while. And how are you?"

"I can't complain."

An awkward silence overcame the room.

"Derrick, let's not pretend. I know you know Tony and I have been going through some stuff as of late. I just came by—"

"You hurt him, Bailey. You really did," he cut me off. "On some level, I can comprehend where you're coming from, though. I'm not saying what you did to Tony was right, but I'm saying I understand."

There was no need for me to ask him to explain himself. I read Tony's letter. I knew where Derrick was coming from, too.

"Does he hate me now?"

Derrick scrunched his eyebrows, began to say something then stopped.

"Oh, c'mon. Just tell me. I want to know the truth."

"You sure about that?"

"I'm sure."

"In that case, I've got some news you are going to want to hear, and some you're probably not. First of all, Tony doesn't hate you. This I know. He could never hate you, Bailey. Dude was *in love* with you."

Hearing such a thing would have ordinarily put me on cloud nine. In the context of this conversation however, it made me feel like I was all alone on a desert island.

"As for what you're probably not going to want to hear . . . never mind. I'm not getting in the middle of this."

"Don't do that, Derrick. My emotions are a mess right now. I need to put them to rest. Whatever you tell me will stay between us. I will not say a word to Tony. I promise."

"What I was going to say is, even though you hurt him, Tony seems well on his way to a recovery already."

What the hell is that supposed to mean? "You wanna break that down for me in English?"

"All right. But you didn't hear this from—"

"Yes, Derrick," I snapped. "I told you I won't say a word."

"Tony didn't go to Philly alone."

"No?"

"No."

"Another . . ."

He nodded in the affirmative. Numbness engulfed me.

"*Who?*"

"Black girl. Never seen her before. Tony brought her through here for a hot second before they took off.

Uh-uh. "What did she look like?"

I wished I could've taken that question back as soon as it left my mouth.

"She wasn't exactly the kind of girl I'd picture Tony with . . . but then again, neither were you, Bailey. No offense."

"None taken."

"Tell you what I recall most about her."

"What was that?"

"She had a brick-house body. Bam, pow, *ta-dow!*" Derrick exclaimed, moving his hands in multiple configurations.

If I didn't know any better, I'd swear he was getting some type of perverse pleasure out of rubbing my nose in this. Frankly, I wanted to smack the shit out of Derrick. Numbness had now given way to a smoldering fury.

"What's her name, Derrick?"

"I think I've already said too much, Bailey. Tony ought to be back from his trip in a few days. I'll tell him you stopped by. He's the one you really need to be having this conversation with. Look, Sushi . . . Mylene, my girlfriend, she fixin' to come over here at any minute. In fact, I thought you were her when you rang the intercom downstairs. I'd kinda prefer it if you weren't around when she arrives. She's got a little bit of a jealous streak. No offense."

"None taken. Bye, Derrick."

You know I bawled all the way down the hallway, into the elevator, out the front door of the building, and back to my car, don't you? Pulled out of that parking space so fast my tires screeched. On top of all the shittiness I was already dealing with, add scorned, betrayed, hoodwinked, and p-i-s-s-e-d to my list of sensations. I wanted to kick somebody's ass. Anybody's. A total stranger's. Didn't know what had me angrier. Tony already keeping company with another woman so soon after our breakup, or him doing so with another *black* woman so soon after our breakup. Who was this bitch, and where did he meet her?

"Not his type . . . had a brick-house body . . . not his type . . . had a brick-house body," I mumbled Derrick's words repeatedly through gritted teeth. No. Oh, no. It couldn't be. *Monifah?*

As nauseating a possibility as that seemed, all clues were pointing towards her. The fact that Tony and Derrick both used the same adjective to describe a particular woman. The way she'd slyly flirt with Tony. The way she'd look at Tony, cheesin' like a mouse. The way he'd look back at her, cheesin' like a mouse. And her ghetto-highness had been out of the office on vacation come to think about it.

All I could think about, as I sped up Sixteenth Street driving like a madwoman, weaving in and out of traffic lanes, blowing my horn, and cussin' drivers who weren't moving out of my way fast enough, was Tony in the city of Brotherly Love doing all the things *we* did together, but doing it with Monifah, of all people, now. Shopping on South Street. Gobbling down cheesesteaks. Having dinner at Dante & Luigi's. Visiting the African-American museum. Listening to jazz at Zanzibar Blue. Kissing on the pier at Penn's Landing. *Arrgggh!!!*

Halfway home, I pulled into an Exxon station on Colesville Road, took out my cell phone, and dialed Tony up. Yes, I know he was in Philly, but so what? Eff a roaming charge, okay? A sista needed answers—now! Didn't get any. He didn't pick up. I called Lisa next.

By the time I arrived home, my hurt and anger had subsided somewhat. Credit Lisa for that. I sat in that gas station, in my car, on my cell for thirty minutes venting to her about what I had just learned from Derrick. She was comforting like only a best girlfriend can be. She also told me all the things I didn't want to hear like only a best girlfriend can do. All the stuff I knew deep down to be the truth, but didn't want to admit to myself. Such as: If Tony was indeed intoxicating himself on the bosoms of JB&H's receptionist, I had no one but myself to blame. That I had already cheated on him, so maybe this was as simple a case of my "chickens coming home to roost." Anyway, everything happens for a reason. Isn't that what they say? Perhaps I had reason enough now to put this mission impossible with Tony Gianni behind me for good and move on. It never would have worked out between us anyway. Right?

After a day like today, what a sista needed most was a strong dose of "feel good." Unfortunately, I had no Hennessey in the house and was too spent for a romp to the liquor store. I thought a fine as hell brotha to hold me in his strong arms and whisper sweet nothings in my ear would be a much better elixir anyway. Unfortunately— yet again—there was no one to fill that vacancy for me at the present. No friend, no lover, no fuckbuddy—not even a *placeholder*, for crying out loud. Wait. That wasn't entirely so. There was someone who could fill that vacancy of mine quite nicely indeed. Only problem—he was hundreds of miles away. I'm talking about Kevin from cold-as-hell-Minnesota. I had to call that brotha back tonight if it was the last thing I did. Find out what he was up to. See if he and I could reconnect. Why not? I had no reason to distance myself from him any longer. Especially with Tony off "recovering" so nicely with his new sista-friend. It was time for me to practice a little "recovery" of my own.

Later that evening, I got in the tub and took one last hot and relaxing bubble bath courtesy of the bubble-bath lotion Tony got me as a gift. I say one last because I was tossing his gift out afterward. I have this policy about hanging on to gifts from ex-boyfriends when the relationship ends on what I judge to be a sour note: I don't. (Fine jewelry excluded, of course.)

Anyway, when one door closes another opens I reminded myself as I got out of the tub, toweled dry, and rubbed baby oil all over my damp, lonely body. From that point on, I was going to focus on the bright side of things. Tomorrow would mark a brand-new day and a fresh new start, I told myself. Who knows? Maybe even a fresh start with a new and exciting man.

I crawled into bed and snuggled under my Nautica comforter. Checked the time on my alarm clock: 10 PM on the dot.

Got to call Kevin before I drift off into la-la-land.

Picked up my cordless, scrolled through the caller ID history, found his number, and dialed.

Ring . . . ring . . .

"It's Kev."

"Mmmm. Somebody hasn't heard that sexy voice since

a rainy night you made her toes curl. You do remember
that night don't you?"

"Bailey?"

"My, my. How many toes have you been curling lately,
my brotha?"

He laughed.

"I remember. Vividly. And by the way, I did call. You
just weren't around when I did, and I didn't leave a message. So what do I owe the pleasure?"

"I miss you," I declared without a trace of shame.

My declaration elicited no response on the other end
of the phone.

"Miss me, too?" I sheepishly asked next, fishing for
some type of a reaction.

More laughter. Still no answer.

Oookay . . .

"I've got a proposition for you, Kevin. Why don't you
catch a flight to Maryland tomorrow and come see me?
I'll even pay for your plane ticket. That's how badly I
want to see you right now."

"How are things with you and your friend?" Kevin
asked, breaking his silence and changing the subject.

"Things aren't. I'm over him," I said, sounding braver
than an Indian chief.

"Is that right?"

"Kevin? My proposition?"

"I'm sorry. What was it again?"

"I *said*, will you catch a flight here tomorrow? I really
want to see you."

"As nice as that sounds, and as much as I wish I could,
I'm not gonna be able to do that," he said.

"Okay . . . well, how about I fly out there to see you tomorrow? I've never been to Minnesota before."

All I heard now were the sound of crickets chirping outside my window.

"Kevin? You still there?"

"There's something I need to tell you, Bailey."

Okay. I've been around enough men to know that whenever one utters that phrase to you, it's rarely ever going to be *good* news.

What, Kevin? You've given me a sexually transmitted disease or something? Dammit! I knew I should have made you . . .

"What is it?" I asked, with a lump in my throat.

"Remember when you asked me about Becky Sue?"

"Yeah, what about her? You said the odds of you two staying together were slim. Correction. You said *real* slim."

"Yeah, well, that's what I *thought*, too. Look, Bailey, the thing is . . . I mean . . . the reason it took me a while to get in touch with you is . . ."

"Stop dancing, Kevin. I don't hear any music playing."

He took a deep breath before continuing. "When I got back home, she and I talked. We talked a lot, in fact. And the long and short of it is, I've decided I want to work things out with her. *We've* decided we want to work things out with each other . . ."

As I listened to Kevin blindside me with this, I simultaneously thought back to what Lisa told me in the ladies' room at Copeland's: *Ain't no black man leaving his white woman for a black woman.*

". . . which means I won't be heading back your way for a while. If and when I do, we won't be hooking up again. Oh—and I think it's best if you don't call me anymore."

Dead silence.

Loud crickets.

"That's it? That's *all* you have to say to me, Kevin? You roll into town out of the blue, ask me to pick you up from the airport, get all comfy and cozy with your shirt and pants off in my home, tell me how things ain't working out between you and your girlfriend, tell me how beautiful you think I am, then have your way with me over the kitchen sink, beg me to call in sick the following day so you can lay around all morning with me in my Sealy Posturepedic, let me fix you a scrumptious breakfast of scrambled eggs, sausage patties, toast, and home fries, and all you can say to me now is don't call you anymore 'cause you've decided to go back to your white woman?"

"Bailey. I . . . I . . ."

"'I . . . I' *what*? You know what, Kevin Wayne? FUCK YOU, AND BECKY SUE!!!"

Click.

39

Someone to
Watch Over Me

There was a knock on my office door. I told whomever
it was to come on in. It was Mike Harrison.

"Hey, Mike. How goes it?"

"Just fine. And how are you?"

Truth was, several days later, I was still bummin' over
Tony—and that asshole, Kevin Wayne.

"Oh, I'm managing to manage. What are you doing
here? On your routine security sweep of the premises
again?" I joked.

"Naw. But then I guess you know better than that."

"Sit for a second, please."

Mike took a seat at my desk. "So, are you over it yet?"
he asked.

"Over what?"

"When we had lunch you said you felt bad about something you did. I believe your words were, 'I was a bit of a badass.'"

"Yeah, that. Well, Mike, in hindsight, I'm afraid I was a bit of a *dumbass,* too. But as you so poignantly stated, life's too short for regrets. Right?"

"Right."

"So, tell me. To what do I owe the pleasure of your visit today?"

"I've been thinking. There is a little something I probably should share with you."

"I'm listening."

"I think there's someone else you may want to take to lunch."

"Who?"

"Monifah Jenkins."

"*Monifah?* Why?"

"Because she called the security station and specifically asked for me that day. Told me she thought you might be in a tight spot with some unsavory-looking character that had no business coming to see you in the first place. She asked me to come up to the floor and check on you. She also told me to make up some reason for dropping in on you, because you told her *not* to call security. Her exact words were, 'The last thing I want to do is piss Bailey off, 'cause I know she doesn't like me.'"

"She told you that?"

"Sure did," Mike said, crossing his legs and folding his arms across his chest. "She was genuinely worried about you, Bailey. Me, I was ready to kick some ass if necessary. Now, I wasn't supposed to tell you anything about this. Monifah wanted it to stay between me and her. But after you took me to lunch that day and treated me so nice, well, my conscience started tugging at me a bit. I couldn't keep her part in it from you. And if Monifah is right—that you really don't like her for whatever reason—maybe letting you know the whole story might give you a different opinion about her. Now, I can't tell you who you should or shouldn't like, but I figured I'd at least give you the good word on Ms. Jenkins. Speaking of whom, where is that girl? Didn't see her up at the front desk."

"She's on vacation. And I'm sure she's having a blast wherever she is, and with whomever she's with."

Gol-lee and gee effin' whiz. Of all the people who could have been my guardian angel that day!

Wow. Who knew under all that ghetto-fabulousness lay a pretty okay sista looking out for a sista. Hmph.

"Well, thanks for making me aware of all this, Mike. I'll make sure to thank Monifah and do something real nice for her when she gets back."

Yeah, right. She's probably dining with my leftovers as we speak. That's going to have to be enough thanks for her ass.

"Cool. Look, I better get back to my post."

"I better get going as well. I've got a lunch date I'm really looking forward to."

"Somebody special?"

"Yes. You could say that indeed."

40

Body of Evidence

"Waiter. Another iced tea with lemon, please."

I was getting a bit impatient. Impatient and hungry. But I was equally excited about who I was having lunch with. Rose Braxton. Oh—make that Rose Lassiter. She had taken back her maiden name. She surprised the heck out of me when I got her call the other day saying she wanted me to meet her for lunch, her treat, at Jaleo's on Seventh Street. It was the first I had heard from Rose since visiting her at the hospital. Anyways, she was late. I expected her fifteen minutes earlier. I glanced around the restaurant for the umpteenth time when I spotted a woman I thought resembled her. Upon a stronger observation, I realized it was Rose.

"Yoo-hooo, Rose, over here," I yelled, waving my arms to get her attention. She came rushing to our table, nearly out of breath.

"I am soooo sorry, Ms. Gentry," she apologized.

"There was an accident on Fifty and the backup was horrendous. On top of that, I left my cell phone in the house, so I couldn't call to tell you I was running late. I hope you at least ordered yourself an appetizer while you were waiting."

"Nope, just working on my second glass of iced tea. Please, sit down."

"I will, but first, give me a hug. It's been a minute."

"Absolutely."

Rose and I engaged in a long embrace. When we were through, she reached into her pocketbook and pulled out a card.

"This is for you."

"You shouldn't have."

"Yes, I should have. It's just a little something for putting up with me and all of my drama over the past few months. I know I wasn't always the model client."

"Really?"

We both burst out laughing and took a seat.

"Should I open this now?" I asked referring to the card she gave me.

"Wait until you get home tonight."

"Good enough," I said, and placed it in my purse.

Rose looked good. Check that. She looked great. Better than I expected her to. She had put on some weight. Good weight. Her previously petite and curvy frame now bordered on voluptuous. She was even sportin' a new hairdo. A spiky, short-cropped number. Very funky. I couldn't pull it off, but she was working it.

"You look fantastic, Rose. I love your haircut."

"Do you? I decided to do a li'l som'um- som'um different. You know, to go along with this new phase in my life. You hungry?"

"Famished."

On cue, our waiter came over, handed Rose and me our menus, and reiterated the specials for the day. I had already heard the spiel, so I just sat and listened again.

"Actually, I've eaten here a few times before, so I already know what I'm having. How about you, Ms. Gentry?"

"I'd like the Spanish mackerel with roasted vegetables."

"And I'm going to have the ground beef sirloin."

"And what would you ladies care to drink?" our waiter asked.

"I'll have an apple martini and a glass of water. Bailey?"

"I'm good. This iced tea is fine. I've got to go back to work this afternoon," I laughed.

"Very well." The waiter took our menus and disappeared.

"So, talk to me. What's going on?" I asked.

Rose took a deep breath and let out a big sigh. "A lot, Ms. Gentry. A lot. But I'm feeling much better, I'm glad to say."

"Listen, Rose. Our professional relationship is over. Start calling me Bailey."

"Oh, okay. Bailey. I start my new job next week. I'm excited about that. I was supposed to have started a week ago, but under the circumstances, I just wasn't physically or emotionally ready to do that. Fortunately, my new employer was nice enough to extend my start date. They could have rescinded my job offer instead, so I definitely feel blessed in that regard. Oh, and thank you so much for respecting my request for some privacy. You and everyone else have been great in that regard. I really needed some time to myself in order to begin my own personal healing. I think I'm making big strides toward that."

"Glad to hear it. And how's little Andre doing?"

"That's the hard part, Ms. Gentry, I mean, Bailey. Can

I just call you Ms. Gentry? That's been ingrained in my head for months and I'm just used to it now."

"Oh, sure, go ahead."

"Andre's too young to comprehend all of this. He knows his father is dead, but I'm nowhere near ready to explain the circumstances of his father's death to him in any kind of detail. I mean, how *do* you explain to a five-year-old that his father threatened to kill his mother then ended up killing himself instead?"

"I feel you. I have no idea."

"I'm taking it one day at a time with my son. Answering his questions the best way I can for right now. By the way, I decided to see a therapist after all to help me work through this."

"Good. I think you're going to find that to be a very wise decision as time moves on."

"As much as I wanted to be free of Sydney, believe me when I tell you I never wanted him to die. I never wanted my son to have to grow up without his father. And that was whether we remained married or not. But that crazy fool shot himself to death right in front of me, Ms. Gentry. Can you believe that? Do you realize that's a mental picture I'm going to have etched in my memory for the rest of my damn life? But again, I'm blessed. I know it could have been worse. Sydney could have taken me to the grave along with him, and Andre wouldn't have a father *or* a mother right now."

Maybe *that* was it. The reason Sydney didn't kill Rose that day. I don't mean out of any kind of compassion for his son, but maybe he *purposely* wanted to leave Rose with an awful recollection she'd have to relive over and over for the rest of her life. Maybe this was his way of punishing her for divorcing him. For the controlling-type personality he was, such a scenario would still allow him to exercise a measure of control over her even from the grave. Sick bastard.

"Well, I want you to know, too, that as much as I wanted to get you a divorce and custody of your son, I never wanted to see this case come to the resolution it did. It was a pretty traumatic ending for me as well."

"Not to sound cold or anything, Ms. Gentry, but I do wish there was some life insurance money I could collect on Sydney. It would be a big help to me and Andre right now. Unfortunately, the only coverage he had was through his job, and he quit that."

"Don't lose sight of the *manner* in which your husband died, though," I told her. "He committed suicide. Therefore it's unlikely his insurer would have paid out to his beneficiaries even if he hadn't quit his job."

"You're right. I hadn't even taken that into consideration. But enough with this talk. I didn't come to lunch with you to be depressed. Let's talk about something more pleasant. What's been going on in your world? Working on any new cases?"

"Two, as a matter of fact."

"Divorces?"

"One's a divorce, and the other's an adoption proceeding. So I've got plenty to keep me busy now that I'm no longer representing you."

"Speaking of which, since you're no longer my attorney, I don't feel as funny about telling you something, and asking you another."

"What's that?"

"Well, the something I've wanted to tell you, but never thought it was appropriate to do while you were handling my divorce case, is that I admire you. I mean, look at you, Ms. Gentry. You're a beautiful, sexy, stylish black woman. You're a professional, making good money, you don't have any crazy man drama going on like I did—least I don't think you do. You're a young black woman going places. I'm jealous," Rose laughed. "And I'm nosy, too. There, I admit it. Which brings me to my other thing. I asked you a while back if there was a man in your life and you told me there wasn't. Frankly, I think you were just trying to play the humble role. But c'mon. A sista like yourself has *got* to have brothas beating down her door."

Beating down my door? Now that was funny. (Hardy-har-har-har.)

"First of all, thank you for the compliments. But in regards to my love life however, let's just say it's not what you might think. Pretty nonexistent is what it truthfully is."

"There's *nobody?* Not even a prospect?"

Rose made me think about Tony.

"Well, there was someone fairly recently. Things just didn't work out, though. Nevertheless, being a lawyer, I work a lot, as you know. Long hours most of the time. I don't even have the *time* to devote to a serious relationship right now."

I was lying through my teeth. What I just told Rose was nothing more than the same old time-honored bullshit-of-an-excuse professional women like myself—who either don't have or can't find a man—tell anyone gullible enough to believe.

"Well, that's too bad, because I happen to think you deserve a good man in your life."

"Dammit, Rose, so do I!"

We both hurt ourselves laughing.

Our lunch arrived. It looked good. Smelled even better. We each said a silent grace and proceeded to get our eat on.

"Got any plans to go out of town or do anything fun before you start your new job?" I asked.

"Actually, I just got back into town. A quickie trip. Nothing big. But I had so much fun. It was just what the doctor ordered."

"Oh, yeah? Where did you go?"

"Philadelphia."

Seems like a pretty popular destination these days, I thought to myself.

"Oh yeah I was there, too. Over the Fourth of July weekend. Do you have friends up there?"

"Not a one."

"So you took your son with you."

"Oh, no. Wasn't quite that kind of party," she laughed. "I had my girlfriend in Takoma Park watch Andre for a few days. You're probably gonna think I'm crazy, Ms. Gentry, but I met this guy recently, and he invited me to go there with him. I was hesitant at first, but then I got to thinking, why not? I've been to hell and back over the past few months. How bad could going out of town with a guy I barely know be? Besides, I needed a diversion. I think he needed one as bad as me."

"Well, you did say you weren't wasting any time getting back on the dating scene. Guess you weren't playing around, huh? Man, this fish is excellent. How's your beef sirloin?"

"Ditto."

"See any potential with this guy?"

She stopped chewing for a second, leaned back in her chair, and grinned.

"Oh, I'd say there's potential all right. But he's different. He's not like other guys I've dated before."

"Hmph. Been there done that and got the T-shirt already. So, he's not a roughneck, drug-dealer type, huh?"

"Heck, no. I told you. I'm not going down that road again. No, this guy's on a *completely* different tip. One I've never experienced before."

"Well, shucks, Rose. You make it sound like the brotha's from another planet or something."

"Almost."

"Huh?"

"He ain't a brotha."

"No?"

"Uh, uh."

"What is he?"

"He's white."

"You serious?"

"Mmm-hmm."

"Whoa. Well, let me tell you, Rose. I have a bit of exp . . . on second thought, never mind. That's a story for another time. So, what's this guy's name? Is he cute?" I asked, lifting my tall glass of iced tea with lemon to my lips to take another sip.

"Better than cute. He's *fine,* and his name's Tony."

The glass fell from my hand and crashed to the table, spilling my drink over everything: our table, my plate of Spanish mackerel with roasted peppers, and my Anne Klein suit. Rose leaped from her seat and rushed over to my side of the table with her napkin as we both worked frantically to absorb the liquid mess I had just made.

"Can we get some help over here, please?" she shouted to a busboy who was clearing a nearby table for its next occupants. He rushed over and lent us his assistance.

"That's a bad suit you've got on, Ms. Gentry. Why don't you go in the bathroom and get some water on it before it stains."

"Good idea."

I scurried off to the bathroom, grabbed a bunch of

paper towels from the dispenser, and began patting my suit with them. Soon as I got it sufficiently dry, I stopped and splashed some cold water on my face and wondered if I heard Rose correctly.

Did she say his name was Tony?

I returned to the dining area to find order restored at our table. My ruined lunch had been taken away, and a clean dry cloth covered our table.

"Sorry about that. I'm such a klutz," I said to Rose.

"Hey, happens to the best of us. How's your suit?"

"It'll need to see the dry cleaner. No major damage, though."

"They're going to bring you out a fresh plate."

"Good. I was enjoying that."

"You want another iced tea while you wait?"

"Uh, no. That's okay. I might lose my grip on that one, too. But you go ahead and finish your lunch. Don't wait on me."

"You okay?"

"Yeah, why?"

"You look a bit flustered."

"I'm just a little annoyed with myself that's all."

Rose proceeded to finish her lunch. I proceeded to pump her for more information. "So, um, finish telling me about this white guy you said you met. Did you say his name was Tony?"

"Uh-huh."

Uh-uh.

I was almost too afraid to ask Rose my next question. Probably because I didn't know how I was going to react if she gave me the wrong answer. I was liable to reach across the table and put both my hands around her . . .

"He, um . . . wouldn't happen to be Italian would he?"

"How did you know?"

Wrong answer, Rose. Wrong answer!

No. This couldn't be happening.

Lawd, please tell me Rose isn't the bitch Tony's been off "recovering" with!

"Um, j-just a wild guess," I stuttered. "W-where did you two meet?"

"Actually, I met Tony a few months ago. We met in that café downstairs in your office building that you suggested I have lunch in before our meeting that afternoon. I was in there eating lunch, and he was doodling away on his laptop at the table right next to me . . ."

"I'm going to stay here, grab a sandwich, and do some personal stuff on my laptop before I head back to work."

". . . Ms. Gentry?"

"Huh?"

"You listening to me?"

"Uh, yes, Rose. My mind wandered off for a second there. I'm sorry. You were saying?"

I was beginning to feel warm. Woozy. Sick to my stomach. Where was that busboy? Amigo's services might be needed again real soon. Thought I might hurl at any moment.

"So he and I make eye contact, right, and I'm thinking this dude's fine," Rose went on. "And he must like what he sees 'cause he's sure 'nuff clockin' me. He says hi, and I say hi back. Now, I'm not into white men, but this one I could make an exception for. He stops pecking away on his laptop for a second, comes over to my table, and asks me how my day is going. I tell him not so good, but I don't go into any detail. Don't discuss my business with strangers. Fine or otherwise. So anyway, I asked him if he worked in the area. He told me no. Said he just finished having lunch with a friend of his and was killing some time before going back to work . . ."

A friend? Is that what he referred to me as? After we just agreed to do the committed relationship thing not ten minutes earlier. A *f-r-i-e-n-d?*

". . . and that was pretty much it. Oh. Except for one other thing he said to me that I thought was so sweet to hear given how I was feeling at the time. He told me I was the most attractive woman he had seen all day. Following that, he slid back over to his table, closed up his laptop, and walked his fine, white-boy ass right out the door.

"He told you that?"

"'Scuse me?"

"He actually said *you* were the most attractive woman he had seen all day?"

Rose looked at me, perplexed, her eyes moving around like loose marbles inside her head.

"Is that so hard to believe? I mean, I'm not exactly—"

"Of course not, Rose. I'm sorry. I didn't mean that the way it came out."

"Are you *sure* you're okay?"

"*Yes,* Rose. Why do you keep asking me that?" I snapped, not meaning to, but unable not to.

"Because your mood's changed ever since you came back from the restroom. You ain't turning schizoid on me, are you?" she chuckled.

(I didn't find that funny.)

"Did something happen in the restroom?" she went on.

No, Rose. Something's happened right here. Right here at this table!

"I'm just hungry. I get cranky when I'm hungry."

"Okay then. I won't ask you anymore."

"So, um, Rose. Your encounter with this guy . . . I-I feel like I'm missing something."

"What's that?"

"You say he just walked out of the café after proclaiming you the most attractive woman he had seen all day? You guys didn't exchange numbers or anything?"

"Nope. He didn't even ask for it."

"Then how in the world did you two end up going to Philadelphia together?"

"Madame," our waiter interrupted at that moment, and placed a fresh plate before me.

As good as that dish was, and as much as I was looking forward to finishing it, I couldn't eat another bite of it. My stomach was in knots. The only thing I was hungry for at the moment was an explanation of how my ex-client and my ex-boyfriend managed to hook up right under my nose.

"Funny you should ask," Rose chuckled. "Believe it or not, we recently ran into each other again. I didn't mention this to you before, but a few days after I was released from the hospital, I made a trip downtown. I woke up that morning feeling pretty low. Like straight-up, unadulterated shit! I just needed to get out of my apartment and get some fresh air. I really felt the need to talk to someone even though I told everyone to leave me alone for a while. I was just wandering around downtown taking in the sights and sounds of the city when I somehow found myself in front of your office building. I decided to come upstairs and see if you were at work. Say hello and maybe chat with you for a little bit if you weren't too busy. I was also hungry, so I stopped inside the café first to get the biggest blueberry muffin they had, and a cup of herbal tea. Well, guess who I see in there drinking a cup of coffee and reading the newspaper?"

"Tony."

"Crazy, ain't it? So I go over to him and I'm like, "Remember me?" And he goes, "Wow, of course I do," and invites me to sit down and join him. Now, this is one good-looking white boy, Ms. Gentry. Believe me. I wish you could see him. But that day, he ain't looking too good. In fact, he looks awful. Like he hasn't slept in a few days or something. His hair's uncombed, his eyes are red. If I didn't know any better, I'd think he may have been crying. I could relate, though. I cried myself to sleep the night before and wasn't looking too tough myself at the moment.

"Anyway, we're both sitting there looking at each other like two people who've just had life kick them in the ass for different reasons. I ask him what brings him to this part of town again. Is the coffee really that good in this establishment? I don't think he realizes that's a joke because he doesn't even crack the slightest smile. He tells me he's about to try and talk some sense into his ex-girlfriend, who recently dumped him out of the blue without warning. And get this. He tells me she works upstairs in *your* building somewhere. So, I decide to be his sympathetic ear for a hot minute. I mean, given all the drama in my life, I figured it'd be nice to sit and listen to somebody else's for a change. Well, you're not going to believe what he tells me, Ms. Gentry. He says his ex is a sista, and she told him he had to get to steppin' because she needed to be with a black man. At first I thought he was just messin' with me. Like maybe this was his attempt at a little humor or something. But then I saw the pain in his face and it was real. Then I realize this must be the reason he's in this café again looking all tore-up and what not. He didn't go into any more detail about this woman or their relationship, and I didn't pry. Mm, mm, mm. I can't believe some sista dumped this fine-ass man just 'cause she wanted to be with a *black* guy? How about just being with a *good* guy? I'd sure like to meet this ex-girlfriend of his. What a *fool!*" Rose said, laughing hysterically.

I could barely breathe.

"Maybe you shouldn't judge this ex-girlfriend of his too harshly. There's two sides to every story."

"I suppose."

"But go on, please. I didn't mean to interrupt."

"Okay. So he wants to know why *I'm* looking so glum. I told him. The truth. I said, did you hear about the woman who was held at gunpoint by her estranged husband in an office building on Connecticut Avenue a few weeks ago? Maybe in passing, he says. Tells me he hasn't been following the news, or reading the newspaper of late. 'The only channel my TV's been on of late is ESPN. Why do you ask?' he says. 'Well, *I'm* that woman,' I tell him, 'and my former husband ended up turning the gun on himself and committing suicide right before my eyes.' He was floored. His entire demeanor changed in a snap. He starts telling me how sorry he is to hear that. How sorry he is that I had to experience something like that. And just like that, this stranger I only met briefly one time before is trying to comfort *me* even though he's obviously in some pain of his own. I didn't go into anymore detail about my ordeal, and like me, he didn't ask anything else. Except if I had a job to go to after finishing my blueberry muffin and herbal tea. I told him I was in between jobs at the moment and that there was no particular place I needed to be. 'Me either,' he said. 'Let's get out of here.' So, I'm like what about your ex-girlfriend? Don't you need to go talk to her? He just looked at me, shook his head, and said, 'Not anymore, I don't.'"

I could visualize Tony's letter in my hand. I could even feel the texture of the paper it was written on on my fingertips. And something now made sense to me that didn't when I read it the first time. I'm speaking of the part where Tony said he made it as far as the café, but that something prevented him from getting on the elevator and coming up to see me like he had planned on doing. Wasn't exactly *something* now was it? It was more like *someone*. Rose. If I didn't know for a certainty that I was wide awake at the moment, I'd swear I was in the middle of another awful nightmare.

"Where did you guys end up going?" I asked, no longer scared of what Rose's answer might be, but resigned to hearing whatever else was to come out of her mouth—no matter how unbearable.

"We spent the afternoon walking around D.C. talking— about everything but our individual issues. It was quite stimulating I must say. He finally cracked for the digits before we parted company. A few days later, he calls me on his cell. Tells me he's headed to Philly for a few days to visit his folks and do some hanging out, and if I'd like to join him. Says he'll book us separate rooms in a nice hotel if I agree. Sounded like a plan to me. He picked me up, we swung by his apartment, he introduced me to his roommate . . ."

"Black girl. Never seen her before. Tony brought her through here for a hot second before they took off . . . she had a brick-house body. Bam, pow, ta-dow!"

I stared across the table at my former client. Her lips were still moving, but I wasn't hearing a thing she was saying anymore. I wanted to lay my head down on the table and cry. Couldn't. Not now. Couldn't stand to hear Rose ask me one more time if I was okay.

"Sounds promising. Hope things work out for you," I said to her as I wiped away a tear I felt forming in the corner of my eye.

"Are you crying, Ms. Gentry?"

"Only because I'm happy for you." Not sure whether I was being sincere or not at the moment.

"Aaah. That's so sweet of you to say. But listen. It's not like me and Tony are an item or anything. It's way too early for all that. Besides, I'm sure he's still got some unresolved feelings for this ex-girlfriend of his he needs to work out, though. I'm just going to take things slow with him. Let things flow. Hey, you haven't touched your food. I'm sorry. I must be talking you to—"

"No, no. It's okay. All of a sudden I'm just not that hungry anymore. Think I'm going to have the waiter box this up for me. I'll eat the rest for dinner later this evening."

Under dimmed lights and the aroma of spice-scented candles, I put on Sade's *Love Deluxe* CD and curled up into a ball on my sofa. Lay there and mulled over all the things I was going to say to Tony whenever I saw him face-to-face again. I was going to "fix his little red wagon," as my Grandma Lucy Pearl used to say. I couldn't *wait* to tell him that I knew all about his new friend. Knew her quite well in fact. I could already picture how the conversation would go.

Bailey: Hey, Tony. I met your new girlfriend, Rose.
Tony: Huh? What?
Bailey: Huh? What? That's right. I even know about the trip y'all took to Philadelphia recently.
Tony: H-h-how did you find out about that?
Bailey: She told me all about it. Rose is my former client; the "high-maintenance" one. Remember her? Surprise! Small world ain't it, Ton'?

I could just imagine the look that would be on his face. I was going to have to make it a point to bring along one of those throwaway cameras just to capture it.

Anyways, however I chose to break the news to him, I knew I had better do it sooner rather than later. Obviously he hadn't told Rose about me. But suppose she brought my name up in conversation? I certainly didn't want her to be the one to break the news to Tony that we knew each other. No! *I* wanted that privilege. I wanted him to hear it straight from my lips. My lips done up in the same shade of Bobbi Brown lipstick he thought looked so good on me the night we met! Okay, okay. Let me guess. Y'all think I was behaving like a petty, vindictive bitch right about now, don't y'all? Hmmm. You're right. Oh, well . . .

As I lay there in emotional soreness listening to Sade sing "Feel No Pain" to me, I remembered that the card Rose gave me earlier that afternoon in Jaleo's was still in my purse. I got up, retrieved it, and returned to the sofa. Tore open the envelope. Inside was a blank thank-you card. The kind that allows the giver to express his or her own personal sentiment to the recipient in their own handwriting.

Dear Bailey,
    Thank you so much for helping me to get my life back. And for not only being my attorney, but someone I could count on to do the right thing. You've made me realize that I do deserve happiness after all. You're a true friend.
    God bless you,
    Rose

It took me few moments to absorb what I had just read. Wasn't expecting it. I slipped the card under the seat cushion of my sofa and shut my eyes real tight. My head and body began to converse with one another. My head uttered a familiar phrase it had said to me more times than I count.

Chill, Bailey. Let it go.

Of course, my body had something to say about that.

For once, I agree with your head.

HAPPY NEW YEAR
2003

Epilogue

Options

There you have it. That's my story. Wow, look at the time; 12:25 AM. And a very Happy New Year to you, too.

So, here we are, two years into the new millennium, and I'm still single, looking and hoping. *Thirty-seven,* and still single, looking, and hoping. I can sum up my sentiment in this regard in one phrase. Say it all together with me, people: *Gol-lee and gee effin' whiz!* If someone—anyone— would have tried to convince me eight years ago that *this* would be my love status come the year 2003, I would have had this warning for 'em: *"Crack kills.* Just say no!"

I swear something's got to change here. (And I'm not talking about my age, either.)

Do I question my state of mind and some of the decisions I made back in Ninety-four? Better believe I do. Since about my thirty-fifth birthday give or take. All day, every day, as Tony Gianni liked to say. Did I do like Spike—do the right thing and kick Tony to the curb because of his

Caucasian nature? Or would the right thing have been for me to hang on to him *in spite* of his Caucasian nature? When white seemed right, was a sista wrong? If nothing else, the years since then have given me plenty of time for reflection. Reflection on my best friend Lisa's repeated warnings to me, for one. I can hear her big mouth now, just like back in the day . . .

"Don't get caught short, Bailey. Mr. Right doesn't always come to us the way we think he will. What we got to do is recognize the package however it comes, or else one day we're going to find ourselves sitting around frustrated, getting fat, and bitching about why it is we ain't got nobody as our biological clocks tick, tick, tick away."

Oh, shut up, Lisa!

Now that I've shared my personal trip down memory lane, I'm sure there are a few things you all are still wondering about. Don't fret. I think I know what those things may be and I won't leave you hanging.

Yes, Tony and I did cross paths again. Briefly. At my request, we met for a drink downtown inside the Grand Hyatt hotel one Friday after work. He bought me a glass of Hennessey. What else? I wanted to meet him to tell him one thing and one thing only: "If my name ever comes out the mouth of a woman you happen to be seeing in the future, you don't know me and I don't know you. We've never met. Furthermore, I think it would be best if you never mention my name to a woman you happen to be seeing in the future."

Of course, Tony had no earthly idea why I was telling him this. But that's all I would tell him. Said my peace, finished my glass of Hennessey, gave him a hug, and left the Grand Hyatt hotel, never to see or speak to him again. Tony was a bright guy. He'd put two and two together, and make sense of my cryptic message if and when the time called for him to do so. So you see, I didn't go out like a petty, vindictive bitch after all. I wasn't going to make myself a fly in their ointment—accidentally or on purpose. If Tony and Rose could make interracial magic happen where I couldn't—or wasn't willing to—more power to them both. I do regret, however, not telling Tony before I walked away for good, that he did indeed raise the bar to my heart. Now only if I could do something about all the brothas since him—the Victors, Keiths, and Myrons of the world—who keep ending up *under* it for one reason or another.

As regards to the woman formerly known as Rose Braxton, we eventually lost touch with each other as well. We last spoke a few months after our lunch at Jaleo's. She did tell me at that time that things between her and Tony had gotten "hot and heavy." Consequently, for all I know, those two could have relocated to Philly and are married with children by now.

Am I forgetting anybody? Ah! Rex. Remember him? The wannabe rap mogul? Can't forget about my boy, Rex. What a funny dude! Wouldn't you just love to know what happened with the two of us? I'll tell you. *Not a cotton-pickin' thing!* I ended up tossing his phone number in the first trash can I came upon after leaving Farrugut Park that afternoon. *Boriquas,* me got no "problemo" with. We're darn near sistas anyway. But Rex lost major Brownie points for that admission of affection for "Caucasian and Asian honeys," too. Despite this, though, he still may have had a chance with me—albeit a very slim one—if not for his explanation of why he was still living at home with his parents at the age of thirty-three. Bruh's *fatal* admission. The *coup de grace.* Feel me? I didn't care if he was on the verge of becoming the next

Russell Simmons and Puff Daddy all rolled into one. Call me pretentious, but that was simply *unworkable* to a sista.

Be that as it may, Rex's psychiatry into the mindset of the single black woman did have me wondering if I had been stricken with "got-to-be-itis." If I had symptoms of any ill-ness, I'd say it had to be "want-to-be-itis." All I ever wanted back then, and still do today, is a good black man—with a few choice extras such as good looks, more-than-average loot, and exceptional lovemaking skills. *Is that a crime?* Am I just another black woman expecting too much?

I don't know if Rex ever did reach his musical aspira-tions. But with the way my luck with men tends to go, for tossing bruh's number in the trash, I'm probably going to turn on my TV one day and see his skinny, dreadlocked ass on BET or MTV getting *paid*. I will say this much: Rex was dead-on about two things he said to me in the park that afternoon. Black men do exercise their options, and a woman only gets so many chances to snag Mr. Right.

Well, maybe it's time for me to exercise my options as well. Maybe. As Tony's roommate pointed out, I'm a black woman. And for me and many more like me, loy-alty to our men runs so deep. But I won't lie. For every day that comes and goes that I still find myself by myself, I have to wonder if that same loyalty is keeping me to-gether or simply holding me back. I don't know the answer to that. But I know this. If another Tony Gianni were to enter my life today, I might have a very differ-ent story to tell.

Anyway, I've listened to every cut of *Who Is Jill Scott?* And furthermore—despite my intent not to—I've sat here and polished off an entire pint of Häagen Dazs mint chip run-ning my mouth with y'all. A shame, given that I also made it clear from the get-go of this conversation that I can't let these sexy thighs of mine get away from me.

Go ahead and call me crazy already. But even though my love life since Tony Gianni has mostly played out like a Teddy Pendergrass song—one love TKO after another—a sista's not quite ready to throw in the towel just yet. I haven't given up hope that I'll meet my kind of Mr. Right—my ideal box of chocolate—very soon. A vertical genius with a horizontal that's off the hook. My brotha, if you're out there, just know that there's an intelligent, attractive, funny, adventurous, self-sufficient, and very spunky sista who's still waiting on you to knock on her door or buzz her intercom.

Take your time, but hurry up. Because a sista does have options, you know.

Acknowledgments

My heartfelt thanx to the following . . .

My agent, Audra Barrett, for making it all come together and tirelessly working to help me reach my goal of becoming a published novelist.

My publisher, Urban Books.

Richard "Big Guy" Lampl for taking me under your literary "wings" back in the early 1990s and being the first to recognize my gift. (I can only hope to have one-third the energy you've got when I'm eighty years old.☺)

The editors at *Today's Black Woman*, *Black Men*, *Heart & Soul*, *Upscale*, and the *Baltimore Sun*, for the privilege of being a contributing writer to your publications.

Dr. Audrey B. Chapman for always being accessible and for having me on your morning radio show in D.C. a time or two. (Always a blast!)

My dear friend and neighbor Susan Payton for all your editing assistance over the years—free of charge at that.☺

Jami Shepard, Carla Germany, Trish Harvey, and Je'ree Hamlet, for reading and critiquing *A Box of White Chocolate* in its many phases of creation.

Truly Herbert . . . for the wonderful tip you gave me.

My dear, longtime friend and fellow author, Valerie Love: We did it! We *finished*. Now we're just getting started.

Finally, you the reader, for buying this book and supporting my efforts.

Love you, Boo-boo.

Daamon
Email: tds_writes@verizon.net
Web: *www.daamonspeller.com*